Provincial Justice

Kay Scarpetta, Amelia Peabody, and Anna Pigeon, make room at the table for Kate Mahoney. Gerry Hernbrode's elementary school principal turned sleuth is street wise, gutsy, and dedicated to the welfare of her young charges, qualities that put her in grave danger and keep the pages of *Provincial Justice* turning. Though this is pure fiction, you know by the sharp details and keen observations that Hernbrode has lived the life, which bodes well for the future adventures of Kate Mahoney.

—Gayle Jandrey, author of the novel, *A Garden of Aloes*

Kate O'Brien Mahoney is the kind of elementary school principal that many parents and grandparents would like to see in charge of the education of their own children and grandchildren. She supports her teachers and staff, and uses "tough love" wisely to help her students—many of whom come from unstable homes—learn to be responsible citizens. When Saguaro Elementary becomes a murder site and a first-grade teacher becomes the primary suspect, Kate goes to extraordinary lengths to protect her school, her students, and her teachers. She is less careful about protecting herself. *Provincial Justice* reveals the external politics and internal interactions that complicate school life for teachers, students, and principals. Readers will find Kate's adventures engrossing.

—Greta Morine-Dershimer, Ed.D., Professor Emerita, Curry School of Education, University of Virginia

Provincial Justice

Provincial Justice

Gerry Hernbrode

Published in the United States of America by:

Imago Press
3710 East Edison
Tucson AZ 85716

Library of Congress Cataloguing-in-Publication Data

Hernbrode, Gerry, 1935-
Provincial justice / Gerry Hernbrode.
p. cm.
ISBN-13: 978-1-935437-16-1 (pbk. : alk. paper)
ISBN-10: 1-935437-16-X (pbk. : alk. paper)
1. Ex-nuns—Fiction. 2. Women school principals—Fiction.
3. Murder—Investigation—Fiction. 4. Inner cities—Fiction. I. Title.
PS3608.E76866P76 2010
813'.6—dc22

2010007326

Book and Cover Design by Leila Joiner
Cover illustrations: Virgin silhouette at backlighting © photooiasson
chalk brush 4 © Spauln
orange plaster © charles taylor

ISBN 978-1-935437-16-1
ISBN 1-935437-16-X

Printed in the United States of America on Acid-Free Paper

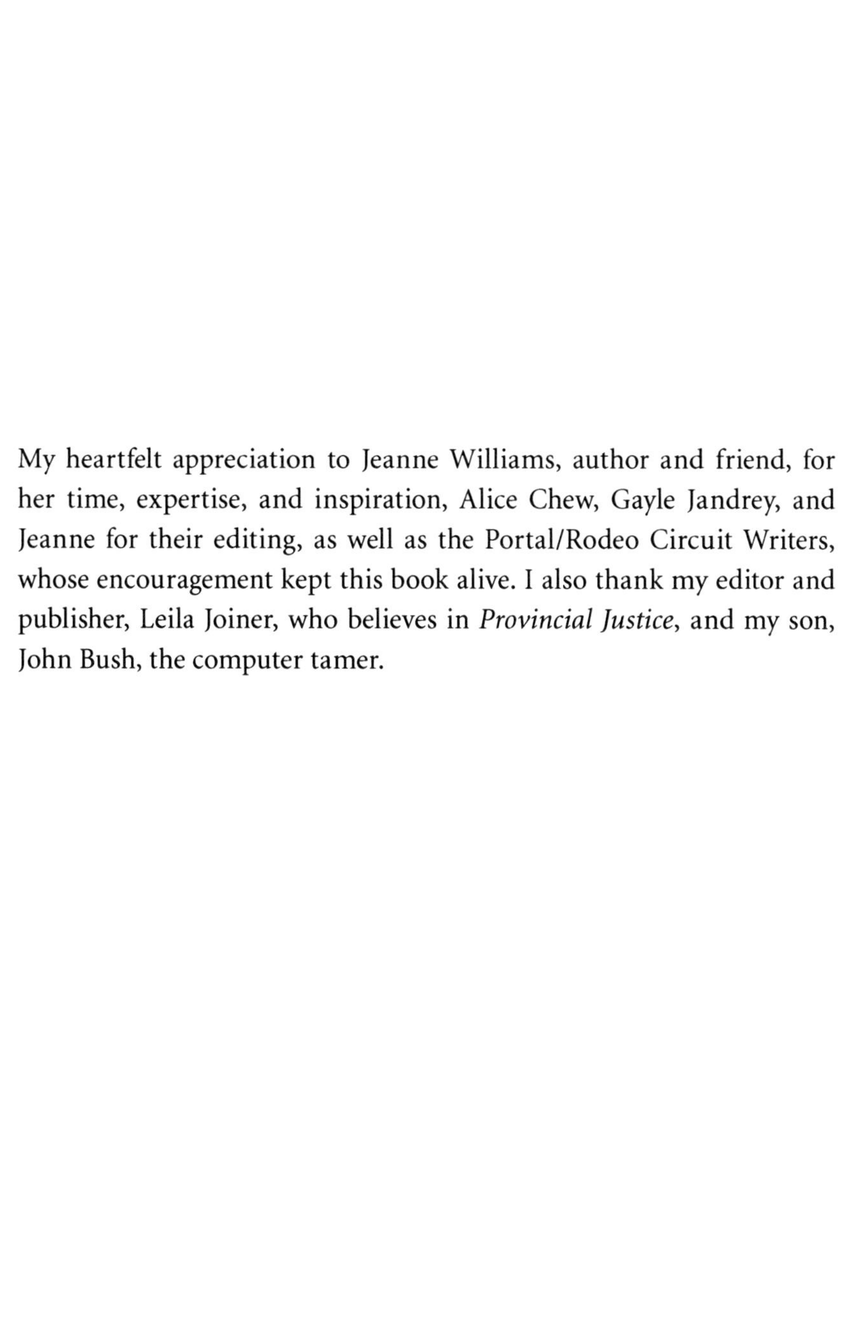

My heartfelt appreciation to Jeanne Williams, author and friend, for her time, expertise, and inspiration, Alice Chew, Gayle Jandrey, and Jeanne for their editing, as well as the Portal/Rodeo Circuit Writers, whose encouragement kept this book alive. I also thank my editor and publisher, Leila Joiner, who believes in *Provincial Justice*, and my son, John Bush, the computer tamer.

To my friend and mentor, Jeanne Williams
and to Inner City Kids
and the Educators who love them

In the Refectory...

Sister Katherine O'Brien's legs felt like ice as she knelt by the nuns' dining room entrance waiting to beg forgiveness from her sisters. It didn't make sense. It was summer. The brown terrazzo floor wasn't cold. She was wearing the novice's habit, sixteen pounds of black serge, yet her legs were still freezing.

It's just another distraction. I will concentrate on my penance. I must get better at this.

Having shed her black work apron, lowered her scapular to the floor, and concealed her hands in oversized prayer sleeves, she fingered the cold instrument of transgression hidden in her sleeve as she prepared to beg her sisters for prayers.

The cloister bell loosed a flow of silent nuns. Observing "modesty of the eyes," she could see only their feet, but she could tell the professed sisters from the postulants and novices by their shoes. Beginning sisters wore name brand dark oxfords they'd brought from home. All sixty professed sisters at this provincial house-novitiate wore the same black, mannish style, purchased in bulk. They had rubber soles. For silence.

"Sister, please pray for me."

"Yes, sister." Some touched her shoulder gently.

They feel sorry for me. They've done this, too. But I'll never get used to it.

"I'll pray for you, sister." The novice felt the hand of Mother Provincial rest on her shoulder. Not daring to look up, she could feel the towering, thin Mother Philippa Manning inspecting her over rimless half glasses. Ramrod straight and so lithe the novices whispered she kept a perpetual fast. The postulant who served her head table set them straight. Mother Provincial ate heartily.

Mother Philippa Manning, despite her absolute power over the six hundred nuns in her province of the Congregation of the Celtic Cross, had a deceptively gentle touch. Lifting her hand, Mother moved silently on.

Mother Provincial wouldn't be distracted. I'll never be that good.

A black Rockport oxford, that of her best friend, Sister Casey Whitehall, nudged Sister Katherine's knee. The kneeling novice remained a statue.

A stronger nudge—

Casey won't make it. She doesn't take anything seriously.

A kick! The penitent raised her eyes to see Casey slowly lower a dark lash over an eye the blue-gray color of a winter sky.

A wink! What if Mother Mistress is watching?

Sister Casey floated on.

At the sound of the second bell, Sister Katherine moved to kneel in front of Mother Provincial's head table for the final phase of her penance. Her black serge habit buffered her knees on the hard terrazzo. The novice's starched wimple, designed to squelch vanity, concealed unruly auburn curls while emphasizing azure eyes, delicate features, and full lips. Not what the founding mothers had in mind.

Sunlight muted by opaque windows brushed the black kneeling figures, then settled upon the Pieta, Mother Mary with her Crucified Son, above the head table. The Book of Kells Calendar by the lectern read July 25, 1970. She'd been here eleven months and two days. *Oh, to be anyplace but here!*

Following Mother Provincial's lead, the sisters rose.

They're all waiting for me!

Her mouth dry, she forced the words, "Mother and sisters, I beg your forgiveness for destroying the congregation's property." She pulled the offending stainless steel utensil from her prayer sleeve. "While working in the kitchen, I used this dipper to tap impatiently on the glass door of the food lift. It…I…cracked the glass."

She kept her eyes lowered and waited. The penance was a long time coming. She flinched as she felt a hand under her elbow. Mother Provincial stood at her side.

This never happens. This isn't according to custom.

"Stand up, Sister Katherine, and look at me."

The novice obeyed.

"Give me the dipper. The glass door is unimportant."

Mother Provincial is breaking all tradition!

"I'm entrusting a poor soul into your care. Elijah Jeremiah. There will be a murder. Remember...Elijah Jeremiah. Say his name."

"A murder? Elijah Jeremiah? Mother, I don't know anyone by that name."

"You will soon. And Boomer will help. Remember that child's name...Boomer."

"Boomer?" Sister Katherine felt her face grow warm. "But there are no men here. How can I help a man I don't know?"

"Don't worry, my daughter. Your lover will help you defend him."

At the word "lover," one hundred twenty-six nuns abandoned modesty of the eyes and stared.

Intoning "Oremus, Domine. Let us pray to the Lord," Mother Provincial returned to her place and began grace.

1

"I don't have a lover!" Kate O'Brien Mahoney shot upright in her bed. She rubbed her arms. *No prayer sleeves!* Felt her legs. *No serge pleats!* Good. It was safe to switch on the lamp. Same damn dream. Her nunnery days were twenty years and a murdered husband ago, but still this convent hangover.

She fished for slippers, banging into Winnie, her corgi, burrowed deep in the down comforter that had slipped to the floor. No wonder her legs were freezing. She glared at the alarm clock as if it were the offending party. Two-thirty!

Winnie interrupted his stretch to receive a reassuring pat.

"Elijah Jeremiah! My Elijah Stewart?" Surely, not the jet black, six-foot six-inch first grade teacher she had at her school. Elijah was as far from convent material as you could get. Was his middle name Jeremiah? As for a lover, it'd been a long, long time since Shawn—

Kate shook those thoughts away and moved to the kitchen, Winnie in her wake. Warm milk would get her back to sleep. To the kitchen, and then to the bay window seat that overlooked the lights of Tucson. They twinkled like a Christmas tree full of promises.

She pressed the mug against her cheek to enjoy its heat, sank into the pillows on the window seat, tucked her legs under and inhaled the warm, comforting steam. Now her dream would go away and leave her in peace.

But it didn't. Her legs remembered the weight of the nun's habit with pleats that had to be redone every other year so the serge would wear evenly. Her serge habit had lasted longer than her vocation.

By the night-light she studied her false nails. Not too long. A bit over the tips of her fingers. Expensive to keep up, but Saguaro Elementary's principal needed to look well turned out. Out of respect for the mission…and the kids. Left on her own, all she could produce were short, hangnailed stubs. The fakes were worth it. Yesterday: penitential black. Today: phony fingernails.

The warm milk wasn't working. Convent dreams were nothing new, she'd had them on and off for twenty years, except for the five years when she'd been with Shawn. He was a rookie cop, she a teacher. So much in love. She turned her mind away from him and tried to feel sleepy.

Elijah had been roaming her subconscious because of his run-in with the superintendent, Dr. Julie Mason—Kate's last worry before she fell asleep. Last evening, home from a Department of Ed meeting in Phoenix, Kate had returned a call from Pat Jackson, a fifth grade teacher. Though they taught different grade levels, Pat and Elijah were tight. Because they shared an office, they could see into each other's classrooms.

Pat's concerns had been high pitched. "I was correcting compositions, and Superintendent Mason came into Elijah's room unexpectedly. Probably because you were out of the building." Pause for the principal to explain her absence, which Kate didn't. "Anyway, it was a surprise evaluation visit. Elijah got nervous—and you know what happened."

Everybody knew. Elijah stuttered when he got nervous. Never with the kids or their parents. Only with administrators. Kate had solved that problem by keeping administrators off his back. Until today.

"And," Pat continued, "it was a bloody shame. A good teacher like that. Word is that Dr. Mason's after him 'cause he's black. At the very least, she probably thinks he's too tall to teach first graders. The way she talked to him in front of the kids. It got my hair on fire!"

Kate doubted whether Julie Mason cared one way or another about the color of Elijah's skin or his height. The superintendent had heard about the stuttering and accused Kate of protecting him because she "feared the NAACP and the Civil Rights lawyers." The possibility that Elijah was a good teacher who spent most of his time squatting so he could teach his charges eye to eye was lost on Dr. Julie Mason.

"And then," Pat's voice rose, "he got disgusted and left the class. Left the superintendent with his kids!"

Abandonment. How to get around that one?

"As if that wasn't enough—"

"There's more?"

Pat's tone rose. "When she finished with Elijah and his kids, she went to the office and enrolled a mentally retarded fifth grader into my class. Totally bypassing the Special Ed placement process."

The snubbing of this federally mandated process was surprising, even for Dr. Julie Mason. Kate held the phone away from her ear as Pat continued. "No Child Development Team to decide whether the placement's appropriate. No weaning in from the ten student Special Ed class to my overcrowded class. There he is. Boomer! His name is Boomer." The teacher paused for breath. "His file is on my desk. Look for yourself. There's no process documented. See what happens when you leave the building?"

Boomer? Pat's disclosure made the dream niggle like a mental itch.

Mother Philippa Manning, a woman she would never forget, was answerable only to the Mother General in Ireland. Before her death a couple of years ago, she'd ruled two colleges, four large hospitals, and fourteen schools. Total power over six hundred nuns. Zero power over Kate.

Kate leaned over and patted Winnie. Rotating like TV antennas, his ears shifted toward her.

It seemed so real. Boomer? A child Kate was going to meet, whose file she planned to check out. Still—was Elijah's middle name Jeremiah? Was this the Elijah that Mother Provincial wanted her to protect? Kate pictured the tall first grade teacher. Thin as a Watusi and just as black, he was young and athletic. He could be mistaken for an NBA center. A graduated Oasis High School basketball star, he was a local hero to his Saguaro Elementary fans. Kate had hired him for the first grade position, the only one open that summer, after he'd proven that "I...I...I can d...do it." She'd watched him in action with a summer school class. Impressive.

Elijah Jeremiah will be involved in a murder. Hardly. The worst the superintendent could do was fire him. Kate emptied the mug and poked around the cupboard for a wine glass. Murder? Not even Dr. Julie Mason could pull that off. The thought of the meticulous superintendent in jailhouse orange brought a smile. Substituting burgundy for milk, Kate took a sip, and then, compliant as a novice, she placed the wine glass in the refrigerator and found herself in her bedroom pulling jeans and a "Pierre's Pub" sweatshirt onto a body that refused to relax. With a heavy steel flashlight in one denim jacket pocket and pepper spray in the other, she headed out the garage door. Winnie nearly tripped her as he squeezed by. She opened the front passenger door, and he jumped in.

"This is crazy, Winnie, but I've got to find out if Elijah's middle name is Jeremiah." The corgi yelped approval.

Did the command of a Mother Provincial still demand her obedience? Ridiculous. Still, if any personality had the power to span twenty years it would be that of Mother Philippa Manning. There'd be no sleep until she checked his full name on the teaching certificate hanging in Elijah's office. Kate pushed the button that locked all car doors, put the pepper spray on the dash, and backed into the street.

She wouldn't let teachers come to the school at night. The square mile served by Saguaro Elementary had five homicides and eight unexplained deaths last year. But she'd occasionally come back herself, usually to gather information about a problem that would otherwise keep her awake. To safely get into the building at night, she used the automatic door opener that accessed the cafeteria loading bay.

No one respected the night shadows at Saguaro Elementary as much as the three evening custodians who went off duty at eleven. They went about their business avoiding the dark, ignoring any sounds coming from it. Ed Meyers, the day custodian who came on duty at 5 a.m., wore rubber gloves when he made the morning rounds of the playground, gathering up the needles and condoms of the night.

This truce between the custodians, drug dealers, and prostitutes continued night after night, year after year, broken only by the occasional police raid. Then, sirens and helicopters were the signal for the three evening workers to gather in a cement block classroom, where they'd sit on the floor to avoid a stray bullet through a window. They'd call Kate on a cell phone, and she'd remind them not to answer a knock on the door. They'd settle down to a game of hearts until the coast was clear, and then go home early to compensate for wear and tear on their nerves. Nancy, the primary wing custodian, carried a deck of cards in her hip pocket, always prepared.

Thinking of them, Kate felt like a proud mother whose kids had become accustomed to living in the shadow of danger. Never considering themselves heroes, the night custodians—Raul Martinez, Nancy Ferguson, and Hassan Mahem—sidestepped trouble on a routine basis so kids in this neighborhood could go to school in a clean building. Kate felt this admiration every day, watching the folks in this part of town go about their business. The staff, the poor single mamas, the kids: all were skilled at skirting trouble. She felt proud to be surrounded by such taken-for-granted courage.

There it is. My lover! Kate'd been wedded to the two-story concrete block school that loomed through the darkness for four years now. The structure encompassed three sides of a city block, wrapping itself in a U shape around the middle courtyard and opening out into a playground now shrouded in black. *A demanding lover devouring all my time and energy.* It looked like a black fortress in the glow cast by the few streetlights that hadn't been broken. *An abusive lover? One day I'll leave him and his stresses. Maybe. What was the fascination?*

Elijah's Four Runner and a district van were parked in the teachers' lot. What were they doing there? Strange. Nobody ever left a car overnight, for fear it would be missing tires or a battery in the morning. Kate circled the block to get a better look.

Lights in Elijah's classroom shone through tissue paper ghosts his first graders had taped on the windows. Caspers smirking through a sinister darkness. Why was Elijah here?

Kate's Toyota Corolla rolled into the cafeteria parking lot, where she activated the remote control. The cafeteria loading bay door rose, hesitated, then silently swallowed the car.

Winnie barked. She'd have to keep him close to keep him quiet.

Kate's flashlight beam bounced off the kitchen's stainless steel sink and across a serving table loaded with dry cereal. In about four hours, the faint smell of dishwashing soap and disinfectant would be muted by the scent of baking cinnamon rolls. Morning cinnamon rolls put people in a good mood, Maria Martello, the cafeteria manager believed, so they were there by the coffee pot in the teachers' lounge each morning.

In the blackness of the cafeteria the beam picked up tables set in precise formation like planes with attached benches for wings. In five hours, about two hundred and fifty kids would be climbing on these benches ready for free breakfast. Eighty-five percent of the six hundred and fifty kids at Saguaro Elementary got free lunch, and the poorest qualified for free breakfast, as well. This was everyone's favorite room in the school. Some kids cried when holidays came. No school equaled hunger.

Excited by the scent of hundreds of kids, Winnie sprinted between tables, stopped suddenly, and was silent. The flashlight beam sought him out.

Too late. He'd already lifted his hind leg and left his mark. Mrs. Martello would hang anyone who brought a dog into her spotless cafeteria. Let alone this!

Kate backtracked to get paper towels, bleach, and water from the kitchen. By the time she'd erased Winnie's work and was satisfied that the only thing she could smell was Clorox, she'd become more comfortable with the deserted building. Winnie stayed close by her side as they padded down the darkened hallway. The scent of fresh wax told her Hassan and Nancy had been faithful to their cleaning schedule.

So familiar, yet something didn't feel right. Silly to feel threatened. Still, she was glad she'd find Elijah in his room at the end of the classroom hall. He'd probably stutter up an excuse, and she'd counter that it was too dangerous. Then he'd growl under his breath, and they'd leave together after Kate had seen the name on his teaching certificate.

In three hours, Ed, the morning custodian, would be coming on duty. This nighttime visitation gave her an insight into the early morning world he inhabited. Did he ever feel threatened?

Kate reached for the knob on Elijah's door, but froze when she heard a woman's voice. Julie Mason's voice? What was the superintendent doing here at this hour?

She turned the master key in Pat Jackson's door instead, planning to slip undetected into the adjoining office for a peek into Elijah's room.

Pat's classroom was chilly. The heat didn't come on until seven-thirty these October mornings. Tense, Kate's senses sharpened. The classroom smelled of glue and furniture polish, odors soon to be replaced by the scent of sweating fifth graders after first recess.

The lights from the first grade classroom cast a bright glow into the shared office. A dim reflection through the office window cast shadows across Pat's classroom. Kate could make out desks clustered in groups of four and neat writing on the chalkboard near the sink. Probably the daily assignments, but it was too dark to be sure.

She knelt on one knee and slipped her hand over Winnie's nose, buying some time to listen. When Winnie squirmed, she tightened her hold on his jiggling dog tags while gentling her grip. Her thoughts were anything but gentle. Damn it! Kate was responsible for the well-being of the children in this school. And Elijah was a good teacher. What the hell was Julie Mason doing behind her back? Whatever the explanation, it had better be a good one.

Through the partially opened office door, she heard Dr. Mason's humorless laugh. "This isn't what you expected, is it?"

No answer. Something solid and soft like a body banged against the movable wall that separated the two rooms. A woman's scream cut through the air like a filleting knife, sharp and thin.

Releasing the dog, Kate flew to the office door, pepper spray in hand. Her left hand was on the doorknob when a shot rang out. Winnie stood frozen, his front paw lifted, paused in midair.

Suddenly, the fifth grade classroom became unreal. The doorknob felt like dry ice. In slow motion, Kate withdrew her hand and grasped the side of a student desk to steady herself. She had a terrifying premonition that the movable wall was going to open of its own will and expose something horrible. Her legs and arms felt heavy as she bent over, grasped Winnie in her arms, and moved with what seemed maddening slowness to the concealment of the bookcases in the reading corner.

A growl built in the dog's throat. Kate muzzled him and whispered in his ear. She strained to hear what was happening in the next room.

Julie's high-pitched scream was followed by heavy thuds. Kate visualized the superintendent's face, the porcelain features. With each blow, the face altered in Kate's imagination, becoming torn and horrible. Suddenly, the beating stopped.

The hair on the nape of her neck and on her arms stood up, away from icy skin. Winnie strained to be free, the growl rising again in his throat. Kate held him so tight, he had trouble breathing. "Sh…sh…sh."

The silence following was more horrible than the blows. Had the attacker heard her movements? Would she be able to keep Winnie quiet? *Oremus, Domini!*

Using the switch by the office, somebody turned off Elijah's classroom lights.

Good! No lights! Good!

The attacker was coming through the office door, choosing the fifth grade room as an exit.

To avoid the blood. To avoid the contamination. Or had he heard Winnie?

As he crossed the room, Kate saw his silhouette framed in the window against the streetlight. He was tall and had a full haircut. An Afro?

Oh, Elijah! Don't find us! Go on by!

Winnie tensed. He'd defend his mistress. Kate held him so close, her arms ached. The figure moved with long strides to the classroom door, then slammed it shut behind him.

For an eternity, Kate waited, afraid to breathe. She strained to hear the retreating footsteps or sounds from the other room. Would the classroom door reopen? The attacker return? Would the wounded superintendent stumble through the teacher's office?

No. That wasn't going to happen. Kate fought the sickening feeling that Dr. Julie Mason wasn't going to be walking anywhere. She waited—and waited. Twenty minutes by the classroom clock. When she finally released the barking Winnie, he shot with pent up force through the office doors into the next room, growling as he went.

Kate followed. What she saw in the beam of her flashlight made her stumble to the sink to heave.

Winnie whined, circling the body of Julie Mason. His small paws made bloody prints as he retreated from the beaten tissue of her head.

Kate forced herself to approach the body. She felt the radial pulse in the left wrist. Nothing there. No breath escaped the pulverized nose, the beaten mouth.

The flashlight beam exposed a small, pearl-handled revolver that had been thrown against the blackboard. Kate recognized it as a Derringer .41. Stylish and deadly, but a single shot. The kind of gun she'd expect Julie Mason to carry. The superintendent wouldn't expect to miss—but she probably had. The departing figure hadn't been limping. No trail of blood marked his path. The pepper spray in her hand felt impotent. Winnie whined softly. Kate agreed. She got sick again.

How could Elijah do this?

Numbly, she moved toward Pat's desk and picked up the phone. Winnie trotted after her. With each step, his red paw prints became fainter on the carpet.

She reported the homicide to 911 and asked them to notify Keith Taylor, the School Resource Officer. She knew the cop on the beat would respond first, followed by detectives in plain clothes. Keith and her assistant principal, Pop Jonesy, would help her hold the school together. Morning bell was only five hours away.

Pop sounded half awake when he answered the call.

"It's only four-fifteen. Don't you ever sleep?"

"Julie Mason is dead. Murdered in Elijah's classroom." Her trembling voice belied the calm she was trying to project. "I need you, Pop. The children will be here soon, and we can't let it be horrible for them."

"Did I hear you right? Julie—dead?"

"Yes, Pop." Kate nodded vigorously as if he could see her.

"I'm on my way."

For a couple of minutes, Kate stared at the workbooks on Elijah's desk with unseeing eyes. Without conscious thought, she reached up and touched the framed certificate above his desk. Encased in a plain walnut frame, it authorized "Elijah Jeremiah Jackson" to teach in the state of Arizona.

A new chill worked its way down her spine.

"Stay here. I'll have questions." The first officer to arrive looked her over. Sizing her up for jailhouse orange? She remained by the phone, feeling heavy as a statue.

She knew the cop on the beat, Officer Rodriguez, who came next and began cordoning off the two classrooms with yellow plastic evidence tape. The press would be buzzing about the death of the superintendent of Oasis District, so the police public relations officer had arrived on the heels of the beat cop. A rotund Hispanic in pressed uniform, he stood against the office doorjamb, looking at the crime scene and suppressing a yawn. Kate guessed he'd been called out of bed to tell the press there were no juicy details yet. Detached and drowsy, he'd change his stance when the press arrived.

The third officer to appear looked like he'd been sleeping in his rumpled overcoat. A man in his early fifties, he had the powerfully built body of a laborer with broad shoulders and chest. A little less than six feet tall and wearing a fedora, he could've been a villain from a gangster movie. Except he was wearing rubber gloves.

He walked the perimeter of the first grade classroom a couple of times, hands behind his back, looking from one vantage point, and then another. Heavy drooping brows gave his brown eyes a deceptively sleepy look. He didn't go near the body. Having been married to a cop, Kate knew he didn't want to destroy the physical evidence the Crime Lab Unit would collect.

Instead, he walked to the sink. His nose twitched as he surveyed the contents.

"Somebody's got a nervous stomach." For the first time, he looked at Kate. "You?"

Kate nodded, irrationally wishing she'd rinsed out the sink before calling the cops. But she knew better. Never touch anything at a crime scene.

"For a principal in this part of town, you're a little delicate, doll."

Kate glared at him. Officer Rodriguez must have identified her. In no mood for this "doll" bit, she countered, "I suppose you can work a scene like this, and then go out and have a Big Mac."

"Two. With catsup and onions."

Kate took a deep breath.

He reached into an inner pocket in his overcoat. For a moment, Kate thought he was going to pull out a gun. Instead, he produced papers and a pen.

"As chief honcho, you'll need to sign this consent form." He placed it in front of her with surprising gentleness. "We've impounded the two cars in the parking lot. The Four Runner has blood on the steering wheel. Driver's door open. Like somebody left it in a hurry. Yours?"

A shake of the head.

"Whose?"

"You've probably already run the plates. You know whose car it is." Kate didn't want to say it was Elijah's.

"Car belongs to Elijah Jackson. Whose blood?"

Please, not Julie Mason's!

She read the form before her. Usually, such legal papers had to go through central office. Under the circumstances, Kate signed it. After all, the superintendent wasn't going to be around to give her hell anymore.

"You're turning green, doll." He took her by the elbow. "Let me get a chair for you out in the hall."

"Don't call me doll." Kate was surprised by the smallness of her voice.

"Oh, one of those, eh?"

Kate felt too weak to ask what "one of those" referred to. A feminist? A lesbian? A man hater? After she gave this macho cop her statement, she'd never have to see him again. She thought to ask his name, but decided it wouldn't matter. Better not waste what little energy she had on him.

He kept talking as he resettled her. "What's your name, principal?"

"Kate Mahoney."

He began to scribble. "That name sounds familiar."

"I was married to Shawn Mahoney."

The writing stopped. His eyes took their time to brush across her face as if memorizing it. They were neither hostile nor friendly. Just curious. His lips curved into a strange little half smile. "Oh. *That* Kate Mahoney!"

Kate's body stiffened, and her cheeks burned. Of course, they all knew about Shawn, a fellow officer who'd been shot in a convenience store holdup. Even though it was eight years ago, they'd remember him.

Remember her, too. The way she'd gone to the press when the cops couldn't find his killer. The way she'd embarrassed the department. But past history didn't need to be dragged up at a time like this.

"Well, Kate Mahoney, tell me. What were you doing at school in the middle of the night?" The smile had slipped away, and his full attention was on her. For some inexplicable reason, Kate was glad he was using a note pad, not a laptop. She told him about her insomnia and her curiosity about Elijah's middle name.

"So you come to school in the middle of the night to find out your first grade teacher's middle name?" The officer's dark eyes burrowed into her space, his tone sarcastic, designed to make her squirm. Kate searched for an explanation. Following up on a dream about a Mother Provincial? That wouldn't cut it, and she didn't want to volunteer information about Elijah's quarrel with the superintendent. Not yet. So she said nothing.

His hawk-like eyes, suddenly alert, kept on target as he pulled out a cigar, bit off its end, and shoved it into the side of his mouth.

Anticipating the cigar smoke, Kate felt her stomach lurch. *If he makes me heave, it'll be in his lap!*

As if reading her thoughts, he didn't light the cigar. "How'd you get here?" he asked.

Kate told him about her car in the cafeteria loading bay. The officer jotted notes as she recalled the sounds she'd heard during the attack. His eyes, clouded with disbelief, kept asking the question, "And why were you *really* here tonight?"

Kate blushed and wished she hadn't identified herself as "that Kate Mahoney." The last thing she needed right now was animosity. Or, worse, sympathy. She yearned to be away from this whole night.

"Mrs. Principal Mahoney, we'll impound your car. Routine police procedure. If lab officers find it's clean, you'll get it back in a few days." He returned the notes to his pocket, his eyes withholding belief.

"What's your name, detective?"

"Theo Buloski. I'm not a detective." He tensed. "Just helping out. Anything else you want to tell me?"

Boomer will assist.

Mother Provincial's words provided the only card she had to play. "I'd been told by Pat Jackson, the teacher in that classroom," she motioned over her shoulder, "that the superintendent had enrolled a mentally retarded fifth grader in her class yesterday while I was away in Phoenix."

The officer switched his cigar from one side of his mouth to the other, his eyes in neutral. He didn't reach for his note pad. "So?"

"I couldn't sleep last night, so I decided to check it out. To see whether Dr. Mason had made the placement without going through the authorized channels. I came here to check out the registration file that I knew would be on the teacher's desk."

"So that's what you principals do at night—worry about kids. Worry about some poor mentally retarded kid who doesn't fit into 'authorized channels.' I'm touched. I'm really touched."

She recognized the interrogation technique: use anger to break out the truth. But she still wanted to hit him. Instead, she just told the truth. "We teach all of our kids, handicapped or not. But a mentally retarded boy who hasn't been prepared for the regular classroom can be lost in a large class. Can disrupt a class. And, yes," her icy eyes stared at the enemy, "I do lose sleep over a situation like that."

For a long moment his eyes continued to bore, then he shifted the unlit cigar into its original position and rose. "What's the boy's name again?"

"Boomer."

"Boomer what?"

"I don't know."

A couple of men carrying a camcorder and photo equipment brushed by, trailing the whiff of darkroom smells behind them. Theo Buloski rose abruptly and moved through the classroom into Pat's office. He scanned a file that lay on the desk, pulled out his notebook, and still looking skeptical jotted something down. Then he stepped over the yellow tape and entered the crime scene.

Boomer had assisted. At least for now.

The evidence team, all wearing rubber gloves, were measuring distances and putting anything that might have been touched into plastic evidence bags. The water glass was placed in a paper bag, so the plastic wouldn't mold around the glass and rub off prints. Even Julie Mason's hands were in evidence bags drawn around the wrists by rubber bands. Some of the assailant's blood might be found under the nails.

Kate struggled to pull herself together. How to protect the children and staff from the horror of a murder in school—this neighborhood's one safe place? She needed help. Where were Pop and Keith?

Fifth-grader Louie Castillo rubbed his nose and steadied his balance atop the climbing tower. Jet-black hair that needed a trim stuck out from beneath a U of A baseball cap worn backwards. Normally, he'd be waiting for the playground monitor to look the other way so he could challenge comers to push him off his king-of-the-mountain perch. Tall and thin, he lacked the low center of gravity of pudgy rivals, and it was tricky for him to keep his throne.

Most times, Tamoni, sitting one bar below, would have challenged, but this wasn't a regular morning. The kids, the majority of them Hispanic with a smattering of African Americans, Anglos, and Asians, had been hustled off the playground early. Mrs. Jackson was herding Mr. Stewart's first graders into the library, so she told her class to wait on the climbing tower until she could find another room for them. This suited the fifth graders just fine. They welcomed involvement in the most exciting of inner city sports—watching the police in action.

"As good as TV! All the cop cars with their blue and reds going! Man, did you ever see so many lights?" Tamoni ran ebony fingers through cinnamon hair the texture of chenille. "More lights than when they had the shootout at Sunburst Apartments. Three brothers dead that time." Brown eyes looked upward to check Louie's reaction. "I lived there then, man. Were we scared or what?"

Louie didn't bother looking down. "You're lying." His eyes never left the entrance to Mr. Stewart's first grade classroom.

"You calling me a liar!" The challenge was loud enough to draw the attention of the others.

Louie changed the subject. "Mr. Meyers says it's a woman who's dead. He says it's Mrs. Mahoney's boss. That's all he'd say."

"She's White. I asked." Tamoni was willing to swap hostilities for a little attention.

"Dead is dead. White. Brown. Black. If they're dead, they're dead." Louie shoved his glasses to the bridge of his nose and sighed. "You sure are into color, Tamoni."

Tamoni accepted Louie's remark as a compliment. "Did ya ever notice? Dead people are always Black or Brown. Well, this one's White. And if there's gotta be somebody dead, it's Whitey's turn. Probably killed by a white woman, too." He stared at his rival. "Bet Mrs. Mahoney did it."

"What?" Louie glared at the newcomer to Saguaro Elementary.

Tamoni beamed. "Nothing against Mrs. Mahoney. But nobody likes a boss."

"What?" Louie weighed the satisfaction of smashing Tamoni's big mouth against the inevitable consequences. Over the years, Mrs. Mahoney had gotten to him. *You fight. You pay the price.*

All eyes on the climbing tower focused on Tamoni. He couldn't resist. "Man, she's mean enough to kill anybody! If you ever looked in her eyes when you're in trouble, you know she's one tough dude." Tamoni lowered his voice to a whisper. "I bet she's even killed kids. Lots of 'em."

Detention be damned! Louie wiggled off his perch and worked his way toward the slanderer. A shrill cry from the lower level of the tower stopped him.

"Look! The cops are bringing out Mr. Stewart!"

Horrified fifth grade eyes watched as Elijah Stewart, his hands cuffed behind him, walked between two officers to the waiting patrol car. Mrs. Mahoney passed between the teacher and the students, trying to shield him from their eyes, but it didn't work. Everybody saw Mr. Stewart being taken away for the murder of Mrs. Mahoney's boss.

"Always a Black!" The silence was broken by Tamoni. "What'd I tell you. Always a Black Man!" He jumped from the tower and went screaming after the teacher, "Elijah! Elijah!"

A small voice from the bottom of the tower asked, "Who's Elijah?"

Louie knew. "That's Mr. Stewart's first name."

"How come Tamoni knows that? He's new here."

Louie shrugged.

In the Sacristy...

Lulled by incense, the provincialate chapel slumbered in the quiet of the warm afternoon. Sun filtering through stained glass windows bathed the altar in a kaleidoscope of color as Sister Katherine removed spent votive candles from their stands, genuflected before the tabernacle, then padded around the altar and back into the sacristy.

Enjoying the genial, petitioning smell of candle wax, she placed the votive holders in a pan of scalding water and began removing the wax. Silently, Mother Provincial appeared beside her. The novice dropped the votive, splashing hot water. "You!"

"Yes. Me." Tying on a black vinyl apron, Mother selected a red votive holder from the hot water, scraped out the wax and returned it to the felt-lined tray. Tongs in hand, Sister Katherine plucked the same red holder from the tray and submerged it into a second pot of boiling water. After the wax had fully melted, she retrieved it, rubbed it dry with a cotton towel, and returned it to the tray.

"Why did you do that, Sister Katherine? Why the extra work when the next candle will get it waxy, anyway?"

The novice's lips tightened as she gentled in a blue votive. "Everything about the chapel should be especially perfect."

The elder religious wiped up the splash. "Especially perfect. As differentiated from moderately perfect? Is that what Mother Mistress is teaching you?" She fished out another votive. "Only God is perfect. Give me common sense over human perfection any day. Common sense—

that's what you lacked when you went to Saguaro Elementary in the middle of the night!"

"And who sent me down that road? You, with your talk of Elijah Jeremiah."

"Which proved to be accurate." Mother wiped her hands, and then took Sister Katherine by the shoulders. "I'm sorry you were in the next room when it happened. But you'll be all right. Unfortunately, we can't say the same for Elijah." Mother loosened her hold. "Find out where he was during the murder and get him to explain why his car was in the school parking lot. Why was Dr. Mason in his classroom at that hour?" She handed the tray to the novice. "You'll have to replace these in the chapel yourself."

"Yes, a Mother Provincial doing manual labor would blow her image." Sister Katherine found herself smiling. "We don't want that to happen, do we, Mother?"

"I prefer to think in terms of religious decorum—of a stratified sort." The nun untied her apron. "My sister, do visit Elijah in jail. Ask him about Jacqueline."

"I'm no longer your sister." Sister Katherine turned abruptly. "Mother Philippa, who's Jacqueline?"

Mother Provincial only nodded, then disappeared through the door into the sanctuary, piddling her finger in the holy water as she went.

2

"Who is Jacqueline?" Kate questioned the dark. Another night, another dream bringing back a sense of being controlled by religious authority. Kate reached for the note pad she kept on a bedside table and jotted down Mother's questions. On balance, Kate wished the dreams would stop.

Investigating Officer Bob McNary coughed, ran his fingers through graying hair, and surveyed the assortment of principals that made up the Oasis District leadership. Typical administrators. Eyes empty, mouths shut. Asses covered.

There were a lot more men than women. Most of the men were balding or graying, but the tanned, younger males looked like they worked out. That would figure. The deceased probably had hired the young ones. Word was, she liked to surround herself with good-looking young men. She tended to hire coaches. The women were mostly in their forties. Only one had gray hair. Probably been around a while.

The males wore business suits, white shirts, and ties. The ties on the older guys were conservative. Predictable. The coach types wore more arty ones. Computer graphics, he guessed, like that crazy Garcia guy used to make before he overdosed. A couple had ties with kids on them. Those would go over big with the kids and parents. Those two must be people pleasers. Hell, they're all people pleasers. In their business, they damn well better be.

All the women wore dresses with soft feminine designs. But every dress had shoulder pads. Damn shoulder pads! Built to make women look strong. Broad shoulders like construction workers. Damn, he hated shoulder pads. Why couldn't they wear the padding where it counted, in the boobs? None of these women were emphasizing that part of their anatomy. But what could he expect from a bunch of principals? He'd had a woman principal once. No boobs there.

One young woman, a beauty with auburn curly hair and fair skin, showed a little leg. All wore earrings, but not the kind that clanked or dangled.

These people were conformists. It hadn't taken him long to learn that their superintendent was disliked by most. Hated by some. Still, these folks wouldn't approve of murder. They'd give up her killer if they knew. Or would they?

He'd noticed a complete lack of mourning. Nobody even pretended. Unusual in a homicide investigation. When the group first gathered, they'd crowded around "Red Curly Hair," the principal at Saguaro Elementary, where the corpse was found. Their mood was restrained, but underneath Officer McNary detected a note of relief.

Dr. Mason was gone. Had one of them taken matters into his hands? Her hands?

The principals looked back at him with poker faces fine-tuned by long hours of practice. As he started talking, he sensed a solid wall of resistance. He was trained to find cracks in walls. These were decent people who probably had committed murder in their hearts. Their guilt was going to get to them. But not soon. This would be a long meeting.

Kate Mahoney looked over the thirty other principals who sat grouped around the perimeter of a giant rectangle formed by joining several conference tables. Dr. Mason had called this her "square table as opposed to round table," and the principals had dutifully chuckled. This formation required a large conference room, but had the advantage of the participants being visible to each other. It kept people from going to sleep and encouraged them to develop poker faces.

Pictures of the twenty-three elementaries, five junior highs, and three high schools were displayed on beige walls. Each school had a picture of its principal alongside it. All, that is, except for Kate's and

Jacqueline's. Kate had been delayed by an emergency when the photographer was scheduled. And Jacqueline? Well, Jacqueline might have avoided the photo session for the hell of it. Jacqueline Stanley, graying principal of Mesquite Elementary, didn't mind strong-arming her teachers to get what she wanted. Tough, at times downright mean. Still, she couldn't be Mother Provincial's Jacqueline. Guilty of mutiny, possibly. Murder, never.

At the moment, Kate appreciated the inscrutable faces. Every person at the table knew about the clash between the late superintendent and four inner city principals, of whom Kate was one. Word of it wasn't public, but the grapevine of principals knew. Yet not one eye was turned toward the four who now sat together. Young Coach Harry Holman from Agave Elementary, more experienced on the football field than in a principal's office. Seasoned, balding Pat Callahan from Prickly Pear Elementary, with his recurring tic and reality-defying optimism. Tough, leathered Jacqueline Stanley from Mesquite, the gray lady in a field of tints.

Why'd we sit together? Not a good idea.

Officer McNary droned on about the "respect for law at the heart of the Principals' mission." Kate had expected Theo Buloski would be here, but he wasn't. At least, Buloski's style had more spice. Officer McNary was going on about how sure he was that any bit of evidence, any whiff of motivation would be reported to him at the break.

At the break! We're going to be here for a while. Not an eye blinked. No one even flinched. *Damn, we're good!*

He revisited the responsibility argument six times, then unexpectedly excused himself and disappeared. To confer with a psychologist? At the sound of the door closing, twenty-seven pairs of eyes focused on Kate and her three colleagues. Some were grateful. Some amused. Some surprised. But no one scowled.

Kate glanced at the three principals sitting by her side. They looked guilty. She felt that way, too. *Big mistake for the four of us to sit together.* She suppressed the urge to get up and move.

When Officer McNary returned, all eyes shifted to neutral. The officer talked on and on about citizenship and the need for law and order, and how the principals were in the vanguard of preserving civilization "as we know it."

Kate's thoughts turned to that day—just last Wednesday—when Dr. Julie Mason had summoned all four "guilty-looking ones." Waiting outside Dr. Mason's office, Kate had studied an architect's sketch of the district's new high school. A few days before, Wallace Talbot, the contractor from Icarus Construction Company, had stopped by Saguaro Elementary to peruse some design features that were working well in the new wing. Dr. Mason, who hadn't visited the school in two years, had brought him to Saguaro. Curious.

Wallace Talbot was a man easy to remember. Tall. Eyes sexy green and intelligent. A scar on his left cheek accentuated his craggy good looks. He had a worry ridge in his brow too deep for a man of roughly forty years, but keeping building construction on schedule would worry anyone.

Kate had been wondering about him when Jacqueline Stanley and Pat Callahan entered the waiting area.

"An emergency meeting?" Kate asked.

A raised eyebrow from one and an uncontrollable tic from the other answered in the affirmative.

"Anybody know why?"

"Not a clue."

Each principal headed an inner city elementary school that served the underprivileged. Tucson, an hour's drive from the border, hosted thousands of children straight from Mexico. New immigrants, legal and otherwise, these kids usually hit the ground running, and these principals' schools charted their course and provided the running shoes. Great kids. Tough job. These four, like their teachers, usually started the week with a double ration of vitality and ended it drained.

"Coach's already in there." Kate nodded toward the Superintendent's office.

Jacqueline Stanley sank into an upholstered chair and leaned her athletic form forward while coaxing a graying strand back into her bun. Horses were Jacqueline's passion, and she kept herself in shape by riding them. Her perfume suggested red jackets and jodhpurs: the elite trailing behind their hounds far, far away from the inner city school she headed.

"Eleven o'clock." Jacqueline checked her watch. "I should be in the cafeteria about now, keeping my little beasties in line. If she's trying to intimidate us—calling us in one by one—Coach would be the first one she'd call in." She flashed the look that unnerved Mesquite's teachers. "Julie underestimates Coach. He didn't break football records by being a pushover. Still, having fallen from grace, he may be weakened."

Kate tried to like Jacqueline. It took guts to let gray hair stay gray in the youth-conscious competition of school administration. And she was right; Coach Harry Holman was vulnerable. A year ago, he'd been principal of a shiny new elementary in the suburbs, where his sculptured good looks charmed women teachers as well as mothers. Prior to being principal, he'd been track and basketball coach at Oasis High, so his sports record impressed the fathers. A week after getting married in June, he'd received an involuntary transfer to Agave Elementary, an inner city school. Tongues wagged.

"If he doesn't hold his own," Jacqueline went on, a twinkle contrasting with the wrinkles around her eyes, "he'll give Julie a false sense of security. She won't be prepared for me."

"Ahem—" Chubby Pat Callahan choked. "What makes you so sure it's something negative?" In his fifties, Pat had been in the district only two years, hired when Dr. Mason was on vacation. An experienced principal, he checked his watch so stealthily the others hardly noticed.

"Julie's efficient." Kate pulled herself out of the deep upholstery and perched on the arm of the chair across from him. "If it were good news, she'd tell us all at once to save time."

"Probably just wants to give the personal touch." He adjusted his glasses while the corner of his eye twitched.

For a distraction, the three studied the sketch of the new high school. "They say she's really proud of the plans." Pat tried to sound enthusiastic. "It's going to be the Taj Mahal of high schools. A showplace that will put her leadership on the map nationally."

"I'd be happy if they'd cut a few corners and reroof my north wing," Jacqueline volunteered.

The office door burst open. Coach Harry Holman shot out, handsome face red and contorted with anger. He charged by his colleagues with nary a sideways look.

Jacqueline and Kate exchanged troubled glances. *If even-tempered Body Beautiful comes out in such a huff, what hope for us mere mortals?*

"Pat, please step into my office," directed a cool voice.

Pat entered, his forefinger masking an eyebrow.

Kate and Jacqueline called their schools and cleared their lunchroom schedules. In twenty minutes, Pat Callahan exited, his face like a zombie's. He moved slowly and mumbled something about looking for a job in another district. Any other district.

"Kate."

Jacqueline's last.

Dr. Julie Mason moved with a rigidity muted by her natural grace. Most women in authority welcomed the softer styles that were becoming acceptable for professional wear, but there was nothing soft about Dr. Mason's appearance. A tall, thin blond, she chose a fitted black suit that accentuated her exquisite figure, while her beige shirt and long, narrow tie looked appropriate for a state dinner—or a funeral. Her short blonde hair was clipped close to the face, accentuating large, cold hazel eyes. She was beautiful. She could get away with severity.

The superintendent beckoned to Kate to sit while she stood by her walnut desk, arms folded across her chest.

Oh shit! The confrontation posture!

"Have you seen the morning papers?"

Kate shook her head "no," though the truthful answer was "yes."

A first page article was thrust under her nose. The headline blared, IOWA TEST OF BASIC SKILLS REVEALS ARIZONA STUDENTS BELOW NATIONAL AVERAGE.

Kate studied the page slowly, buying time to gather her wits. Oasis District students, on the whole, had scored above the national average. Predictably, Saguaro Elementary students, most of whom spoke English as a second language, scored below.

"Taking into account my students' unfamiliarity with the English language, I'm pleased with the results." Kate tried to return the paper.

The superintendent refused it. Their eyes collided. "You'll notice they're up to grade level in math calculation that doesn't involve language."

"What?" Dr. Mason moved so close Kate could feel her breath. "Your students perform this poorly, and you're pleased?"

Anger flashed in Kate's eyes and warmed her cheeks.

"Pathetic!"

She was on her feet. "I'll tell you who's pathetic. Our lame-brained legislature that expects fifth grade kids straight from Mexico to read English in one year, and then take the test on fifth grade level. It took their fifth grade Anglo counterparts five years to read that well."

Dr. Julie Mason towered over her fuming subordinate.

"You inner city principals disgust me." She flicked a piece of lint from her jacket sleeve. "When you, as school leaders, don't think minority students are as smart as Anglos, of course the expectations of your teachers will be substandard."

Kate wanted to hit her. She maneuvered around behind her chair and dug her fingers into the upholstery so hard they whitened. Having widened the distance between them, she struggled to clear her thoughts. "After they've been a year at Saguaro, the law says our kids take the test on grade level, even if they can't read it." Kate's voice was calmer now. She'd studied this testing problem from all angles. "Remove the test scores of all the kids who speak Spanish at home and who can't read on grade level yet and average the remaining scores. You'll find our students are doing well. I can compile that data for you."

Dr. Mason sighed. "Exactly what I'm saying—low expectations." She tapped a pencil on the polished walnut desk.

Kate's temper sizzled like water drops on a hot griddle. "My life is devoted to my students. I expect their best. But no matter how hard they work, it takes time for them to learn a foreign language." Kate knew she was yelling, and she didn't care.

The superintendent leaned over her papers, looked Kate in the eye, and flicked at another speck of dust.

I am that dust!

Every blonde hair on Dr. Mason's head remained perfectly in place. There was no sign she was doing battle, except for her eyes. They narrowed as they took Kate's measure and found her wanting. "You're not afraid of me, are you?" Her voice was barely audible. "That's a mistake, Ms. Mahoney."

Kate shook her head. No, she wasn't afraid of the superintendent. Still, she felt sweat moisten her armpits. Her knees felt rubbery, and her jaw was clenched so tight it hurt.

I'm afraid of myself—afraid I'll leap over your spotless desk and strangle you. Hell, yes, I'm afraid of me!

What happened next surprised even Kate.

"The public expects all Oasis District schools to perform well." Dr. Mason's eyes calculated Kate's response. "I expect all of our schools to perform above average on standardized tests and," she rested both hands on the desk and moved forward, "if you can't deliver above average scores, you'll be replaced by a principal who can."

"You're asking me to have the teachers teach the test answers?" Kate's mouth fell open in disbelief. "That's what you want, isn't it?"

"I'm not asking. I'm telling you. The tests will be given again in the spring. Your students will perform up to grade level or your contract won't be renewed."

Kate felt like she'd been kicked in the stomach. She clenched the chair for support. "My teachers are professionals. To ask them to cheat would gut the trust that holds us together."

Dr. Mason smiled. "Gut. How dramatic!" She moved toward the door and paused with her hand on the knob. "Well, then, if they don't want to cheat, they'll just have to do a better job of teaching."

She opened the office door, her thin lips tightened across her mouth. Her look of dismissal for Kate was also her summons for Jacqueline Stanley.

As the second hour wore on, the principals' neutral facades began to fray. There were suspects among them. Worse yet, the police knew it.

Veronica Pena, Oasis High School's principal, removed her half glasses, massaged between her eyebrows, then stood and confronted the police officer. "I'm certain you've no legal right to detain us here."

Dr. Doug Ellis, now acting superintendent, rose and reminded his subordinates that the police were calling the shots. The district expected the captives to remain with good grace. Officer McNary, the only one smiling in the room, excused himself and left. Kate wondered whether he had a bladder problem.

She shifted in her chair to study Jacqueline, who rested her elbows on the table, cradling her tanned chin on interlocking fingers. Steady hazel eyes were noncommittal, but her lips smiled like the canary-eating cat.

Jacqueline, a murderess? Always the nonconformist. Professional to the core. Would Jacqueline consider it a duty to get rid of an unprofessional superintendent? That smile. If Jacqueline murdered, she'd get away with it. Kate was toying with this ugly notion when the subject of her musing turned and beamed at her. Then gave a nod of approval.

She thinks I did it! Kate jerked her eyes away, only to let them rest on Coach. Here was a man who expected to win. He'd played by the rules, and it had worked for him. How would he react to being forced to cheat in order to survive? His golden boy good nature disguised the interior of steel and discipline that had made him a sports hero.

Coach Harry Holman's ease turned jovial as he whispered to a colleague. Then they both laughed and turned to look at Kate. A cruel look lingered in Coach's eyes as he cupped one huge hand around the other to conceal his thumbs up sign.

He suspects me! Or is he savoring his own sweet victory? Why did Julie make him a principal? He didn't know an elementary school from a football field. Was he one of her lovers? No. A lover wouldn't be relegated to a tough inner city school. Or would he? Maybe, if the love turned sour. If the lover married someone else. Can't get much more sour than that.

Deliberately, Kate maintained eye contact. Coach kept his steady glare on her. When she refused to break eye contact, he reddened and looked away.

A headache pounding in her temples, Kate turned to Pat Callahan. Leaning back in his chair, hands behind his head, he looked content. No tic. He caught Kate's eye and sent her a wink. Without thinking, Kate shook her head. He nodded with a grin.

Why do they all think I did it? Or are they covering their own tracks?

The officer reentered. He moved to the far corner and reached up to remove a small object from the loudspeaker. "What's that?" Veronica Pena queried.

Phlegmatic Officer Bob McNary suddenly came to life. "It's a camera. My superiors have been evaluating my performance." He glowed. "I'm sure you use video cameras to study your teachers now and then." He turned to leave the room. "With their permission, of course. Don't worry, my boss had mine."

It was only a matter of minutes before he returned.

"You all may go with the exception of Ms. Mahoney and Ms. Stanley, Mr. Callahan and Mr. Holman. You four stay in your seats, please."

It was three-thirty by the time Kate got back to Saguaro Elementary. The crossing guards were rolling in the 15 MPH speed limit signs, and only the kids in the after-school program were on the playground.

McNary and another detective had interrogated each inner city principal separately. Kate remembered her husband Shawn telling her, "Find out what motivates the person you're questioning and lean on it." These cops knew the principals were thinking about problems at their schools that could magnify in their absence. Time was gold for these principals. So the questioning was separated into slow and easy segments with plenty of lag time in between.

Still, Kate hadn't told them about the achievement testing threats, and she doubted that her colleagues had. The first thing inner city principals learn is to use their ears more than their mouths. If the testing came out as a possible motive, Kate already had a pat answer: "You think somebody would murder over that?"

But she couldn't get Jacqueline out of her mind. Nor could she forget Coach's cruel satisfaction. So out of character for him. Or was it?

With twenty minutes to go, the office staff was wrapping up. Terri Alvarez, Kate's secretary, flipped her single long blonde braid over her shoulder. It swung into place in the middle of her back. Six feet tall and a body builder with a figure that impressed daddies as well as little boys, Terri could handle just about anything that got thrown at her. Today, Kate guessed, she'd had a lot to handle.

"Hi, stranger." The secretary pushed a floppy into her computer to download the day's work. It would join the other computer backups in the fireproof safe. "We were beginning to wonder if we'd have to visit the jail to get your signature on these letters." She nodded toward a pile on the desk by the principal's office door. On especially hectic days, Terri didn't let important items get lost on the principal's desk. She kept them in plain view, where she could be sure they'd be attended to. "Tough day, eh?"

"Not nearly as bad as it was for Elijah." Kate moved toward her office. "I've got to get down to the station to see him."

Terri smoothed crinkled plastic covers over her computer and printer and tucked the edges under. "Don't waste your time. Pop tried all afternoon to get in touch. No luck." She sat on the edge of her desk, crossed her legs, and raised her skirt from force of habit. Body building results should show. "Keith's in his office, and he wants to see you before he leaves. He's been by a half dozen times looking for you."

"Did you tell him his buddies were working us over?"

Terri had her compact out and was freshening her lipstick. "You're not crazy about cops, are you?" She pressed her lips together, satisfied by what she saw in the mirror.

Kate rolled her head and kneaded the muscles at its base. "Only in emergencies. Then nobody can fault their two-minute response time for schools." She reached out and touched Terri's arm. "Thanks for keeping things together here."

Terri brought her braid to the front and studied the effect in the compact mirror. She could handle the heavy loads because she had fun playing with the light stuff. "Pop worked out of your office all day. We got a substitute teacher to cover his class. That's what assistant principals are for, right?" She snapped the compact shut, reached for her purse, and rose to her full six feet. "He's got a list of folks who need to talk to you, including Wallace Talbot. Wallace insisted he had to see you right away. I told him the cops had you."

Kate wondered what the contractor for Icarus Construction would find so urgent. Dr. Mason had given him the master key to Saguaro when she'd introduced him. He planned to use the designs of the Saguaro bus and parent pick up zones for the new high school. Why would he need a master key if the design work were outside? Julie had gone out of her way to help the handsome contractor. Unless there was a good reason, Kate wanted that master key back.

"Wallace is interesting. It isn't often I meet a man I can look up to." Terri fingered the blonde strands at the end of her braid. "He's divorced. Positively deadly green eyes. Sexiest eyes I've seen in a long time." The tall blonde flashed a coy smile. "Be sure I'm around when he comes in tomorrow. He wouldn't set an appointment time, but that's what two-way radios are for."

Kate shook her head. "Be careful what you wish for." Unwilling to admit Wallace Talbot had made an impression on her as well, Kate watched her right-hand lady head out.

Keith's office door was open, so Kate let herself in. Theo Buloski sat at the school resource officer's desk, fedora on his head and smoking a cigar, while comparing a pile of papers to the notebook he'd used at the crime scene. He didn't look up.

Kate coughed. No response.

"Officer Buloski."

The policeman squinted, pushed his hat back, and gestured toward the single chair with the hand that held the cigar. A trail of gray smoke pointed the way.

"Mrs. Mahoney."

This officer knew smoking in public buildings was against the law in Tucson. Irked, Kate coughed again.

The policeman took another puff, then put both hands flat on the desk. The cigar, firmly anchored between two fingers, continued to belch out smoke. "Two coughs in ninety seconds. Are you trying to tell me something, Mrs. Mahoney?" He slowly rose, walked to the door, and placed the burning cigar on the cement walk outside.

"Not there. A child might pick it up."

The officer's eyes, under drooping brows, pierced the principal. He smashed the cigar with his heel and kicked it into the grass, then returned to his place behind the desk to study the woman before him.

"Officer Buloski, I'm looking for Keith."

"Mrs. Mahoney." The officer shuffled his feet under the desk and folded large hands on top of it. He took off the hat and hung it on the computer, exposing a bald, sunburned pate. Kate sensed an uncomfortable man taking a stand she felt she wasn't going to like.

"Mrs. Mahoney, please call me Theo." His face blushed to match his bald dome. "Since I'm going to be around for a long time, we'd better dispense with the formalities."

"Why would a homicide detective be on campus for any length of time, Officer Buloski?"

"I told you the other morning, Mrs. Mahoney. I'm not a homicide detective. Keith Taylor tried to see you today to let you know I'm taking his place as School Resource Officer stationed at Saguaro." Theo Buloski leaned back in his chair, hands behind his head, waiting for the reaction.

She just looked at him.

His body stiffened. "It seems we may have a little trouble with communication, ma'am, but we better get used to each other, so I can help you with the kiddies' problems."

"Officer Buloski, don't insult my intelligence." Kate stood and leaned over the desk, looking down her nose at the cop. "You might use the School Resource Officer cover, but I know you're here to investigate Dr. Mason's death. My staff members aren't guilty of this murder, so the sooner you find the real killer, the better. Is Keith really gone for good?"

"Been reassigned to the high school." The cop's face inched closer to Kate's. The smell of the cigar enveloped her like a sinister mist.

"Where does that leave me and my kids?"

"I told you. With me."

"You've been sent here to spy on us, and you expect me to hand our students over to you!" Kate could feel her face flush, her jaw tighten. "I doubt you've been trained to work with children."

"I know how to work with kids. I'll talk with them nice and reasonable like, and if that doesn't work—"

"Yes?"

"If that doesn't work, ma'am, I beat the crap out of them till they do what I say." A smile crept into his eyes. "I'll be a big help."

Kate's tone was low and threatening. "Touch one of our kids, and you'll regret it."

A robust laugh exploded from the cop. "Just checking out your sense of humor, little lady, and I find it woefully lacking. Lighten up. I might be good for the kids."

“And if you call me little lady in front of my students, I’ll—”

“You’ll report me to my superior, Lieutenant Rawlins.” A toxic twinkle sparked in the officer’s eye. “And that’ll do you a lot of good, since you’re one of his favorite people, aren’t you, Mrs. Mahoney?” The business-like neutrality Kate had sensed at the crime scene replaced the mirth in his eyes. “Whatever you think of me, Mrs. Mahoney, we share a common enemy. I crossed Rawlins, too, and that’s why I’m here. Put out to play with the kids my last two years before retirement. Rawlins couldn’t demote me for some trouble that I handed him, but he did take me out of the real action.”

Kate hesitated, then moved back to her chair. The mention of Rawlins drained her energy like air from a punctured tire. She sat staring into space, seeing Shawn’s face vibrant with life. Fourteen years ago, she used to take her finger and trace the lines around his eyes, feeling the little wrinkles at their corners. Across his brow, smoothing out the worry lines. Down his cheeks, round and Irish. Over his full, sensual lips and along that stubborn jaw into the dimple on his chin. And the blue eyes—so honest and full of love when he looked at her. Thirty-one was too young to die. Twenty-eight, too young to be a widow.

Officer Buloski had softened when their eyes met again. “Mrs. Mahoney, when I was assigned here, I read the police report and newspaper clippings about your husband’s death. I can understand why you felt the investigation was lacking.”

Kate felt numb. She’d been over this territory before, too many times. She listened with little grace.

“You burnt the bridges when you took your story to the press, and the furor turned Captain Rawlins into Lieutenant Rawlins. Knowing Rawlins as I do, I imagine he took the easy way out and called the investigation off too soon.”

Kate repeated the details out of habit. She’d gone over the facts so often, they were part of her being. “He responded to a 911 call at a mini mart on his beat. The thief fired two shots into Shawn’s chest. The police officer with him returned fire and killed the thief instantly. There were no witnesses. What Rawlins chose to ignore were the threatening phone calls Shawn had received the previous week. Shawn hadn’t taken them seriously. Neither had Rawlins.”

So much energy to discuss Shawn's death. Why was she wasting it on Buloski? "I want Keith back."

The impassive look on Theo Buloski's face said that wasn't going to happen. "I admit Keith Taylor is a whole lot cuter than I am. Kind of a Ken Barbie doll." A half smile curved his lips. "He's a nice boy. Your type, I bet."

Kate bristled and changed the subject. "What is Elijah's status? Can I see him if I go down to the station?"

"He's being held on suspicion of murder. They've read him his rights, and he's got a lawyer—a Mohammed Duncan, I believe." The neutral, business-like look had returned. "They'll be questioning him now. Maybe you can get in tomorrow morning."

Kate got up to leave, thought better of it, and sat down again. "Officer Buloski, I must accept you as Rawlins's gift. The only thing we have in common is Rawlins as an enemy. But let me make two things perfectly clear. First," Kate pointed her index finger at him, "I believe you've been planted here to work this murder from the inside. You'll find my teachers are innocent, but far from fools. They'll know what you're up to. Second," two fingers this time, "I've seen police brutality. Hurt one of our kids in any way, and you'll find that I'm no Barbie doll. Do you understand, Officer Buloski?"

Theo Buloski pulled out another cigar and lit it. "Yes, ma'am. In the future, I'll screen my jokes."

The embers at the end of the cigar had begun to glow when Kate rose slowly, deliberately put the chair back in place and left, closing the door behind her. Let him suffocate in his own smoke.

After the traumas of the day, Kate could hardly wait to settle into the womb of her townhouse. She planned a simple dinner with wine followed by a TV show so dull it wouldn't tax a single brain cell. As she drove home, she pushed the worries of the day down as fast as they popped into her consciousness. Oh, for the nirvana of the mindless.

With a tinge of irritation, she surrendered her hope for privacy when she spotted Ralph Breckwood, Junior, her sixteen-year-old neighbor, leaning over the adobe stucco wall that separated her patio from his family's. Bare to the waist, he directed a steady stream of water in the direction of her Texas Ranger, a gray-green bush that would be called a weed in most parts of the country. Texas Rangers can survive almost anything, but Kate's neglect had nearly done it in.

It was a toss-up as to which was more neglected, the Texas Ranger or Ralph Breckwood, Junior. The tall, lanky lad fended for himself most of the time. He and his M.D. parents had moved to Tucson from Chicago ten years ago. Mom was the chief physician in the community hospital emergency room. Dad had become a popular gynecologist with a legendary bedside manner. Their incomes could finance a move to a gated country club community, but they stayed next door, probably because their time and energies were concentrated on work. It would take family togetherness to plan and execute a change, and this family didn't do anything together.

Over the years, Kate had taught young Ralph how to ride a bike and how to swim. He watered her patio plants and made her laugh, and she opened her refrigerator to his grazing. Kate wasn't home much, either, but when she was, she listened—at least a little.

Ralph slipped down to turn off the water, and then vaulted the wall to her patio. Kate, tired to the bone, wished she had his energy. She wouldn't mind having his tan, either. He'd developed into a desert wildflower, tough and showy. Didn't seem to need much care.

"I wish I could do that." Kate handed him her packages as she put the key in the lock. "I can hardly get in the door."

"All of you strong women…" the way he emphasized strong made Kate think he was talking about his mother, "…wish you could have our physical strength. Penis envy replaced by muscular envy, now that science can get babies out of test tubes."

Winnie bounced around them as they entered. Delighted at the sudden wealth of companionship, he rocked back on his short rear legs, begging for a proffered pat on the head. Kate gave the excited dog the obligatory attention, while Ralph dropped the packages on the coffee table, headed straight for the refrigerator, opened it and groaned. "How do you survive? Nothing good's in here."

Kate directed him to the meat tray and some luncheon meat she'd bought to keep him supplied. He coupled it with a slab of cheese and slapped them together with mustard and mayonnaise between two slices of bread. As it reached his mouth, he paused. "Want one?"

Kate collapsed at the kitchen table and murmured a feeble, "No, thanks, and I don't want a regurgitated serving of Freudian male superiority, either. You need to update your sources, Ralph."

"Murdering teachers got you down? Am I right, oh, Sexless One? It's all over the news."

"Where is it written that kids between the ages of eleven and nineteen must be obnoxious? What's with this, 'Oh, Sexless One?'" The moment she asked the question, she wished she hadn't.

Ralph shrugged, his attention divided between the baloney and the cheese. "That's what Dad calls you. Says you didn't stay married long enough to find out what marriage is really like, so you idealized your dead husband, and nobody else can measure up." He opened the freezer. "Mind if I help myself to a little ice cream?" He pulled out the carton. "Wouldn't you know it? No real ice cream. Well, frozen yogurt will have to do."

"Mighty big of you, Ralph, to accept my humble frozen yogurt." The Sexless One remark irritated her. "Don't you have any food at home?"

"Well, we do and we don't." He jabbed into the white yogurt cylinder, causing the muscles on his right arm to tense, then stepped back, letting the ice cream drip on the white ceramic tile. "Everything here tastes better."

"Mind the scoop." Kate dove for a paper towel, knowing it would be better parenting to have him clean it up himself. But hell, she wasn't his parent, and she liked a clean kitchen.

"Don't get all hot about the 'Sexless One.' Anyway," he shot her a wicked glance, "I could change all that."

Kate sat up, her hands on her hips, and stared at him.

"Don't look so surprised. I saw you looking me over out there by the gate."

"I was checking to see whether your diapers had been changed. Out!"

Gathering the makings of his second sandwich, Ralph headed out the door, protesting that he was just kidding. Kate had put up with a murder, an investigation, a mouthy cop, and she was in no mood for overheated hormones. Besides, she had the nagging fear he was taking after his dad, with his famous bedside manner.

In the Robery...

Sister Katherine O'Brien forced the tapestry needle into a cross-stitch that held the heavy layers of the habit's black serge pleats in precise rows. Pleats that would fall gracefully when the skirt was let down for chapel. No interior fabric layer could slip or the hem would hang unevenly.

Two novices were guiding black serge slowly into the needles of the robery's two electric sewing machines. The treadle machine sat idle, awaiting Sister Katherine, a novice of lesser sewing ability.

Across the robery, three postulants wearing long black dresses and caps sewed silently at a high wooden cutting table. They wouldn't wear the wimple until they became novices after their six-month probation period. They were mending cotton nightcaps and cotton chemises, long tunics that were worn under the habit. Chemises were washed weekly, the habits only once a year. Postulants sewed cotton. Only novices were permitted to sew the black serge in preparation for making their own habits.

"Well done, Sister Katherine." Mother Provincial pulled a high stool to the robery table and inspected the cross-stitches.

"Why am I here?" Sister Katherine whispered in deference to Low Silence and to avoid disedifying the postulants. "We both know I don't belong here." She jabbed the needle into a pincushion.

"I'm the one who doesn't belong." Mother Philippa's tones were sweetly reasonable. "It's your dream, not mine." She retrieved the needle and continued cross-stitching. "I repleated my habits every two years, so the pleats would wear evenly. Thirteen times until I became Mother Provincial. Then the novices did it for me." She chuckled softly. "One of the reasons I agreed to remain so long as Mother Provincial."

"Murder. Mother, we need to talk murder!" Sister Katherine glared at her companion. "Do you know what happened to Elijah?"

"Poor young man. He's in jail for a crime he didn't commit."

"Who did it, Mother? Who killed Julia Mason, if it wasn't Elijah?"

The postulants looked up. Mother nodded their way, and they returned to their sewing. "I don't know, sister." Her thimble forced the needle through an inch of serge. "I knew that Elijah would be unjustly accused of murder, but I don't know who did it. Being dead is vastly overrated, when it comes to enlightenment. I know about Elijah because he's my responsibility."

"Why is that?"

Mother Philippa shook her head and threaded the needle with the white thread used in temporary cross-stitching. "Black on black is hard on the eyes. I'm only helping you with this easy part."

"Mother, this isn't my habit." Sister Katherine's voice rose. "When I took off my habit, I was done with it. With you!"

"A consoling illusion." Mother handed over the newly threaded needle. "Just like the ties that bind Elijah and me. It's not that easy." She slid off the robery stool. "Try to find Jacqueline. She's a key. Not the only one, but important."

Mother Provincial gently removed the hand that Sister Katherine had placed on her sleeve. "Good night, Sister Katherine."

3

The computer screen stared back at the principal, its innards churning up mischief. Kate shot the machine a dirty look, rubbed her neck and buzzed for Terri. “You’ve got to help me, or I’ll shoot the damn thing.”

Terri shrugged. “Face it. You and computers live in two different worlds. What do you want?”

“To pull up the names of all persons associated with Saguaro who are named Jacqueline.”

Terri waited for an explanation. Getting none, she took the chair and began to restore order. “You want all the Jacquelines?” She turned to the woman leaning over her right shoulder. “All the Jacquelines?”

Kate ignored the implied “Why?” and nodded. “Yes.”

In minutes, Terri’s flying fingers tamed the monster. Kate plucked the list of twelve Jacquelines from the printer. She recognized the nine students, but the names of the three mothers were new information. Was one of them a lead? Was she moving in this direction to avoid checking out her colleague, Jacqueline Stanley? Or was she losing her mind, following the commands of a phantom Mother Provincial? Leaving decisions to religious authority. Again.

“Want anything else?”

When Kate shook her head, Terri rose to leave, but she had to ask, “Why do you want them?”

Kate sidestepped the question. “To be sure we’ve got them all, send out a memo requesting staff to list the full names of any Jacquelines connected to the school.”

"The computer got them all."

Kate sniffed at the monitor. "I don't trust the damn things. Let's verify the old-fashioned way."

Terri flipped her braid and left the room.

The iron cot creaked as Theo Buloski spread his legs and stretched. He could feel springs through the thin, plastic-covered mattress. The only place in the cell to sit, it was too low for Elijah's six-foot, six-inch frame. The teacher leaned against the stainless steel sink, its naked plumbing squeezed in beside a lidless toilet.

"Ever been in jail, Theo?"

The gray concrete wall had been sandblasted to remove obscenities, but new graffiti overlaid the cleaned areas. From a vertical window too narrow to need bars, a slip of Tucson sun slid across the brown linoleum floor. Theo's nose twitched at the faint smell of disinfectant. He was thankful it was fall. It had to be hotter than hell during a Tucson summer. He'd been in hot jails. A bitch.

"Never in an American jail."

He was weighing how much he wanted the tall, skinny Black to know. Few knew about his CIA work. He wasn't about to reveal that he and two comrades had received the Congressional Medal of Honor for covering the ass of his squadron as they escaped from a Viet Cong ambush. Three medals were given, two posthumously.

After the war, he'd worked in Europe as a double agent, ending up in Australia one step ahead of the KGB. The Aussies were scrupulous about whom they let on their island. They saved his hide, if not his soul.

No, he wasn't going to tell Elijah about that, but he did volunteer, "Was in a Turkish hell hole once. Cell was bigger. More men in it. Crowded with men and rats. And an open urinal." Even now, he shuddered.

The gaunt prisoner had begun to pace. Theo wondered whether he was from a Watusi line, way back. Three paces carried Elijah from wall to wall.

"Tucson's jail may be fancier, but it's the same feeling." Elijah stopped and fished in the baggy pocket of his orange jumpsuit for a pack of cigarettes. "Makes you feel like a trapped animal." He took one and tossed the pack to Theo. "What were you doing in a Turkish jail? Selling hashish?"

Theo almost lied. Bad habit acquired in the CIA. Instead, he shook his head and took the offered smoke.

Getting no feedback, Elijah snorted, inhaled deep and long. "Funny, the only things they let you keep in here are these cancer sticks." He flicked an ash on the floor. "Things that will kill you. Cost effective for life sentences." His lips began to smile, then changed course and turned down at the ends. He snorted in disgust.

Theo leaned forward, blowing smoke into the communal fog. "That's why I'm here, Elijah. To get you out." He assessed the level of trust in the jailed man's eyes. Found none.

"Strange, you showing up as School Resource Officer, right after the murder. I'm not talking."

It pissed Theo off that he couldn't think of a new approach. Something to get the guy to tell where he was the night of the murder. To say why his car was there. Maybe explain the superintendent's nocturnal visit.

"Kate and the folks at school really want you out of this mess."

Elijah nodded. "I'll bet Kate doesn't trust you, either."

Theo managed a crooked smile. "Nah. I smoke cigars on school property and threaten to beat up her kids. She wants her Keith back." He snuffed out the cigarette, immediately sorry that he had. A prisoner offers you a cigarette, you ought to do him the courtesy of finishing it. He'd bring Elijah a carton next visit.

"Elijah, I'll tell you why I'm here. I embarrassed my lieutenant, so he took me out of the action and sent me to play with the kiddies. Still detective pay, but not where the action is." He watched Elijah. The man was halfway believing him, probably because he was lonely and wanted news of the school. "Well, I'll do the school thing. But on the sly I'm working on this case. If I can crack it, they'll have to put me back where I belong."

The creases across Elijah's forehead lessened. Not much. His arms still hugged his chest. He picked up yesterday's paper off the cot and studied the front-page headline again: OASIS SUPERINTENDENT KILLED. TEACHER IN CUSTODY.

"They've got me tried and convicted. Mason's blood on my steering wheel convinced the judge to deny me bail. Why would I touch the steering wheel, but not use my car to get the hell away?" Elijah turned toward the patch of blue sky visible through his window. "How can I teach again in this town, even if they do find me innocent?"

"The district hasn't tried you. They think you might be innocent, or they wouldn't be giving you paid administrative leave."

Elijah's lip curled. "The district may be paying me for getting rid of a rotten boss."

"It says there might have been an eyewitness," Theo said, then watched for a reaction and got none. "Kate didn't see the murderer. This damn rag will say anything to sell papers."

"It doesn't say who the eyewitness was." Elijah propped himself against the cement wall. "But anybody watching the TV footage of the crime scene would have seen Kate there. Who else has the master key and night access? You'd better watch her, Theo. The murderer may think she knows more than she does."

Theo folded the paper and slipped it under the pillow. Keeping an eye on Kate Mahoney would be as much fun as guarding the queen bee in a hive. Opportunity for plenty of stings.

"The best thing you could do to protect her is tell me why your car was in the parking lot and where you were during those early morning hours." Theo eyed the slender giant. "For Kate's safety, we've got to find the real murderer. I need some facts—and you've got them. Maybe you're taking the fall for somebody else. Maybe you've got a suspect yourself."

Elijah's eyes brightened, then looked away.

Theo persisted. "Who're you protecting?" Someone more important than a principal.

Elijah banged on the bars, summoning the guard.

On a hunch, Theo produced the name that Kate had distributed to staff. "Are you protecting Jacqueline?"

For the first time, he saw fear in the tall man's eyes.

"Guard, this gentleman needs to be escorted out." Elijah faced his visitor, who could smell the fear. "And he isn't to come back!"

Theo left contented. He'd learned more than he'd expected.

For three days, yellow tape had cordoned off Elijah's first grade classroom and shared office. A substitute teacher and the school psychologist moved his first graders to the library. Pat Jackson was left to deal with thirty-one curious fifth graders in the room next to the crime scene. With her office also off limits, she had no place to stash away memos, like the one she now read for the third time.

To: All staff
From: Kate

Please send me the name and description of any student, parent, or person associated with Saguaro by the name of Jacqueline. This includes district personnel who work here occasionally. This request is of the greatest importance. The names should be in my office by noon tomorrow.

Noon tomorrow! Who had time to look through the files? Pat believed that poor kids have only one possession—time—and she used it like a miser, filling every hour with as much learning as she could cram in. How to save time? She'd have the children write down mother's first names. That would have to do.

Giggles by the movable wall claimed her attention.

"Louie." Pat nodded toward his empty seat.

Louie Castillo disengaged his ear from the wall that separated the two rooms. As he wiggled the aviator glasses on the bridge of his nose, they began to slip. Innocent brown eyes gleamed from beneath long black lashes. "Just getting a book that fell down behind the bookcase."

Gladys tittered and fingered the soft collar on her indigo velvet dress, crossed her legs, and swung matching velvet slippers. The other kids wore ragged jeans and faded tee shirts, so Gladys with her long blonde ringlets was different. She didn't care what the other kids thought. Except for Louie. She sent him an approving smile that sobered under Ms. Jackson's gaze.

During this final study period, Pat moved on cat feet around the room getting fakers back on track. Tamoni's kinky black head was bent over his work—practicing gang graffiti. Pat picked up his practice sheet with one hand and opened his spelling book with the other. He groaned and dropped his head into folded arms. He'd been that way since Elijah had been put in jail. No motivation. No interest in school.

Maybe a short break would get him going.

"Boomer." She motioned to the new student.

Navigating his awkward one hundred and eighty pounds between desks, Boomer bumped into Louie, dislocating a baseball cap. Their eyes met. Louis mouthed, "It's okay." They knocked heads as they dove to retrieve it.

Rubbing his forehead, Boomer stopped in front of his teacher. Half African American, half Anglo, his dark brown hair was coarse. An uncoordinated hulk, he placed both feet rigidly together in a conscious effort to keep them out of trouble. Clasping his hands firmly, he lowered his head to check whether his other extremities were under control.

"Boomer, would you do water fountain duty?"

Keeping his head bowed, he looked up at his teacher through cinnamon eyelashes.

"Yes, Mrs. Jackson."

"You did a good job yesterday, Boomer." The innocence of the lad brought a smile to her lips. "You keep the water on at a steady pace. That's what the classroom council had in mind when they gave you the duty of keeping the water on while students get their drinks."

Boomer beamed, turned and moved gravely toward the object of his responsibility.

"Table four, you may get a drink."

As she expected, Tamoni was first out of his seat. He sprang for the water fountain and landed on Boomer's foot. The big boy responded by increasing the flow of water as Tamoni bent down to get a drink.

Eyes full of water, Tamoni lashed out. The gentle giant picked him off his feet, laid him carefully down on the carpet next to Gladys's desk and sat on him. Gladys placed a velvet slipper on Tamoni's hand and pressed down. Hard. The howling boy struggled to get to her. Immovable as a sumo wrestler, Boomer kept his head down, shaking it slowly while his eyes sought out the teacher.

"Who saw what happened?" A roomful of eyes said "yes," while the heads shook "no." A firm hand on the Hercules's shoulder brought Tamoni's release.

"She was in on it, too." Tamoni fingered Gladys, who looked up wide-eyed, pencil poised midair. "Look at this!" Brandishing his reddened hand, he pointed at Gladys. "You sneaky little bitch!"

Gladys arched her eyebrows. "Where did you ever learn to talk that way, Tamoni?"

The class snickered. Everybody in this neighborhood knew how to talk that way.

"I can't imagine what he's babbling about, Mrs. Jackson. He's interrupting my studying. Can't you make him behave?"

The teacher gripped Tamoni with her left hand and Boomer with her right. She motioned with her chin for Gladys to follow as she hauled the boys out the door and released them on the sidewalk. How she wished the cops would give her back her office!

"All three of you know the rules." She positioned herself between Tamoni and Gladys. "Ms. Mahoney handles all fights. And believe me," she eyed Gladys, "she has no mercy."

"Yeah, here people just get murdered," smart-mouthed Tamoni.

Gladys put her hands on her hips, stuck her nose up in the air, and turned away, while Boomer began to whimper. The teacher reached out to soothe him, then pulled her hand back. No fights—just like the other kids.

Comforted by the inadvertent touch, the large boy stopped sniffling, aligned his feet and hands and scowled. "Bad boy—mean to Boomer. Bad boy—Jacqueline will get you."

"Who's Jacqueline, Boomer?"

The boy lowered his eyes and became silent.

"It's important." Pat tried to look Boomer in the eye. Impossible. "You must tell me, Boomer. Who's Jacqueline?"

A hint of recognition flashed across Tamoni's eyes, and he almost smiled.

"Who's Jacqueline, Tamoni?" Her tone demanded an answer.

"Beats me." He looked away.

Kate Mahoney scanned piles of papers arranged on her desk. The largest stack had to be handled today; the second, sometime this week; and the third was fodder for long reports for Central Office. She pushed the third behind her computer, pretending it wasn't going to eat up her weekend.

At the moment, she was focused on Mr. and Mrs. A. J. Rogers, who were being ushered in by Terri. "These are Rosella Rogers's parents, Mrs. Mahoney." The tall secretary shot Kate a warning glance as she closed the door behind her and went on her way.

The shapely Mrs. Rogers was in her twenties and wore tight blue jeans. Her scrawny neck rose from the French-cut neckline of a plain white tee. Her face looked weary from miles traveled more than years lived. Her eyes, outlined in black, flashed indignation. The rhythm of her gum set her tempo. Feet apart, she held her arms akimbo. Long red fingernails tapped impatiently on thin hips, keeping time with her gum. Nothing unusual there.

What concerned Kate was Mr. A. J. Rogers. About five feet two inches, a couple inches shorter than his wife, he wore a long, studded denim vest over a dirty white undershirt and stood in front of the door, blocking it. His scowl, made sinister by the droop of a dishwater blonde mustache, mirrored his wife's displeasure. The tattoos on his arms were the kind cons got in prison. Kate worked with dads like him every day, but something about him made the hair on the back of her neck rise.

"Won't you have a seat, Mr. and Mrs. Rogers?"

The wife began to sit, then glanced at her husband, who tightened his arms across this chest. She remained standing and increased the pace of her finger tapping.

Something kept Kate standing behind her desk. Again, she felt her flesh prickle. She'd learned to trust gut feelings, so she shifted mentally to the worst-case scenario. Every inch of the man's stance threatened physical harm. But how much harm could he do? He didn't weigh as much as she did. If they both attacked her, she could hold them off until her screams brought the office staff. Terri, the body builder, could deck the mister, and she'd take the wife. They'd sit on them till the police arrived.

"I'm Kate Mahoney, Rosella's principal. How can I help you?"

The man's growl was low and mean. "After what you've done to our kid, you got your nerve, standin' there all sweet and honey-like."

Rogers. Rosella Rogers. Kate's face remained "sweet and honey-like" while her brain ran at warp speed, reviewing recent discipline infractions. There was a Rogers there somewhere, but she couldn't place the child. Must be new to Saguaro.

"Wouldn't you be more comfortable sitting down?" The mother hesitated, then sat, digging the heels of her cowboy boots into the carpet. Kate was glad she wasn't wearing spurs. "Would you be kind enough to tell me what's bothering you?"

"You disgraced our pore Rosella, and you're standing there high and mighty." Father's eyes were cold and heartless. Used to prison life. "You need a whippin'."

Arizona Revised Statutes made it unlawful to threaten an educator in a public school. Kate didn't intend to inform him. He was so small. He could be handled.

"What's offended you, Mr. Rogers?"

"Listen to her, Mama." The tone to his wife was strangely tender and caring. "Actin' like she didn't humiliate our darlin' terrible. Pore little thing'll never be the same."

"Not likely," the mother nodded.

What's going on here? Kate wondered. Then she remembered. After lunch, Rosella Rogers, a third grader, had been eating bagged potato chips out in the playground. Kids were supposed to finish eating in the cafeteria. Kate made her sit by the cafeteria wall till she finished eating. Experience and Mr. Rogers's stance kept Kate from laughing aloud. *There's more to this than meets the eye.*

The mother began to sniffle. "To think that my little Rosella had to sit there—with all the kids staring at her. Laughing." She blew her nose loudly.

It would be useless to assure these parents that none of the kids even noticed the little girl finishing her lunch. This wasn't about Rosella. It was about these adults. What was going on?

Guessing that dad had been in the pen, Kate began to talk about a subject dear to every ex-con's heart—safety. She told them about the promise she made to every child and parent that Saguaro Elementary would be a safe place for children. How the principal and staff worked together to enforce zero tolerance for fighting. Their tension eased as they heard how older students were trained to mediate as Conflict Managers on the playground.

"That's what I want for my kid. A safe place!" By now, Dad's hands were on his hips, although he didn't leave the door. Ex-con dads valued safety for their kids above all else. "Maybe we oughta forgive this here principal, Ruby." He moved over to his wife and put his arm around her shoulders.

She beamed up at him.

"She's doin' the best she can. She's got a hell of a job."

The wife sighed, her fingers stopped drumming. Those on her right hand curled around his wrist. She fastened reddened eyes on Kate. "It's so good to have Jake home from the Big House. He done two years for assault and battery." The offense was disclosed with pride. "He knows how to protect people."

Kate felt a cold shiver creep up her arms. Time for this parental conference to come to an end. They exchanged pleasantries. As she ushered Mr. and Mrs. A. J. Rogers out the door, she saw what her nervous system had sensed. Two hunting knives hung from Mr. Rogers's belt. Hidden by his vest, one was about ten inches long, the other twelve. She steadied herself against the doorframe and took a deep breath as the two lovebirds departed, then turned her attention to three fifth graders.

"They've been fighting. Mrs. Jackson brought them in." Terri nodded toward the offenders.

The three were a study in contrast. Gladys and Tamoni huddled together, smiling at each other and practically holding hands, while Boomer stood apart, isolated and miserable. Hostile enemies often congealed into a cooperative mass when faced with a real and present danger: the principal. Boomer wasn't bright enough to play that game. She read Pat's description of the foray and motioned the children into her office.

Gladys scooted into the upholstered chair until her back rested against its plush support. Her legs dangled awkwardly. Taking his cue from her, Tamoni shifted continuously in his chair, grasping both armrests with a white-knuckled grip. Boomer remained standing, assuming the only business-like posture he knew—feet aligned and monitored, hands grasped in front and controlled.

"*Stand up!* This is *not* a social meeting." After the previous encounter, Kate would have liked to gather these chicks in her arms, give them each a warm kiss, and send them on their way, mentally thanking them for being so uncomplicated and forgiving in their hostilities.

But that was not to be. Fights, when she'd arrived at the school, were mandatory. Everyone had at least one fight per day. No more! A fight with a classmate meant a fight with the principal. They were increasingly rare. Kate intended to keep it that way.

Thinking of what made her maddest in the entire world—child abuse—she drew from a rich supply of adrenaline, transferred her anger to the case at hand, and gave them her most withering stare. "*What* did you think you were *doing*? Fighting stands for everything this school is against!"

The two froze. Boomer remained unmoved. In emergencies, he had one card, and that's the only one he played.

Face blanched, Gladys squeaked out the story she and Tamoni had agreed upon.

"It was all just a silly mistake, Mrs. Mahoney." She gulped, wet her lips and continued. "Tamoni stepped on Boomer's foot by accident." Another breath. Lying takes oxygen. "Then Boomer," she leaned close to the principal and whispered, "you know how he is."

Kate scowled. Gladys drew back, stricken but undaunted. "Well, Boomer got mad. We can't blame him; he doesn't know better. He picked Tamoni up and threw him on the floor, right by my foot." She sneaked a sideways glance at Tamoni, who was nodding frantically, rubbing his injured hand. "Well, with all the commotion, I jumped up and by accident landed on Tamoni's hand." With a final rush of breath, she scrambled to the finish. "I didn't mean to. Forgive me, Tamoni."

Silence. For a full minute, the three sizzled under Kate's glare. Finally, Boomer broke the stillness. "Bad Boy. Bad Girl. Bad Boomer."

Kate touched his shoulder. "It's good to know somebody is telling the truth. What do you have to say, Tamoni?"

His eyes focused on the ceiling, the boy shuffled nervously. "He's telling the truth." He stole a sideways peek at Gladys and shuddered at the return glare. Kate suppressed a smile.

"You all know we don't allow fighting here at Saguaro." Kate's tone became that of a detached judge. "The three of you will report for noon-time detention tomorrow and four more days." She turned to Gladys. "You get an extra day for lying. Go back to the classroom. The boys will follow shortly."

Kate wanted the little lady to cool off before she encountered Tamoni alone. After Gladys minced out, Kate cupped Boomer's chin in her hand, unsuccessfully trying to establish eye contact. "If someone is bad to you, Boomer, you tell the teacher. She'll make them be good to you."

A hum, and then, "I sit on them."

So do I, Boomer, Kate thought, *so do I.*

When Coach's figure filled her office door, Kate glanced at her watch. Still school hours. Strange. This was the first time he'd stepped inside Saguaro Elementary.

"Got a minute?" Before Kate could answer, he'd closed the door and moved a chair up to her desk.

Kate tried not to stare. The man before her looked and smelled as if he'd been on an all night drunk.

"You haven't been back to your school like this."

He shook his head.

"Thank God!" The kids at Agave Elementary saw enough "hung over" adults in their neighborhoods. The principal had to be the steady rock in their unsteady world. Not this one. Not now.

"I called in sick. And I am." Body Beautiful looked sick. Bloodshot eyes underlined with blue bags. His shoulders sagged, and his blonde hair needed a comb. Probably a wash.

Kate waited. So did Coach. Finally, she guessed. "You haven't been sleeping?"

He nodded.

"You've been drinking. A lot."

Another nod. "That's all I've been doing since—"

"I saw you at the interrogation at Central Office. You were okay then."

Coach's large frame relaxed a little. He reached for a cigarette, then, remembering where he was, shook his head. "I've been drinking since the police worked me over that day. You...you didn't tell them about the shit Julie gave us for low test scores, did you?"

Kate breathed a sigh of relief. "No. I'm pretty sure none of us did. If that's all you're worried about—"

"That's not all. There's more."

Kate didn't want to hear it. Confessions go with confessionals. She remembered kneeling in a stuffy, airless closet heavy with the garlic of the previous penitent, squeaking out her sins to the God substitute on the other side of the curtained grill. Was the heat in the confessional because of a warm day, or was it a premonition of things to come...in a very hot hell? No, Kate didn't want to hear confessions. Especially, she didn't want to hear about mortal sins. Like murder.

But Coach wasn't about to accuse himself of murder. Otherwise, why would he be careful about the testing leak? Not murder. Motive for murder? She didn't want to hear it. But the human being on the other side of her desk was so miserable, she heard herself saying, "Want to talk about it?"

Coach cleared his throat and began.

In the Classroom...

From her window seat, Sister Katherine O'Brien considered the novices gathered for Mother Provincial's homily on the vows of poverty, chastity, and obedience. Their innocent faces, so vulnerable...sacrificial. A sea of trusting lambs. Eyes intense. Jugular veins exposed. She was the exception. The one goat.

"In summary, my daughters, you'll find that poverty is the least painful of the three vows. All of your needs will be met. The perfection of this vow is in your internal detachment from small things.

"The vow of chastity implies a discipline that you've all demonstrated. You'll transform your sexual desires into the love of Christ and service to His children. He will protect you."

Sister Katherine studied the lambs. *Do they know what they're giving up?* Veiled eyes gave no clue.

"But then there's the vow of obedience. Obedience: submitting your will to the will of another for the love of God. I guarantee you'll feel the pinch of this vow every day."

Oversize beads hanging from Mother's waist clicked against the desk as she rose. "My daughters, pray for me as I pray for you daily. You are dismissed. Sister Katherine, please see me."

The novices, observing Great Silence, waited for Mother and Sister Katherine to leave the classroom, then proceeded to their duties. Hushed as mutes.

Mother Provincial led Katherine into Mother Mistress's office, where she closed the door and sat at the desk. Its surface was empty except for a small crucifix that stood upright, as if it were a tree growing out of the wood. She nodded the novice toward the only other furniture in the room, a straight back chair. The faint smell of candle wax suggested a spent votive.

"My daughter, is something troubling you?"

Sister Katherine walked to the chair, but remained standing. "You know bloody well! Kidnapping me so I'm under your power. Again! I want out of this dream! Now!"

Slowly, the elder nun placed her hands on the desk. Her unpolished nails were neatly trimmed. "There's no need to be discourteous, sister. I don't control your dreams. I merely participate in them. In a manner of speaking, we're both acting under obedience, aren't we?" Mother commented dryly. "But we need to put this little row aside and get on to more important matters."

"What could be more important than my freedom?"

"Your life, Sister Katherine…your life." Mother rose and moved around the desk. "Your life is in danger, sister." She reached for the young nun's arm.

Sister Katherine withdrew it. "You're not scaring me!" The novice sounded terrified.

Sadness clouded the Provincial's eyes. "All right, I won't call you by your religious name if you wish, Katherine."

"Kate."

"Kate. Evil persons believe you saw Julie Mason's killer. They plan to eliminate you."

"Eliminate?"

"Kill."

Sister Katherine gasped, felt for the chair behind her, and sat down.

Mother's voice gentled. "You need to seek sanctuary in a hidden place until this murderer is found. I suggest our Irish Motherhouse on the Aran Isles in Galway Bay. You'd be safe and welcome there."

The novice moistened her lips. Her eyes flicked as she gripped the edges of her chair. "You'll do anything to control me. Well, I have no vow of obedience, and I want you out of my life."

Mother touched her sleeve. "Kate. I want to protect you. Please listen. Listen…"

4

It was raining on Superintendent Julie Mason's funeral. A slow drizzle turned rivulets on the pile of dirt next to the casket to mud, forcing the clusters of mourners, principals, central office administrators, and secretaries to the other side.

The gray sky dripping down over concrete tombstones didn't dampen spirits. In voices not subdued enough, the educators chatted about the identities of the few friends who had turned out for the occasion.

Rain was unusual in Tucson in October. In this desert city, where daily sunshine is the norm, this surprise shower caught most participants without umbrellas. The principals, used to getting down and grubby with the kids, wore washable garb. Even the central office administrators in their dry-cleaned attire tolerated the sprinkle with good grace.

The smell of rain and wet earth is the perfume of choice for desert dwellers. Kate felt her curls tighten and her makeup disintegrate. She didn't care. Life was good. Her annoyance with last night's dream was gone, its message ignored. Even her guilt over enjoying the funeral didn't diminish the day.

"All your principals turned out except one."

The voice at her elbow was familiar; only the cigar was missing. Kate felt the drizzle cease as Theo held an umbrella over her head.

"Isn't your investigating here a bit obvious, Officer Buloski?"

She turned to face him. With her under the umbrella, Theo was out in the rain, a situation she made no attempt to remedy. Drops splashed off his bald crown and worked their way down along his ears and nose.

The turned up collar of his trench coat kept the flow from soaking in, making him the only waterproofed mourner.

"Don't school administrators watch the weather report?"

"We don't have time," she murmured. When Theo moved in to listen, Kate shifted to the far side of the umbrella. The police officer edged into the space she'd surrendered.

"Why are you here?" she stage whispered. "Homicide detectives don't belong at funerals. Mourners need a degree of respect."

His guffaw attracted the attention of the principals at hand. Kate glared. When the stares had subsided, the officer continued in hushed tones. "Don't give me a bad time because my grief doesn't match that of your fellow mourners. If I'd known her, I'd probably be as happy as the rest of you."

"I repeat...why are you here?" Kate wouldn't be pacified by a mere umbrella. Neither would she reject it.

"Like I said, I'm checking out who's here and who's missing."

"That's investigating. Consistent with your undercover work at Saguaro."

"Nope. This is unofficial. I'm going to solve this murder on my own time, more or less," he whispered into Kate's ear. Had she been less curious she'd have put some distance between her ear and that cigar breath.

"You're supposed to be working for the school right now."

"Look at you. The only negative person at this funeral. I'm working...to get your teacher back and me out of your school. What's not to like about that?" Drips off the umbrella that he tipped in her direction caused Kate to move closer to him. "Now look around. Who's missing?"

A quick look told her the only principal missing was Jacqueline Stanley. *Jacqueline? Could she be Mother Provincial's Jacqueline? Impossible. Damn! That nun had planted seeds of distrust.*

As if reading her mind, the cop echoed her thoughts. "Jacqueline Stanley. Bull's eye!"

"How do you know so much about the principals?"

"Study. Study. Study."

"She didn't do it."

Theo took a cigar out of his breast pocket. Sniffed it and returned it. "Probably not. If she'd done it, she wouldn't risk sticking out by not showing up. Probably just an independent spirit. But from what I've heard, independent spirits irked Her Majesty, Queen Mason." He tightened his coat collar.

Coach had his beautiful, pregnant wife at his side. His eyes met Kate's, and he turned away.

Theo was looking in the other direction. "Who's that tall guy over there with the cutie on his wing?"

Kate had noticed Wallace Talbot from the moment he and his blonde companion had exited their BMW. Her mint green silk suit was streaked by droplets that followed the ample curves the cut of the suit was designed to display. Her tight curls were relaxing with the rain. As the rain watered down her makeup, it revealed a beauty who was no youngster. Probably in her early forties. Wallace held a newspaper over her head.

Theo insisted, "Who is he, why is he here, and who's that with him?"

Kate glanced at the casket. "Dr. Mason often made friends with business partners. I don't know the blonde. Might have been an acquaintance of the deceased." For the first time that morning, Theo took a notebook from his pocket and jotted a few lines. Then he settled into a silence that Kate considered blessed.

Dr. Mason, not one to share the spotlight, liked her male business contacts without ladies on their arms. The mint green suit kept brushing against the gray striped business suit. Probably not casual acquaintances. Kate planned to get an introduction.

Thunder growled. The drizzle threatened to turn into a deluge. Since the only immediate family member, a sister from Yuma, had already arrived, the undertaker began on time. The service was over in fifteen minutes. No eulogies from grieving family or colleagues. Singing Julie Mason's praises wasn't worth a soaking. Theo and his umbrella followed Kate like a permanent appendage as she approached the sister to offer sympathy and continued at her side when she attempted to chat with Coach and meet his wife. Seeing her approach, Coach took his wife by the arm and moved in the opposite direction. Kate wasn't surprised.

She turned her attention to Wallace Talbot. Suspecting that everyone who came in contact with Theo was under surveillance, Kate chose her words carefully.

"Nice of you to come, Wallace."

The tall buxom blonde stepped between them and peered into the principal's eyes with a look of exaggerated confidence, almost smugness. "I'm Flora Anderson, Wallace's executive secretary at Icarus Construction."

The secretary's handshake was strong, the large diamond ring on her right middle finger twisted inward and pressed painfully into Kate's palm. She suppressed a wince and looked down at the secretary's big boned wrists. This woman was strong, despite her thinness. Thin, except for curves in the most fortunate places. "Kate Mahoney, principal at—"

"Saguaro Elementary. Wallace has told me *all* about you. I hear you do wonderful work with the poor little kiddies in *that* part of town."

Flora's ability to antagonize was immediate, not a plus for an executive secretary. Wallace extended his hand past Kate to the man at her elbow. "Wallace Talbot."

"Theo Buloski, a friend of Kate's. Glad to be with her in her time of mourning. Sometimes a lady needs a strong shoulder to cry on."

Kate could've killed him. Flora reached over and rested a manicured hand on his arm. "You men can be so helpful!"

Theo blushed and shifted the umbrella to shield Flora. The rain suddenly hit Kate's neck and began to course down her suit. Theo moved under the umbrella toward Flora. "That's my job. I'm the school resource officer at Saguaro. Broad shoulders are a job requirement."

"A cop!" Flora jerked her hand back. With few parting words, the couple headed back to their car. Theo watched them, beaming.

"Well, Flora certainly rang your bells," sniffed Kate. "If you hadn't revealed your occupation, she'd still be fawning over you."

"That's why I told her…to get her reaction." Satisfaction softened the lines in his face.

"I think it's terrible. Sleuthing among mourners at a funeral."

Theo pulled out a cigar with its implied threat. "Nah, Madam Principal, I ain't got no couth. It's downright damnable. Almost—

but not quite—as bad as murder." He bit off the end of his cigar and chuckled.

Ten minutes to six, and Tamoni's mom hadn't shown for the five-thirty conference Kate had scheduled as her last meeting of the day. She wanted plenty of time to talk. The principal hoped to win the woman's confidence, and then bring in the classroom teacher at a future date. So far, the mother had refused to meet with Tamoni's teacher.

What was this woman like? She sounded young and uncertain over the phone, probably little more than a youngster herself. During a home visit, the school nurse had learned that Mom had been on drugs when she was carrying Tamoni, hence his learning disability. Maybe she still used.

The office door cracked open, and Tamoni stuck his head in. "My ma sent me to tell you she can't come. Goodbye." He slammed the door and was gone.

Kate sprinted across the room, out the door, and swooped down on the fifth grader, who was already sauntering across the playground. "You live close by?" She'd checked his address and knew he lived in a large apartment two blocks from school.

The boy's gait quickened. "What's it to you?"

"Is your mom home now?"

He nodded yes, then said, "No."

"Let's go find out. West Wind Apartments, number 32, right?"

The streetlights glowed as dusk set in. Principal and student walked across the playground's browning Bermuda grass that was still watered twice a week to prolong the green. Watered at night to keep folks from having sex on the playground. In the desert summer, it cost nearly two hundred dollars a month to water a piece of grass the size of a double-wide trailer, so the school yard with its own well was an oasis of green amid a square mile of dusty brown.

The wind of October brushed land worn down by the brutal heat of summer. Weeds and grasses that had grown knee high during August monsoons, now dead and brown, lined the streets. Streets with no sidewalks. Giant brown plastic garbage cans dotted the curbs like silent watchdogs. Pointy stalked yuccas and prickly pear cacti were planted under windows to discourage break-ins.

Silently, they passed an empty lot, where high weeds hid an abandoned couch, old tires—a wildcat dump. On Tamoni's block, a single wooden cottage, whose owner was a holdout from the days, a generation ago, when this was a middle-class neighborhood, sat nearly hidden between two large apartment complexes.

On his own turf now, Tamoni's stride turned sassy. Defiance against her intrusion into his world? Or was he enjoying the attention? A little of both, Katherine thought. As they approached the complex, a couple of kids hung out of windows and squealed greetings. Five teenagers wearing the black and gold colors of the Rattlesnake Barrio gang were smoking in the stairwell. A comment made in Spanish as principal and student brushed past brought a low laugh. No children were playing outside now that it was getting dark.

Orange construction paper jack-o-lanterns grinned from one window, while a black witch on a broomstick flew across another. Products of school art classes. TVs blared from nearby apartments.

"What's your mother's name, Tamoni?"

"Mrs. Jones."

"Her first name?"

His pace slowed as he approached apartment 32. "Jacqueline. And don't call her Jackie. She doesn't like that." He stopped two doors short. "Mrs. Mahoney, is this a good idea? If she wanted to see you, she'd have come to school."

Jacqueline! She must meet Jacqueline. Tamoni was fitting his key into the lock when the door opened from the inside.

"I couldn't help it, Mom. She made me bring her here." The black chenille head bobbed under the mother's arm and disappeared into a back room.

Jacqueline Jones wasn't what Kate had expected. Not a kid. Thirty-something. Tall and slender, she had high cheekbones and full, red lips. Her delicate features were framed by fuzzy hair that had been washed, but not set. Freshly manicured nails the color of her lips were coated with flour. She dabbed them against her apron.

"So you came, did you?" She was definitely Tamoni's mom. The same big, brown eyes. The same caution. "Well, now that you're here, you might as well come in."

The apartment could have belonged to a college kid. Oversized pillows, probably picked up at a thrift shop, were stacked together to form seats in front of the TV. A desk cluttered with papers and books took up one corner. The small pile was Tamoni's classroom textbooks. The larger pile—*American History, General Math, Stanford Dictionary*—was definitely not his. A green study lamp illuminated the makeshift desk formed by a flat door laid across stacked cement blocks. Partially burned, fat, chunky candles were scattered around the cramped living/kitchen area. A set of real drums, not toys, occupied the second corner. The overall effect was poor, but tidy.

Jacqueline's eyes followed those of the principal. She nodded toward the drums. "A friend got those for Tamoni. He figured there was jazz in my boy's energy, and he was right. Tamoni can make those drums talk. I'd let him drum for you now, but the neighbors have been complaining." She nodded to a kitchen chair. "Sit down. I've got to finish this bread." Up to her wrists in dough, she continued. "I didn't come 'cause you'll say the same as all the other teachers at all the other schools. Tamoni is bouncy. Don't you think I know that?" She punched the dough, picked it up, and slammed it back into the bowl. "Sometimes, I can hardly stand it. He's never still."

"Mrs. Jones—"

"And I know it's my fault. So don't be telling me. I don't do drugs no more." Another slap against the dough. "But I can't take the harm back, can I?" She gave the dough a final pat, tucked it in around the edges, carefully rounded its top, and covered it with a clean dish towel. "So I try to make life here as good as I can, but I know school's hard for him." Fierce dark eyes snapped at Kate.

Kate looked away. "Maybe it doesn't have to be hard. Work with us, Mrs. Jones. We'll find Tamoni's strengths and run with them." She chose her words carefully. Tamoni would be listening from the bedroom, and she didn't want to echo the mother's pessimism. "You'd be surprised what a bit of confidence can do for a child. Could he bring his drums to school? Maybe I could get him into the school band."

"That's what my friend was going to do, once Tamoni got better." Jacqueline Jones attacked the table with a wet dishcloth. "But my friend can't do it now. He's in trouble." She sat down, suddenly tired, and stared out the window. Tears slid down her cheeks. No facial muscle moved.

Kate reached across the table and touched her arm. No response. They sat in silence for a couple of minutes until the tears stopped as suddenly as they'd begun. "You can call me Jacqueline, Mrs. Mahoney." She patted the outstretched hand, and a sheepish smile curled the ends of her lips.

"And you can call me Kate, but not when Tamoni's around."

The mother's smile held. "I guess you need all the authority you can muster when dealing with my boy."

"You've got that right. I'll talk to the band teacher. Will you give permission for some testing, so we can get Tamoni some special help?"

Jacqueline nodded, and Kate pulled out a permission form that the mother read and signed. "Does your friend who helped Tamoni live in this neighborhood?"

"Doesn't live here—but he works here." Jacqueline corrected herself. "Used to work here."

Kate took the mother's hand. "I hope things get better for him." Her professional work done, she hesitated. "Jacqueline, did you ever meet Elijah Stewart, our first grade teacher? He's taken quite an interest in Tamoni."

Jacqueline didn't raise her eyes. "Elijah Stewart? Never heard of him." Tamoni stuck his head out of the bedroom door, his eyes large and uncertain.

Elijah had mentioned meeting her when Tamoni first came to Saguaro. Was this woman lying, or had she forgotten? Jacqueline Jones's lips were pressed firmly together. No use questioning her further. "Could I use your phone?"

"Sorry, they disconnected it when we couldn't pay the bill. When I got your note, I called you from the neighbor's phone." The mother offered her hand. "Do you want Tamoni to walk back with you? These are rough streets once the sun goes down."

Kate smiled at the implied role reversal. Truth was, she didn't want him out on these streets after dark. "No problem. I'm used to this neighborhood, and it's only two blocks. Stop by the school when you can. I'd like to introduce you to Mrs. Jackson, Tamoni's teacher."

"I've heard she's strict, but fair. Boomer has her for a teacher, too. He lives a couple doors down." The mother nodded in the direction of the stairway.

Kate left with the feeling she'd missed something. Well, at least she had the permission for testing.

The sweltering heat of summer had made Kate forget how quickly chill settled in on dark October evenings. She hugged herself, wishing she'd worn a jacket. As she neared the alley on the final block, tall oleander bushes cut off her view of the houses on her side of the street. Across the street was an empty lot.

She knew she was in trouble when two bullets took out the streetlights on either side of the alley. Simultaneously, doors of what appeared to be an empty black Buick parked at the curb flew open, and three men wearing black ski masks got out. They began moving in uniform step toward Kate. The masked driver moved the car into the alley and got out, leaving four doors open.

Fingers of ice spread down Kate's back. She felt faint. She blinked her eyes, willing the men away. *This can't be happening to me!*

They kept coming.

Instinctively, she knew better than to change her pace. *Act as if nothing unusual is happening. Maybe nothing will happen. Maybe they're just trying to scare me. Slow and steady. They're advancing like tanks in a war zone!*

Their pace continued, machine-like. Deliberate. Slow. To terrorize. Closer. Every step a deliberate evil choice.

They're animals. They'll devour me.

Their controlled pace projected the brute confidence of predators in their prime. They were enjoying themselves.

Run! For God's sake, run! No! Shut up and think.

Her shaking legs didn't want to go on, but she gambled that she looked steady and cool. As if nothing were happening.

God, get me out of this, and I'll never do anything wrong again. It would be so easy, God. Just send a police car around the corner. Or any car! I'd run out in the street and get it to stop. Please, God! Any car!

No car came.

Kate knew they could've waited until she walked by their car, and then dragged her in. This walk was for their amusement. She could hear them thinking, "Is she so stupid she doesn't know what's happening? She'll find out."

I've got to do something. I'm almost up to them, and I don't know what to do! My mouth is so dry, I can't talk. My knees are going to give. I can't stand it. I can't! I can't!

They were an arm's length away. She could smell their brute intensity. They stopped—encasing her in a tight circle of black that slowly eased her into the alley. She felt a knife point at her throat, another at her back

Someplace, Kate had heard of some lower animal that was a gushy blob held together by an external skeleton. Puncture that skeleton and all the guts pour out.

That's me. And these knives will puncture my shell! No, not yet. The sharp blade pressing at my throat isn't penetrating. Not yet! I mustn't move!

"Well, look what we have here. A little chickie. Little Chickie, your Big Daddies are gonna to take you for a ride. Little Chickie Mahoney. You're gonna disappear. But, first, you're gonna spend a little time with us."

The voice was evil incarnate. A mixture of lust and hate. Kate had never heard a tone like that before. The voice belonged to the knifepoint at her back. She turned slowly to face it. The knives yielded to allow the turn.

"There must be some mistake. I'm not Mrs. Mahoney. She's the principal."

Who the hell is talking? My lips are numb. They don't even seem to be moving.

The feminine voice was cool and calm. As if correcting a casual error. "I'm Mrs. Cummings, the reading specialist. I teach Armando Castro. You know his father, Emilio Castro, I'm sure."

The knife points stood down. Emilio Castro, the drug dealer, was the chief authority in this square mile. Word was out that he liked the way the school was run. A private school had given up on his son, Armando, but at Saguaro, Mrs. Cummings was teaching the boy to read. Castro appreciated that, and everybody in the neighborhood knew it.

"What the fuck! No wonder she's not afraid." This from the knife at her back.

Its owner grabbed the gangster to Kate's left by his collar. "You fuckin' son-of-a-bitch. You said you knew Mrs. Mahoney. You said you remember her from when you were there. Take another look."

He thrust the shaken gangster into Kate's face. Only eyes glinted through his ski mask, but she'd recognize those eyes anywhere. Just four years ago, she'd been nose to nose with Juan Ramirez on a daily basis. Many a time, when he'd been in trouble, she'd searched those eyes for the truth. By chance, she'd discovered that Juan was a talented long distance runner, so on weekends she'd taken him to any run within twenty-five miles. Last year at Oasis High, he'd been a track star. Poor Juan. A wannabe betraying his friend to get into the gang.

Their eyes locked for a moment, then Juan pulled back.

"Fuck! So I made a mistake. It's dark out here, man, and Mrs. Cummings looks a lot like Mrs. Mahoney."

The blow from his leader sent him sprawling.

When she looked down at him in the light from the open car door, she saw he wasn't seriously hurt. She also saw that one of the assailants wore hiking boots—MERRELL—black and silver. Strange footwear for this part of town. Stranger still that she'd notice.

"Gentlemen. If you'll excuse me, I'll be on my way." Kate had no idea where the words were coming from. Her brain had been bypassed.

"Don't say a word of this to Mr. Castro." The leader sounded alarmed. "Okay?"

"I don't see why I should. As long as no harm comes to this lad." Kate was pressing her luck, and she knew it. "What was his name?"

"None of your concern. We'll take care of him." The leader's tone made the hair at the nape of her neck stand up. Poor Juan. Just a kid wanting to belong, who ended up with the wrong people. He'd probably get beat up. For his sake, she hoped he'd be thrown out of the gang.

As the men in black moved to their car, Kate realized that her terror had been diminished by concern for Juan. The moment the engine started, it returned. Chilled through, she stumbled in a daze toward the school.

Later, she remembered having a hard time unlocking the office door, then rushing inside and turning on the perimeter burglar alarm system. She'd sat paralyzed for...she didn't know how long. Finally, she pulled herself out of her stupor and called the police and Pop Jonesy.

"Officer, I've told you at least five times. I didn't know any of them. They had the build of young men in their late teens or twenties, but they all wore black ski masks." Kate sat stiffly on the teachers' lounge couch and pulled her jacket tighter around her neck. Still, she shivered. Her hands tried to eke warmth from the hot chocolate mug Pop had given her. The cocoa smell didn't belong here. It belonged in her childhood kitchen, where she was safe and snug even after Halloween adventures. Would she ever feel secure again? Pop stood behind her, his hands on her shoulders. Protecting as best he could.

"Bob, why are you on this call?" asked Theo Buloski, who'd been called in by the police dispatcher. "I'd think you'd have your hands full with the Julie Mason murder."

Tears welled in Kate's eyes, and she blinked them back and sipped her drink. She knew why Officer Bob McNary was there, and so did Theo.

"Don't bullshit me, Theo. You know those guys were after the witness to Mason's murder. That puts me square in the middle of this incident." He held up a hand to ward off Kate's protest. "I know you didn't see anyone that night, Mrs. Mahoney. But the newspapers put you there. Probably that's what these thugs were going on."

Bob McNary sat on the edge of a recliner, his forearms resting on legs that were anchored to the floor by the biggest feet Kate had ever seen. She thought of the four pairs of feet she'd seen in the alley. Three in sports shoes, one in hiking boots—MERRELL—black and silver. Funny, she remembered that. Moisture formed in her eyes. She took out a tissue and used it.

Bending until a lock of gray hair fell over his forehead, Bob McNary re-read his notes. Looking for something. "Very clever of you, Mrs.

Mahoney, to pass yourself off as the teacher of Castro's kid. What made you think of that?" He pushed back the wisp of hair, sat up straight, and relaxed back into the chair, settling in.

Pop's hands pressed harder into Kate's shoulders. She sensed his impatience, and she was tired. So tired. "It just came to me." She wanted to ward off the memory, not relive it. "They were right there. Around me. Close." She shuddered. "I can still smell them…and I kept thinking I needed a plan. Didn't have one. Then all of a sudden this popped out of my mouth. Not from my brain." She shrugged. "It just came out."

The officer scribbled a line or two. "But, you know, I can't figure out why they knew where you'd be? Were you fingered when you went into the public housing?"

"Apartments. We don't call them public housing at our school. Makes them sound too cheap." Kate almost laughed. Calling attention to such a small detail after a night like this. She was beginning to feel light-headed.

"Somebody knew you were headed down that street. Somebody who knew what you looked like must have alerted the thugs. Jacqueline Jones? Tamoni Jones?" He was on the edge of the recliner again. Getting his face close.

Pop's grasp tightened. "Don't you think she's been through enough, Officer? Can't we continue this tomorrow?"

Bob McNary ignored him. "If somebody could finger you, then how did you get away with this mistaken identity ploy?"

Kate wouldn't look up. The first part of her answer was true. "I really don't think Jacqueline or Tamoni had anything to do with it. For one thing, their phone is disconnected. There wouldn't have been enough time to contact those three…beasts. I don't know who those three were." She had to exclude Juan. He wasn't a beast. Misguided, but not a beast. "And, obviously, they didn't know me."

"Three? You had said there were four assailants. What was it—three or four?"

Officer McNary knew she was lying. She didn't have the energy to oppose him.

"There were four. Did I say three? Did I tell you one wore hiking boots?"

The eyes of the interrogating officer never left her face. He put up three fingers and nodded. Kate showed four fingers and stared blankly. McNary shook his head, closed the notepad, and stuck it into his pocket. "We'll continue this tomorrow."

With a sigh of relief, Kate watched Theo usher the officer out.

Several hours later, in bed when she couldn't sleep, she tried to determine what to do about Juan. He'd saved her life. She couldn't implicate him. Still, he was a link to the brutes sent by the murderer. She'd think about it in the morning when her mind was clearer.

As it happened, she never had to decide. It was five o'clock in the morning when the opening custodian found Juan's strangled body on the sidewalk in front of Mrs. Mahoney's office. The cord that killed him had two ends. A picture torn out of last year's yearbook identifying Mrs. Mahoney was threaded on one end. On the other end was a dirty piece of newsprint inscribed with the words, "PRINCIPAL'S PET."

In the Laundry...

With the temperature in the novitiate laundry fifteen degrees hotter than outside, large overhead fans replaced hot air laced with the smell of scorched steam with more hot air. Humidity was so high it could have rained. The weekly six-hour stint in the laundry was enough to try the vocation of any novice, its real function less obvious than clean sheets.

Sister Mary Bridget, the laundress, had the process down to a system, and the young nuns cooperated. Partly through obedience. Partly to finish as quickly as possible. The low silence made the rumbles of the huge washing machines and presses seem louder. The nuns were practicing modesty of the eyes as they worked, meditating while the smell of bleach and soap replaced incense.

The postulants were emptying individual laundry sacks from a wheeled canvas cart onto a sorting table. Sheets went to one washer. Towels to another. Nothing went into the big washers until Sister Mary Bridget said so. It would be a grievous violation of poverty to have darkened sheets because some blue item had slipped into their wash.

Five novices surrounded a long wooden table, preparing laundry for the presses. Some folded cotton caps worn under the wimple, tails on the inside, patted down so they would go through the press flat with the nuns' laundry number visible on the outside of the cap.

As Mother Provincial moved among the young novices, she noticed their wimples drooping. Unconsciously, she felt hers. It had begun to soften. Best to complete this business quickly.

At a large mangle, Sister Katherine and a novice partner fed sheets into the giant rollers. Their timing was synchronized. A sheet fed at the wrong angle ended up crunched. Not perfect. Not even close. So the two novices kept checking each other's positioning of the ingoing sheets. The outgoing sheets had a faint, toasted odor from the mangle.

Did her partner notice the steady stream of tears rolling down Sister Katherine's cheeks? Maybe she thought they were sweat.

When Sister Katherine saw Mother standing beside her, she snapped, "Why are we ironing sheets? Who says it's more perfect to sleep between ironed sheets?"

"Tradition, Sister Katherine. Tradition."

"Christ's sheets weren't ironed."

Mother smiled. "Try telling that to the sisters who've been used to ironed sheets their entire religious life. That's what keeps us all on the same page, sister. Tradition and authority." Mother reached for the novice's hand and felt it jerk away.

The tears started again. "Don't you ever think of new ways? Can't you let some fresh air in?"

Mother motioned to another novice to take Sister Katherine's place and nodded to Sister Mary Bridget, who noticed immediately when a cog was removed from her fine-tuned system.

"A Mother Provincial who doesn't defend the status quo is a contradiction in terms. Come, sister." Mother steered the novice to the garden, where they drank in deep breaths of cool, fresh air. Mopping her face with a plain cotton handkerchief, Mother gingerly fingered her softened wimple. She chose a bench near the grotto, where a concrete St. Bernadette knelt before a concrete Virgin Mary.

Sister Katherine stared at the lush rhododendrons and velvet iris with eyes that didn't see. Tears began again.

Mother drew near. "Juan?"

Agony enveloped the novice. Not a sound escaped her lips, but her entire body was racked with convulsive grief. Mother took the young nun in her arms and rocked her like a baby.

"I should have told them who I was." Sobs blurred her words. "It was my fault. He was protecting me." She let out a wail. "I'll never get over the guilt."

"I know what you mean." Sadness settled over both women. "There's a stab of guilt when something bad happens on your watch, even if you didn't cause it."

Sister Katherine's sobs became fainter, then stopped. She pushed away.

"There was nothing you, Mrs. Mahoney, could have done. Except get yourself murdered, and that was hardly called for. Juan made the decision to join those gangsters. He knew they were dangerous."

"You called me Mrs. Mahoney."

"Yes, I don't want to irritate you further by complicating your identity. Although, Mrs. Cummings worked well for you."

"You! That's where the idea came from!" The light returned to the novice's eyes. "You put it in my head. You're allowed to do that?"

"Don't give me the credit. Your courage carried you through." Mother feigned modesty. "Although, I must admit, I've always been known for my quick thinking."

"But Juan—"

"You must leave Juan to God's mercy. He'll receive it because of the way he protected you." Mother Philippa fingered the Celtic Cross on her scapular. "But you must go into hiding."

"My school needs me. I don't run away from trouble."

Mother Philippa appeared not to hear. "Your dear childhood friend, now Mother General Casey Whitehall, has a room prepared for you at the Celtic Motherhouse on Innis Mor in Galway Bay. The murderers will never find you there. And the sisters have agreed to address you as Mrs. Mahoney and respect your widowed status."

"Never. Never in a million years. All due respect, Mother, but I don't want to set foot in a convent again. Not ever." The wimple folds framing her face had softened into droops.

"Then I can only pray for you, my daughter, for you are in mortal danger." Mother Provincial turned and left Sister Katherine absorbed in thought.

5

Kate, followed by Officer Bob McNary and Theo, hesitated at the door of the faculty lounge. Ed Meyers, the custodian, had brought extra folding chairs, and she had picked up seven dozen assorted Dunkin' Donuts, confident that, as the day wore on, the staff would get its appetite back.

How could she be prepared for this meeting? Every child and teacher knew somebody who'd been murdered within the last few years. Within this square mile, there'd been four murders and ten unexplained deaths last year alone. But Juan was one of their own. Not their pride, but a former student, nevertheless. And he'd been left on the school's doorstep. His death violated the one safe place.

Teachers, cafeteria ladies, aides, custodians, and secretaries filled every niche in the lounge. All the chairs were taken. Some staffers were sitting on the floor. Tote bags, usually open and spilling over with papers to be graded, were untouched; not a red marking pen in sight. Kate had never heard this group so hushed. *Oremus Domine! Help me find the right words.*

Bonnie Roset, the district counselor, offered suggestions to help the children and staff cope. Somehow, the comforting smell of coffee made Kate feel guilty. Juan would never smell coffee again. She wondered how much the shocked staff was absorbing. She needed to pull the group together so they could support each other.

"Please review the 'Danger Stranger' signal that the children have learned to call when they sense trouble. They're to walk home in groups of at least two.

"I promise you, I'll give the solution of these two murders top priority. An excellent teacher has been taken from us. A former student, murdered. We need to help the police in any way possible, but carefully, so we don't become targets ourselves. And please don't talk to the Press camped outside the office door. Central Administration has sent over a person to handle them."

Afterwards, Kate was embarrassed she hadn't counted the death of the superintendent among the losses.

Officers McNary and Buloski stressed the need for relevant information, even if it seemed insignificant. Who were the three gang members who'd been with Juan? Were these thugs covering their own tracks or were they working for someone else?

Kate recalled that Coach Holman had been Juan's track mentor a couple of years back. The same Coach who, in confidence, had revealed his motive for welcoming Julie Mason's death. But Coach wasn't a man to commit murder; he wouldn't use a former student to silence her. No, he hadn't had to reveal his secret affair to Kate. If he'd been guilty, he wouldn't have said a word. She'd keep his confidence secret, but she'd probe the link between Juan and Coach herself. Still, she'd kept Juan's involvement secret, and now he was dead. If he'd been picked up by the cops last night, he'd still be alive. Was she being loyal or full of pride? Putting herself above the law?

The staff's mood had shifted from mourning to smoldering anger. There was that look Kate had seen so often in her people's eyes. It said, "I can do something about this." It frightened her.

"Folks, above all else, I caution you. Be careful. These people are killers."

Nobody seemed to be listening.

It was a great day for Clarissa Mae Fox. Today she was six years old, and there weren't many six-year-olds in Mrs. Woodworth's kindergarten class. Most of them were five-year-old babies.

This morning, Mama had braided her coal black hair into fourteen little pigtails that stuck out from her head like a halo. Each pigtail had a pink ribbon that matched her birthday dress. The dress was made of "or-gan-dee" that poofed out all over. Papa had taken one look at her and let out a low, surprised whistle. "Now, isn't that the prettiest girl I've ever seen."

Most kids don't have papas, so Clarissa knew that she was lucky. He loved her, and he'd never leave her. She wanted to be pretty for him.

When she checked out Papa's opinion in the mirror, she admired the contrast between the white of her eyes and her dark skin. She had pretty white teeth that looked good when she smiled. Papa was right!

But the best part of the day was happening right now. As the Birthday Girl, she got to take the "a-tin-dance" sheet to the office. She walked slowly, thinking about the big boy, Juan, who'd been murdered. His killers must have been really bad to dump him on the schoolyard. She felt kind of bad about that, but she wasn't going to let it ruin her day.

Bad things happen. Especially, men beat up women. Cops came all the time to the Desert Dreams Apartments, where she lived. But her Papa wouldn't hurt her mom or her, though he yelled sometimes. And she was safe here at school.

Before she left the classroom, Mrs. Woodward had reminded the kids to cry out, "Danger Stranger" if anybody they didn't know tried to give them a car ride or offered candy. Juan mustn't have known the "Danger Stranger" yell. Sometimes, it amazed Clarissa, what big kids didn't know.

Today, she was going to take the short cut to the office that only the big kids used. It was a gravel path between the old and new buildings that was so narrow most adults couldn't get through. People said a fat kid had been stuck in there once. The custodian had to grease him to get him out. That story probably wasn't true. Anyway, Clarissa was little. She wouldn't get stuck.

Once she had ventured into the "big kid" walkway, she tried not to think about the spiders and bad things that could be in this dark place. Big kids survived a trip through the short cut, and so could she. The light at the opening near the office became bigger and bigger as she approached it.

She was almost there when a giant at least ten times taller than Clarissa suddenly blacked out the light. She stretched her neck back to look way up to his face. It was almost covered with a black bushy beard. With his feet apart, he completely blocked the opening. He had something big in his hands. When it went flash, Clarissa guessed it was a special kind of gun. She was surprised she wasn't dead. The bullet must have missed her.

She let out a blood curdling, "Danger Stranger!" and tried to escape. It was too late. The giant grabbed her new skirt.

He kept saying, "I won't hurt you. I just want to talk to you," just like the teacher said a "Danger Stranger" would. Clarissa's heart beat so hard and fast, she thought it would pop out of her chest. She kicked and struggled, but she couldn't get away.

"Okay, little girl. Quiet down." He held her with one hand and used the other to pull a candy bar out of his shirt pocket.

The deadly candy trick! It was happening to her. With one final burst of strength, she slipped through his legs. Still he wouldn't let go. She bit him in the thigh with all her strength and hung on like a bulldog.

Tiny Pallado, star reporter for the Associated Press, let out a howl of anguish and released his intended interviewee.

Screaming, Clarissa flew around the corner and into the arms of Officer Theo. "He's back there," she sobbed, her entire body shaking. "He…he almost got me!"

With horror, she realized she'd dropped the "a-tin-dance" sheet. She'd have to go back to get it, but this time she'd have somebody with her. Her new problem distracted her, and her sobs decreased. She spat out threads from the stranger's pants with disgust. "He tastes awful!"

All three hundred pounds of Tiny limped around the corner, holding his aching leg. "Is there a school nurse here?" He gave Clarissa a dirty look. "What I need is a rabies shot!"

Theo knelt down to comfort the kindergartner. "It's all right. He may be a stranger, but he's not dangerous." He shot Tiny a cool glare. "As far as I know." Theo turned Clarissa over to Tiá, and the two went off to find the "a-tin-dance" sheet.

Theo cited Tiny for "Disturbing and hindering the operation of a public school," and the press got a story they hadn't expected.

Donny Adams, the gray-haired manager of West Wing Apartments, had just tumbled out of bed. Dirty jeans nearly covered the bottom half of his long johns, and the smell coming from the top made Kate wonder whether he wore them night and day. With a long time between washings.

He unlocked Jacqueline's door for the second time in twelve hours. "You guys get me out of bed in the middle of the night, 'cause she don't answer her door. So you find out she's gone." He looked up and down the woman with the two police officers. "So what's to see? Don't you guys ever sleep?" Ignored by the cops, he turned to the woman. "I can tell by the color of your skin you aren't related, so what do you want Jacqueline for?"

When Kate started to answer, Theo squeezed her elbow, and she remained silent. TVs blaring in adjacent apartments provided background for the manager's complaints. "I don't know what happened to her. Folks move out in the middle of the night all the time 'cause they owe rent. She was paid up. Don't figure."

The officers moved silently between the two rooms, trying unsuccessfully to turn on lights. The light bulbs had gone with Jacqueline. "Isn't that stealing? Her taking the bulbs? They were here when she moved in."

Ignoring the manager, the investigators resorted to flashlights, pausing now and then to scribble in their notebooks. "How do you remember things, Kate?" Theo asked.

"This," she felt the sandpaper roughness of cinder blocks topped by a smooth plank that had been a makeshift desk, "was piled high with books. Two stacks. One belonged to Tamoni. The others were like… high school texts. American history, books like that. A green desk lamp sat on this end. There were candles around the room."

The departure had been hurried. Hangers lay in the floor of the closet. The refrigerator was on and empty except for a half-filled carton of milk and a container of cottage cheese with a dab left. The TV and the pillows piled in front of it were gone. "There's no smell of baked bread. Jacqueline must have left shortly after me, taking the unbaked dough with her," Kate offered. "Did Mrs. Jones have a car, Mr. Adams?"

The manager assumed the tone of a good citizen. "A little old VW Beetle. Remember those?"

"Theo, it looks like she took all she could in her car. Maybe made two trips. Probably didn't go too far."

"That's why she left the desk. Probably didn't have any help, so she took only what she and Tamoni could carry. Interesting, about those books." Theo opened his mouth to say more, glanced at the manager, and let it go.

Bob McNary moved close to the yawning manager. "Where's the mattress?"

"What—oh, *that* mattress—" He stroked the stubble on his chin.

"That mattress. The new one that was in the bedroom when you let me in last night." He took a step closer. "Where is it?"

"Well, you know," Donny Adams began, patting back his gray hair, "that was a brand new mattress—"

"Yes, it was."

"Well, I'll tell you. To help Jacqueline out, seeing as how she seemed to be having trouble with the police and all, my wife and I took it downstairs into our apartment for safe keeping—" His hands stopped moving. "For her, of course."

"A new mattress?" Theo brightened. "What kind?"

"It looked new. I didn't notice the brand name." The manager fingered his chin again. "Wasn't interested in it, 'cept to save it for her."

Theo warmed to the scent. "She didn't take the new mattress because she had a small Beetle. How does a woman this poor afford a new mattress? They're expensive. Some are real expensive. I want to see that mattress, if we're finished here, Bob."

Silently, they followed the manager, now wide awake and working his fingers nervously, downstairs to his apartment. There, he roused his sleeping wife—up off the new mattress.

"King-sized Sealy Posturepedic. Extra long. Expensive. She had a benefactor. Who?" Theo wondered out loud. A packing tab stuck to the underside stitching indicated it had been packaged the previous December.

The manager's wife, a cigarette in her right hand, coughed. With her left hand, she clutched a frayed chenille bathrobe too small to button.

"I told you that mattress would be trouble." She glared at her husband, backed into the bathroom, and closed the door behind her. In a minute, the toilet flushed.

"Mr. Adams, I'll send some officers over this morning to take that mattress as evidence," McNary deadpanned. "In the meantime, I trust it'll get no further use."

Mr. Adams escorted them to the door, stroking his hair as he went.

The two investigators stopped at the nearest Denny's for coffee and perused the Yellow Pages that Theo had fished from his car. Kate watched while they divided the list of retail mattress dealers to be visited. She felt like an outsider; an outsider who was being baby-sat.

"Gentlemen, I need to get back to my school." She left a couple dollars for the waitress and rose to leave.

"Wait a minute, and I'll drive behind you in my police car."

"I've got the district car, and I'm off."

The two police officers exchanged worried glances.

Ziona closed the principal's office door firmly behind her. The nurse's wide eyes overshadowed the rest of her face. Kate sensed something big was about to break.

The nurse tipped her head to the side and pretended to be put off. "This can wait." She turned toward the door, fingered the knob, hesitated, then opened the door wide enough to let in the office sounds. No feedback. She closed the door and tried again. "But it's really important. Of course, I understand it's been a tough day…with Juan and all." The faint smell of Clorox wafted about her.

Kate slumped in the chair behind the desk and kicked aside her heels. Ever since this morning's call about Juan, she'd felt flat. No energy. As if she couldn't go on. "This just floors me, Ziona. We work so hard to make Saguaro a safe place for these kids. God knows, they think it's safe…until this morning…" She rested elbows on the desk, cradled her forehead in her hands, and murmured, "I'm so beat. Even my teeth are tired."

The nurse shoved papers and a tray overflowing with paper clips aside and perched on the edge of the desk. Kate looked up into eyes that showed no mercy.

"I'll bet you're so down you can hardly plop one foot in front of the other. You need some big time nurturing, baby." Ziona's arms hugged her chest, and she continued in a tone that was anything but motherly. "Of course, every teacher in this school who's ever taught Juan needs strong TLC right about now. And you know what they're doing? They're teaching school and giving their kids the guts to go on. They don't have time to sit around being tired!"

Ziona's glasses had moved so close Kate could see her reflection in them. "You don't take prisoners, do you?"

Ziona shook her head.

"No wonder we don't get along!" Kate felt the corners of her lips twitch. She was rewarded with a twinkle in the nurse's eye. "So what do you want to tell me?"

The nurse slid off the desk, pulled up a chair, and crossed her legs. "Now, I want you to stay seated, 'cause this will knock your socks off, and I don't want you passing out."

Maybe it was just curiosity, but Kate was beginning to feel better.

"Anyway, after work yesterday, I was shopping at the Safeway Grocery that's just a few blocks from school." She nodded to the north. "I came across a man dressed in tight—real tight—black leather pants. He had on leather suspenders, but no shirt. His chest had real black curly hair." She wiggled her fingers in front of her blouse.

"So?" Kate had seen that outfit on the campus more than once. It was Mr. Harrison, who had a son in Mrs. Matthew's fourth grade. No wife. Seemed to take good care of his boy. Shirts were required on campus, but as long as the shirtless Dad came and went quickly, no fuss was made.

Ziona's eyes livened behind huge round frames. "Well, this man was leading a couple of women on leashes. They had big collars around their necks, the kind with spikes, and they were dressed in skimpy outfits like the Playboy Bunnies used to wear, only leather."

"Why am I not surprised?"

Ziona was barely breathing.

"There's more to it?"

The nurse nodded. "One of the women was Daisy McBride…our P.T.O. President."

"No! Oh, shit!"

The two women stared at each other in horror, then collapsed with laughter. They couldn't stop. Finally, Ziona composed herself enough to ask, "Well, what are you going to do about it?"

This brought on another round of whoops.

Kate stammered, "I'm going to pray that Daisy McBride takes little Desiree and moves to another school." Tears were rolling down her cheeks. "What next?"

"Kate, do you really want to know?" Ziona cleared her throat, pulled herself together, and made for the door.

Kate was still chuckling when she noticed that, suddenly, she wasn't so tired. She made a note to talk with the teachers of the Harrison and McBride kids. They needed to know that something might be going on at home. If the kids started acting out, there might be a reason. Suddenly, the "S and M" act wasn't so funny. The threat of the children's possible involvement sobered her. But at least she had her energy back.

Outside, the autumn sun was gentle. So different from the brutal summer blaze. Cottonwoods were turning color, and the recent rain had greened some of the brown. A great Saturday morning.

Inside the Pima County Jail visiting room, the chill radiating from the green concrete block walls iced Kate to the bone. A faint smell of disinfectant rose from the drain in the middle of the floor. Why a drain in a visitor's room? Kate didn't want to know. The heavy metal table was bolted to the floor. So it couldn't be used as a weapon?

Theo seemed right at home, immune to life's emotions. So like the concrete St. Bernadette. A concrete St. Theo. Kate had to chuckle.

"Whatcha lookin' at?" Theo asked.

"Nothing."

Kate's smile faded when she saw the first grade teacher. Nothing had prepared her for the thin form wearing an orange jail uniform that hung as if from a wire hanger. Lank and limp, with little hint that a human body filled it. He'd always been thin. But this? Kate tried not to stare, but she knew the box of Sees Candies she'd brought wasn't nearly enough. He had to get out of this jail…and soon.

Elijah's tone was subdued, a shadow of the robust, optimistic voice she was used to hearing. His eyes skittered around the light green room with its bare tables and benches. The three were the only occupants. The guard outside looked through the small window in the door every once in while.

"I must say, Elijah, orange is not your most flattering color." Kate's casual tone fell flat. "I gave the letters from your class to the guard." She looked up into dark eyes set in sockets deeper than she'd remembered. Concerned eyes, suddenly still.

"My kids know I'm in here?" He got the answer from the faces he searched. "Hell of a role model!"

"Mrs. Robbins, your sub, told them you were away on business." Kate offered. "But word has gotten around, so I told them you've been unjustly accused, and you're detained on police business."

A glint appeared in Elijah's eyes, and he almost smiled. "Detained on police business. Lots of our kids have dads 'detained on police business.' You do have a way with words, Kate."

The tall inmate gave Theo a cigarette, took one himself, lit them both, and chuckled softly as he watched Kate wrinkle her nose in disapproval. "It's not like in your office, where I don't dare light up. In this here office of mine, we can puff away." He handed her the pack of Marlboros. She took it and threw it at him. He caught it, grinned, and tucked it in his shirt pocket

"There you go, Kate. Always strong-arming me. You make me feel like a ninety-pound weakling." He inhaled deeply, and his half smile grew serious. "I heard about your close call. You'd better go into hiding yourself." He leaned down so his nose almost touched hers. "Get out of town, Kate. The cops can't be at your side every minute. I'm safer right now than you are."

"How did you hear about it, Elijah?"

"I've got phone privileges. Keep in touch that way. Teachers at the school and friends. They're all scared for you, Kate. You gotta hide for a while."

Kate ignored his words and chose her own with care. "We've solved one mystery, Elijah. We know who Jacqueline is."

"Damn! I told Theo to leave her out of this!" He started to rise.

Kate tugged at his sleeve, and he settled back down. She wasn't at all certain this meeting was going to be productive. At least, he'd get the Sees Candies.

The two men smoked in silence for nearly a minute. Theo's eyes met Elijah's. "Jacqueline, Tamoni's mother, had a new, king-sized Sealy Posturepedic mattress. Extra long. Still had the packing number on it. It was the same mattress that you charged on your Sears card and had delivered to Jacqueline's apartment about three weeks ago."

Elijah lowered his voice and addressed his principal. "I guess you think that's pretty bad. Me, dating a parent. But, Kate, we just clicked." He looked down at his big hands, at the nails bitten to the quick. "I went there to help Tamoni. After a few times...I stayed the night."

Kate didn't like being mother confessor. "Tamoni wasn't your student. He was a friend. I can see how it could happen."

Theo snorted. "A murder's been committed, you might spend the rest of your life in jail, Elijah, and the goons who did it might ice Kate! You two can sort out your professional ethics later." His voice was rising. "Were you with Jacqueline the night of the murder?"

"I can't answer that."

"You *won't* answer that!" Theo's outburst brought the guard to the glass window. "You know Jacqueline is gone. Where is she now?"

Elijah studied his fingernails and shook his head. "I've no idea where she might be." The teacher sounded so miserable, Kate believed him. He turned to her. "I'm sorry about your scare the other night. That's probably what sent Jacqueline away. Word gets around fast in the apartments. She would never have pulled Tamoni out of school without good reason. And she doesn't scare easy." He cast a scathing look in Theo's direction. "You have no idea what that woman's been through. Drugs. She kicked the habit when Tamoni was born drug addicted. She's been fighting to keep clean ever since. For his sake."

Kate had seen this pattern many times before. Love of a child, often the strongest motivator for a mother.

"So she's studying now to get her GED?" She fielded the question gently.

"She told me she was taking the high school equivalency exam this winter."

"I saw the books. Jacqueline pretended she didn't know you, Elijah. Just talked about how a friend had taught Tamoni to use the drums. A friend who didn't live in the neighborhood, but worked there." Kate leaned forward despite the smoke. "Are you sure you're not protecting a woman who's skipped out on you?"

His eyes gave the answer. He was sure.

Theo lit up a second cigarette and asked in a controlled voice, "Did you leave your car at school often?"

"Every evening. The brothers know it's mine, so word's out to leave it alone. That's one benefit of being a black man." The irony curled his lip. "That and being able to get close to Jacqueline."

"If your car being there fit a pattern, then the person who wanted to kill Dr. Mason knew you'd be a suspect if the death occurred nearby, a prime suspect who'd probably end up in the cooler without bail if it occurred in your classroom. Maybe that person even knew about the threatening evaluation Dr. Mason was preparing."

Despite herself, Kate had to admire the way Theo probed the possibilities.

The sounds she'd heard the night of the murder came back to her. Again, she saw a tall man moving through the fifth grade room. Now, as she sat near Elijah, part of her doubt returned. Had the killer already been found? Was Elijah protecting Jacqueline because she could reveal that her lover had *not* shared her bed during those early morning hours? Had the same thugs who'd come after her gotten Jacqueline and Tamoni? Made it appear that they'd moved?

A chill coursed through Kate. Would Elijah be willing to kill to eliminate a witness? Even a woman he loved? How close was Elijah to the "brothers"? Involuntarily, she shook her head. Her imagination was running away with her.

As Theo and Kate walked down the steps of the city jail, she breathed deeply of the fresh air, then questioned Theo with surprising candor. "Has it occurred to you that Elijah might be the killer?"

Theo guffawed so loud a guard looked his way. "Of course, it's occurred to me. He's the most likely suspect. That's why I subpoenaed his personnel files. That's why I'm going back in there to check the phone calls he made from jail."

Kate's eyes fired up. "You mean that my accompanying you to question him today could work against him?" An image of Mother Provincial flashed before her: *I want you to protect an unfortunate soul, Elijah Jeremiah.*

"Kate, I'm a detective. I'm out to get the killer. That's what I do for a living."

"Even if it's Elijah?"

"Even if it's Elijah." He tipped his fedora back from his brow and stared at her. "Geez! No, I don't have your mind block. Killing is definitely a no-no, Mother Superior! Remember, 'Thou shalt not kill.' Number Five of the Big Ten."

"I'm not going to help you." She turned and headed for the parking garage. Theo quickened his pace to keep up with her.

"You've got to."

"I don't have to help keep an innocent man behind bars." She hurried on, moving toward the car that would distance her from his logic. Thank God, he'd come in his own car. As she moved, she rummaged in her purse for the car keys, cursing the compartment that had swallowed them.

Theo grabbed her arm and spun her around to face him.

"Leave me alone!" She pulled away, but he held tight.

"A minute ago, you asked me whether he might be guilty. You have your own doubts, Kate." He released her. "Have you looked through his personnel files at Central Office?"

"Of course. But I hired Elijah right out of college. All of his professional history has been at Saguaro." Kate continued fishing for her keys. "Theo, he's not the kind of person who murders people. There's nothing professional in the files that I haven't put there—his evaluations over the last five years. I have copies of those in my office."

Kate was both irritated and intrigued by the "gotcha" look in Theo's eyes. She stopped fiddling for her keys. "All right, spill it out. What did you find?"

"Five years ago, when he applied for employment at Oasis district, there was a Jacqueline among his references."

"Yes?"

Theo basked in his smug moment.

"Go on," she urged.

A gloating chuckle, and then, "When Elijah was at the University of Arizona, he worked part time for Jacqueline Stanley, taking care of her horses. She wrote a glowing recommendation, said he was dependable and good with the animals. And—"

"Five years ago, Jacqueline was with Tucson District One. She's been with Oasis district only three years, so her recommendation didn't ring a bell when I hired him. I didn't know her then. Another Jacqueline. And what? What were you going to say?"

"And he worked a couple of summers for Icarus Construction as a hod carrier. Hot, heavy work carrying mortar across the high beams. Probably got a lot of substitute work. Wallace Talbot wrote him a good recommendation. Kind of strange—these two connections. I made a copy of his file. Drop by my office and take a look."

"Coincidence. I'll check his file at the District office."

When they reached Kate's car, she set her purse on the hood and began emptying its contents. The car keys were in her coin purse. "I don't remember putting them there."

Theo smiled. "Stress does strange things to people, even Mother Superiors."

"You called me that once before. Why?"

He held the door as she slipped behind the wheel.

"Oh, I went to Saint Monica's in the Bronx when I was a kid. Spent a lot of time in Mother Superior's office." His eyes warmed. "There's something about you that reminds me of her. I was always in trouble with her, too." He thrust his head inside the driver's window. "Except… Mother Superior would have said the Fifth Commandment should be obeyed."

Kate hit the automatic window button. Faced with decapitation, the police officer withdrew. The principal made a mental note to watch herself. No convent mannerisms.

Ziona's lips were pursed so tight they were bordered with wrinkles. Kate would've kidded her about being uptight had it not been for the sullen presence of Allistar Matthew Mackenzie, slumped in the back seat of the district car. One of the provisions of the contract the sixth grader had just violated stated there'd be no words spoken between the recalcitrant and the principal when she took him home. The manipulator was stripped of his tools. A speedy trip home, the penalty for Matthew's infraction, insured that the parents were immediately involved, whether they liked it or not.

Yesterday, Mrs. Mackenzie had signed the contract agreement in a conference with her son, his teacher, Mr. Nelson, and the principal. Mother had thrown in the disclaimer, "This won't work. Nothing ever works with my boy. He's the devil's own."

A newcomer to Saguaro, Allister had promised to clean up his mouth. A few minutes ago, he told Mr. Nelson to "fuck off and get your hot ass away from my desk." Kate expected that. Contract holders usually tested the agreement. That's why Kate dropped everything to deliver him to his mom.

When Kate asked the school nurse to accompany them, Ziona objected. "Matthew lives in a tough apartment complex. We need Theo."

"Theo's tied up. Allister needs immediate consequences. He has to know we mean business." Kate signed the three of them out on a sheet kept exclusively for that purpose. When staff was out in the neighborhood, the office needed to know with whom, where, and for how long. Too long, and a scouting party would go looking. From her desk, she scooped up the two-way radio that had the attendance area within range.

The lad in the back seat was tall for his age—tall and strong. White eyeballs against ebony skin emphasized his defiance. He was used to getting his way with his only parent. Used to talking his way out of things. This ride didn't fit his M.O., and he was pissed. Good. A few rides like this, and he'd watch his mouth. Contracts with parents and students almost always worked. Maybe not the first go-round, but a second or third trip did the job.

Ziona sucked in her breath as they drove into the graveled parking lot of the low rent complex that was Allister's home. It consisted of two parallel, one-story concrete block buildings facing each other. The doors on either side were separated by a cracked, three-foot-wide concrete walk that divided the steps of the facing apartments. Close. Very close.

Eight big, black party boys who looked like they belonged in the NFL blocked the entrance to the walk. Their game was drugs, not football. Glassy-eyed, one moved slow, like a zombie, through the door of the first apartment to the left.

Kate read Allister's smug expression in the rear-view mirror.

"So you're fuckin' goin' to take me home, are you?"

"That's right. Which is your apartment?"

"At the back of that long line of apartments. Right past the brothers." Another smirk. "And there be no rear entrance."

"Get out of the car, shut the door, and stand by the trunk."

The sneer turned to surprise. He shrugged and got out.

"You're not going in there!" Ziona squeaked as the boy slammed his door.

Kate picked up the two-way radio and got Terri in the office. "Saguaro base, this is Mahoney. Do you copy?"

"Mahoney, this is Terri. I copy loud and clear."

"Terri, keep someone by the radio until we sign off."

"Trouble?"

"Not yet."

"I'm here."

Kate turned to the nurse. "Quiet. I don't want Allister to hear you."

Ziona stage whispered, "Don't go in there. I've always known you'd get into big trouble one of these days." Her voice turned to a low groan. "And I'm afraid that day is today!"

Kate ignored her. "When I get out, you move to the driver's seat. If I'm not back out in ten minutes, tell the office to call the cops. You've got the address...455 Calle Enriquez."

Ziona motioned toward the walkway. "What if they try to get in the car?"

"Drive away and call for the cops."

"What if they get in front of the car?"

"Drive over them!"

"That's not in my job description!" Ziona squealed so loud, Kate was afraid Allister might hear. She checked. He was still standing by the trunk, looking surprised.

"You're going to get hurt, Kate. They're all high." Ziona was pleading. "And you're not even black!"

The principal flipped off the safety on the pepper spray she was fingering in her right jacket pocket. "Right about now, Ziona, I wish I were black as you. But we're not going to chicken out. Allister and his mom have to go by those party boys when they want to get home. This time, I'm going to walk it with him. Ten minutes. Check your watch. I've got 2:07." She swept the contract off the dash with her left hand.

Allister followed. Together, they moved past two giant brown plastic garbage dumpsters that smelled of rotting vegetables and diapers. Trash was piled beside them, level with their lids. If garbage men were running late, this was the part of town they skipped.

Kate's attention focused on the small opening between the two buildings. The men didn't give any sign of stepping aside. On the contrary, their watery stares under half-opened lids hinted they were looking forward to the moment when they'd be asked to do so. The sweet smell of marijuana wafted heavily from the open door to the left.

Allister at her side, Kate maintained a business-like step. She'd nearly reached the point of confrontation when a slim African American wearing a Dallas Cowboy jacket and tight Levis came out of the door to the left. He was smaller than the others, clear-eyed, with an in-charge attitude. This was the man the others had come to visit. A drug dealer who didn't want trouble on his doorstep. Kate recognized him as a parent whose family didn't live in this complex.

Taking her by the elbow, he introduced her to his clients. "This is our school principal. She does a good job. I wish I could say the same for Allister, the young gentleman at her side. Mrs. Mahoney, we've met. Beppo Daniels, at your service."

Kate hated it when dealers were charming. That's the way they sucked in the kids! The onlookers surveying her through glazed eyes were unimpressed, but they parted, allowing passage. The dealer stayed at Kate's side while she knocked on the door with the left hand that clutched the contract.

Mrs. Mackenzie invited her in, but said, "No," when the dealer tried to accompany her. Mindful of her ten-minute limit, Kate explained the infraction and urged the mother to use boredom as punishment. No TV. Mom was not happy. Allister showed signs of fraying at the edges. Kate could only hope.

As the principal turned to leave, the mother whispered in her ear, "This ain't going to work." At least, she whispered this time.

The dealer escorted Kate to the car. They didn't speak. He appeared to be mildly amused at his role of protector, and Kate hated it. But given the alternative...

Ziona had the motor purring when they came down the path. As Kate slipped into the passenger seat, the dealer leaned down to the window. "Mrs. Mahoney, you can take your hand out of your right pocket now."

The nurse slammed on the gas, and the vehicle lurched forward so fast it almost sideswiped him. Ziona's eyes shot fiery darts at her boss. "I am *never, ever* going back to that hellhole."

Kate ignored her, just looked out the window.

"Furthermore, I'm going to tell Officer Buloski about this. I don't like him, but somebody's got to stop you."

If she heard Kate say, "You know, I think Allister's going to come around," Ziona didn't let on.

In the Choir...

The chant rose from her lips in calm measured cadences. Each square note given its own space and dignity became part of the rise and fall of the whole. Sister Katherine didn't read the notes as much as she prayed them. Joining her voice with those of the other choir novices, her heart rose with the swells coursing to the heavens, then gently, regularly, returned to earth. Whispering at the end of each sweep, the great secret...God is here. Not there.

In Gregorian chant, the timing of each note is not indicated on the four-lined staffs, so the nuns' unity depends upon the lifting and lowering of the choir mistress's directing hands. Sister Mary Rosula used both hands like a symphony conductor.

Sister Katherine felt a presence move next to her at the end of the back row, and she shifted her choir book to accommodate the newcomer. The Latin of the next cadence swept higher and higher in carefully planned abandon and began its equally measured descent. All lips closed in unity as Sister Mary Rosula's thumb and index finger met.

All except one. The voice next to Sister Katherine chanted on, drawing to a whispered conclusion in its own good time. Sister Mary Rosula glared at the union of her thumb and index finger as if it were the offending party. "Well, what was that all about? Who believes they can improve upon the cadence bequeathed by Pope Gregory over fourteen hundred years ago?"

The choir looked in Sister Katherine's direction as Mother Provincial moved from behind her. "I'm sorry, Sister Mary Rosula. I got carried away." The nuns slowly bowed in deference. "My place is in the front of the chapel, so I never get to chant with the choir. Your sisters chant beautifully, Sister Mary Rosula."

Faces glowed against white wimples.

"I beg your pardon, Mother. I didn't realize it was you." The choir mistress captured her fluttering hands beneath her scapular. "Sisters, you have witnessed the humility of our Mother Provincial. When her chant was...ahem...slightly different from that of the choir, she acknowledged her...ahem...nonconformity immediately. In contrast, some of you like to go your own way and never own up to it. Thank you, Mother, for your example. Is there anything I can do for you?"

"I need to take Sister Katherine for a few minutes."

Mother Philippa bowed to the directress and left, followed by the novice. Rather than descend the choir stairs, Mother creaked open a seldom used side door and began to climb to the bell tower, lifting her skirts above the dusty steps. Dim light struggled through a cobwebbed window. When the novice tripped in the dusk, Mother turned and handed her one end of the black cord of Aran wool that the superiors wore around their waists to remind them of their connection to the motherhouse on Inish Mor. "Take hold."

Sister Katherine gasped as she climbed. "Mother, you really were humble back there." She puffed on. "Admitting the mistake."

"Not humility. Good politics. And Sister Mary Rosula's flattery had something to do with the request she'll be making soon for new Christmas sheet music."

The novice's heavy breathing kept her from answering.

"Eighty-two steps straight up," Mother continued. "If you take them fast, they'll give you a good workout." Reaching the belfry, she used her handkerchief to brush dust off the bench surrounding the chapel bell.

"So that's why your handkerchiefs are always so dirty. We have to purex them in the laundry, and everybody wonders why they're so black."

"Sadly, I have little privacy." Mother drank in the crisp fall air. "Look at the view."

Sister sneezed. "And the dust! Mother, you didn't bring me up here to admire the view." She parted her back pleats and carefully sat on the dusted bench. "Elijah is losing weight as well as his spirit in jail. I'm not sure he could survive the brutality of prison. You have to do something fast."

"So like his Grandfather Gene." Mother straightened. "Don't talk of prison. We're—that is, *you* are—going to get him out. Kindly remember, I'm dead."

"Who is Gene? You knew his grandfather?"

"Yes, I did, sister. But that's another story. One that's not going to be told. Back to Elijah's innocence."

"How will *we* get him out?"

"Think, sister, think. How did Dr. Mason get to the school that night? Did she come in the District van with the murderer? Was Elijah there to meet her or did he leave the car parked overnight for another reason? If so, why?"

"I'm sure the police have considered all possibilities."

"Sister Katherine, never assume bureaucratic institutions will cover all bases. It's amazing what they miss. Believe me, I know. Tell Theo to check the cab companies."

"You know of Theo?"

"Yes, charming man. Quite unaware of his own grace. The cab companies, sister."

"Charming is hardly how I'd describe Theo."

"To each her own. Mind your skirt on the dust of the stairs. These habits are blessedly hard to clean."

6

Papers for the teacher training in-service covered every inch of counter space in the small Saguaro Elementary office. The luxury of time and privacy that Kate experienced at school on weekends compensated for the nagging feeling that she wasn't out having fun on her days off. She reminded herself that the teachers were at home washing clothes and cleaning, finding satisfaction in providing for their loved ones. And that's what she was doing, putting together cooperative learning packets that would promote a new avenue of learning for her kids. Weekends at the school were her consolation prize for not having a family.

True, she discouraged staff from working at school on the weekends even during the daylight hours. Last year, a teacher had been raped at Mesquite Elementary, a mile away, when she was caught alone one Saturday morning, Xeroxing the week's homework assignments. Saguaro had at least one break-in a month before the unbreakable glass windows were installed. If teachers must come on weekends, Kate insisted they bring someone with them.

As for herself, she felt safe. She had set the office perimeter alarm. Her loaded .38 revolver rested on top of the gray filing cabinet. Theo had done the paperwork, so she had a permit to have a concealed weapon on campus.

Before collating the papers, she studied the work area. It had to be restored to its original state when she was finished. Secretaries hated having their organization messed up. Tiá's attendance sheets sat in the basket ready for Monday morning distribution. The red and green lights of three networked computers and a printer stared at the boss lady from a shelf above the intercom. The intercom itself was uncharacteristically silent and unlit. The year's budget, clipped to a stand next to Terri's computer, was being readied for the central office. Kate savored the order and silence. A far cry from the semi-organized chaos during the workweek.

Her secretaries could duplicate and collate the in-service papers themselves, but it would crowd next week's heavy schedule. Besides, this was one way a principal could accumulate some brownie points. Keep the secretaries and custodians happy, and the place will hum. Get on their bad side, and problems multiply. Kate had good secretaries, and she intended to keep them content.

After a couple of hours spent bending over desks, her muscles yearned for a stretch. Time for another weekend indulgence, a walk around a quiet campus. She dropped the keys in her jeans' pocket. Hiding the .38 in her waistband seemed too dramatic for a sunny October afternoon. Instead, she put her pepper spray in her right pocket and slipped out the nurses' door.

Each time she walked the playground, she knew she'd have to fire Paul, the groundsman. Half the time, he didn't show up, claiming he'd been called to other schools for special projects. When he did make it to the campus, he spent a lot of time sleeping in his truck, complaining, "This is my lunch hour." When Kate tried to nail down the time of his floating lunch, he shrugged as if to say, "You don't have time to fire me." He was right. It took time to check his alibis and document infractions, but she was working on it.

The rosemary under the library windows was brown from lack of water. Weeds struggled up the chainlink fence. Bald spots under the swings, deepened by hours of squealing play, needed more sand. There were brown spots all over the playground, where sprinkler heads had been broken or stolen. Fortunately, the sprinklers were on a timed system, so most of the field and trees got water unless the entire system went down. Then Kate made it a top priority and bullied Paul into fixing it.

The Arizona cypress planted by last year's sixth graders had been leaning at a sharp angle since the August winds. She'd asked Paul several times to stake it straight, but it still listed precariously. Passing grads shouldn't see their tree being neglected. She headed for the grounds storage shed, kept separate from the main school because of the gasoline for mowers. From a heap of tools, mulch, insecticides, and gasoline cans, Kate dug out a six-foot metal stake, a bucket, a rope, and a sledgehammer. What a mess! Paul definitely had to go.

The tree well was dry, and Kate didn't want to mess with the water timing system, so she carried buckets of water from a nearby classroom. When the ground was soaked, she tamped first with a rock, then the side of the sledge, and the wobbly stake stood on its own. Starting with the sledge over her head, Kate managed a full swing that knocked the stake to the ground with an impotent thud. She swore under her breath and was repeating the process when, from behind her back, arms and hands covered hers. Her first reaction was fear. Anything could happen on this playground. She'd left herself vulnerable, alone and highly visible.

She turned to see Theo's face a few inches from hers. Her audible sigh of relief was cut short by the look he sent her. An electricity she hadn't felt since her husband's death coursed through her. By force of habit, she shot Theo the intimidating principal-look that she used when threatened.

He ignored it. "Let go."

She relaxed her grip and slipped from under his arms.

He brought the hammer down squarely. The stake slipped cooperatively into the ground. A couple more blows, and it was two feet in.

When Theo put aside the sledge, his lips betrayed the slightest hint of a smile. Kate felt the heat creep across her cheeks. "Go around to the other side and push the trunk when I say," he ordered. She pushed, while Theo pulled on the rope girding the tree. Slowly, it eased upright. Theo fastened the rope with a knot Kate didn't recognize.

Grinning, he started to walk toward his office in the classroom wing.

"Thanks," Kate called after him. "Theo…"

He stopped and turned, his eyes still smiling.

"Did you check out the taxi companies? About the night of the murder?"

"Done. A long time ago. Nothing. No cabs here." His lips took up the smile as he detoured around the swing sets and walked on.

What had Mother Philippa said about Theo being "unaware of his own grace?" How did the elder nun define grace?

Not that it mattered. What had flashed between them was just random chemistry. She wasn't going to think of it again.

Using work as an antidote for unwanted feelings, she cleaned three drawers in her desk. Besides, she needed a secure resting place for the .38 revolver. The locked bottom drawer would do.

Monday afternoon found Allister Matthew Mackenzie, broken contract on the floor next to him, slouched in the chair outside the principal's office. He busied himself investigating the bottom of his shoe with a pencil.

Kate expected it. Contracts take time to kick in. Moving past Ziona's door, she asked Mrs. Tiá Mendez, the Spanish translator and parent advocate, to come into her office. As they passed the nurse's door, Ziona leaned against the threshold, arms folded. She rolled knowing eyes and stage whispered, "Tiá, don't do it!"

"You don't miss much, do you, Ziona?" Kate shot her a barbed glance.

"Almost nothing. I know trouble when I see it." With the grace of a cat, the disapproving nurse slipped back into her office and shut the door.

"What was that all about?" With full red lips, Mrs. Tiá Mendez flashed the smile that won her the affectionate name, "Tiá-Aunt." Parents about the same age as Tiá—early thirties—looked into her hazel eyes and trusted. Children looked into them, saw a loving aunt, and obeyed her. Dangling star earrings bounced against the background of her full black hair. Warm and motherly, she could be tough as nails, which is why Kate needed her now.

Kate recounted the events of the last visit to Allister's home with the assurance, "I doubt we'll run into that situation again."

"So now the party boys know who you are. They'll leave us alone because their supplier won't want trouble on his doorstep." Sounded reasonable.

Relieved, Kate sent her to get Allister while she unlocked her bottom desk drawer and removed the .38 revolver. She carried it concealed under a pile of papers into the restroom and, in one of the stalls, slipped it into the shoulder holster hidden under her blue suit jacket. She fastened the single jacket button. A couple of times she practiced drawing the gun until she was confident she could reach it instantly.

With luck, she'd never have to draw the gun, but she needed it as backup. Dopers would never suspect that the lady principal would be carrying a piece. There lay her advantage.

It would be a whole lot easier to avoid this home visit entirely. But Allister would know she was taking the easy way out. If she wanted him to do the hard work of keeping his contract, she had to do her hard part as well.

When they arrived at 455 Calle Enriquez, a party was in progress, featuring many of yesterday's players. Kate checked the rear-view mirror. No smirk this time. Allister's forehead was creased with a line between his brows. The corners of his lips turned down. Worry mixed with a little chagrin. After he'd stepped from the car, the principal repeated for Tiá the directions she'd given to Ziona the day before.

"Ten minutes." Tiá checked her watch.

"What would you do if one of them tried to stop you from driving away?"

"Run over him."

Kate nodded. She'd brought the right lady.

The men parted slightly as she approached. Reluctantly, as if it were an effort, Allister slipped in front of her to make an opening. Though she tried to look nonchalant, the muscles across her shoulders tightened. She kept her eyes down, seeing only the men's shoes. One leaned toward her, so she had to brush against him as he slurred, "Little Chickie from the school. Big Daddies oughta do this one right."

"Little Chickie. Your Big Daddies gonna take you for a ride." The same voice that Kate had heard that night! She felt nauseated. No matter how hard she'd tried to scrub that voice from her soul, it kept coming back. And now, here!

The hair at the nape of her neck stood on end. Would he hear the loud thump-thump of her heart? Sense her chill? She forced herself to notice what shoes this "Big Daddy" wore. Black hiking boots! Unusual in this neighborhood. "Big Daddy" stood next to a smaller pair of Tony Lama cowboy boots. Handmade and expensive.

Kate followed Allister like a zombie. Barely able to speak, she simply handed Mrs. Mackenzie the contract with her left hand and began a spasm of coughing. She used her cough as cover to turn from the door to study the men.

The owner of the hiking boots wore jeans and a red and black plaid hunting jacket. An Anglo, he was a few inches taller than Kate, but had a muscular body like a construction worker. Probably over 200 pounds. A black beard and receding hairline suggested he was in his forties. His narrowed eyes glared back at the principal.

Looking up to him, A. J. Rogers in his Tony Lama cowboy boots was stammering through a drug-induced haze. There was nothing hazy about the two large knives that still hung from A. J.'s belt.

"You need a glass of water, Mrs. Mahoney?"

Not daring to risk another look, Kate leaned against the door, still coughing, and nodded. Having emptied the glass, she headed back down the walk, the weight under her jacket a slight comfort. This time no one spoke, and she didn't look up. Just noted shoes. The hiking boots had the brand name, MERRELL, in black and silver on the outer side.

"You had four minutes left." Tiá glanced at her boss as she turned the ignition key. "You look like a ghost. What happened?"

The principal shook her head and gave no answer. They drove in silence for a couple of blocks before Tiá spoke. "I'm with Ziona. I never want to go back there again."

"Me neither, Tiá. Me neither."

"I've never heard of anything so damn stupid."

Kate moved across the office and closed the door. "Please lower your voice. There's no need for the neighborhood to hear you calling me stupid." Controlled anger spilled out from the corners of her calmness.

Theo, from the top of his shiny, bald head to his clenched fists, radiated heat. Was he going to have a heart attack? Or hit her?

"Not only did you put yourself in danger, but you exposed Tiá." His fists flew up in the air.

Kate backed away. "Sit and calm down." Her teacher tone was losing its sweet reasonableness. "You're going to have a heart attack the way you're carrying on."

He stood where he was. "Did you take the revolver with you?"

At least, she'd done something right. "Of course, in a concealed shoulder holster."

Theo slapped his forehead with his broad hand, let out a "Geez!" and stood shaking his head in disbelief. "You're walking through those goons. To hear Ziona tell it, squeezing through those homeboys, all of whom are in la-la land with their brains turned off and everything else turned on. Armed to a man, you can bet your life on it."

He moved forward with menace in his eye. Kate stood her ground. Let him hit her. She'd get him for assault and battery.

"And they spot that piece you're carrying." He leaned down so his nose was within inches of hers and glared into her eyes. Like she did with the kids when they got into big trouble.

"Back off. I'm not a kid."

He repeated, "They spot that piece you're carrying." He touched his index finger between her eyes, "And boom! No more Miss Priss."

"I don't have to listen to this." She got up and headed toward the door, but he blocked the way.

"I'll bet Allister was scared stiff. He knew he might get caught in the middle."

"Then he won't break his contract again, will he? Don't tell me how to run this school, and I won't tell you how to be a spy." She moved toward him. He didn't budge. "I'd no idea the assailant from the other night might be there, or I wouldn't have gone. Not even for Allister. I should never have told you I'd seen him talking to A. J. Rogers. That's what set you off. I should have gone to Officer McNary directly."

She was glad for the hurt in his eyes. He'd called her stupid and practically attacked her, when she was only doing her duty. Let him take some of his own medicine. "Shawn trusted me and my judgment. He didn't live long enough to get cynical and burnt out." Her look said, *like you.*

"Oh, better a dead rookie than a burnt out has-been."

Kate knew she had it coming, but that didn't diminish the pain. She felt like she'd been slapped across the face.

"I'm sorry." Theo's voice softened. "I was out of line saying that."

"Get out!"

"I'm sorry. Wish I could take it back."

"Out!"

Theo turned and disappeared through the door.

Officers McNary and Buloski were among the police who raided 455 Calle Enriquez one hour after the visit of the school personnel. None of the clientele were wearing hiking boots.

Beppo Daniels and A. J. Rogers were interrogated by McNary and Buloski for two hours and detained for another go-round.

After hours spent in the small interrogation room with no windows, it was a relief to sit for awhile in the police conference room. An esthetics wasteland, beige on beige, it wasn't saturated with the scent of fear, like the interrogation room.

"Going to tell the school about this?" Bob McNary took a handkerchief out of his hip pocket and wiped his neck, then stretched.

Theo shoved his fedora back on his head and savored the cigar smoke. "Nothing much to tell. Those goons are tight. We need to find something to hold over Rogers's head. We've already got 'possession to sell' on Daniel's back. He might cough up a name for leniency." Theo blew a circle with the cigar smoke.

"Hasn't worked so far. They're scared of the guy in the hiking boots." McNary interlaced his fingers and studied the effect. "How can you stand it?"

"Oh, she's okay most of the time. The kids like her." Buloski exhaled. "She's too wrapped up in that school. Never takes time out for anything else."

McNary's eyes betrayed amusement. "What are you talking about? I ask you how you can stand the gosh awful smell of cigar smoke, and you go on about some female. What's her name?"

Buloski flushed. "Kate Mahoney, the school principal. Had a row with her yesterday about going into that drug den without an officer."

"If we get a lead on her assailant, you can let her know. That should make her happy." McNary snapped his knuckles and smiled with satisfaction.

"I'm thinking you'd better do the talking. She'd be on my back for antagonizing two parents." He got up and paced the room. "No matter how it turns out, you tell her about the drug raid. Our boys in there," he nodded toward the cell block, "probably know about the 'hiking boots' connection to Kate and put her visit and our raid together. Kate may end up with two more enemies. She needs to know it."

McNary didn't answer. He was concentrating on knuckle snapping. With one hand on the doorknob, Buloski turned and asked, "Want me to get you some coffee or something?"

No answer. McNary was busy.

Kate was out on the lunchtime playground when Ziona caught up with her.

"He's done it again. Allister is in your office, broken contract in hand."

"Well, at least he made it three days this time."

"Thanks for small favors." The nurse waited for Kate's reaction the way a hawk waits for a rabbit. "Tell me you're not going back."

Kate smiled. "Have you noticed how some of the first graders are walking too close to the front of the swings? They're liable to get hit." She played to the nurse's pet peeve: playground safety. "We need to get some swing guards installed, so they'll have a better idea of how close is too close."

"Nice try. You can't change the subject. Nobody will go back with you, Kate. Everybody heard Officer Buloski yelling at you after the last visit."

"Leave Allister in the conference room. I'll tend to him myself."

The nurse snorted. "You go alone, and I'll kill you before the druggies get a chance."

Kate walked the length of the swings, gauging how close was too close.

"Ziona, please get Ed to measure the length needed for swing guards. Be out here while he does it, so you can explain the area to be secured.

Then call Benny at the warehouse and see if there are any extra guards of the right length that some school's discarded. If there are, put in a work order to have them installed. If not, get a playground equipment catalog from the P.E. office and let me know the prices." She smiled at her scowling sidekick. "Got that?"

Allister sat at the end of the conference table, fortified on three sides with textbooks, a binder with papers bulging out of every orifice, and a grimed forest green backpack. Only his eyes showed over the barrier when Kate sat down to talk with him.

"Well, you made it three days this time, Allister."

He started to answer, then closed his mouth.

Good. A cuss word that didn't make it out.

"Did you notice the cop car out in front when you came in?" *Liar, liar, pants on fire!*

Suddenly alive, the dark eyes flashed. "No."

"Well, I have to work with the police and Officer Buloski on an emergency. Can you study here for a few minutes till I get back to you?"

The youth was visibly relieved. "Guess so."

Passing through the office, Kate whispered to Tiá, "I'm going to be in the classrooms all afternoon. In about an hour, I want you to tell Allister there's been a broken water pipe in the kitchen, and the plumber needs the principal there. Be apologetic that I'm not yet available to take him home."

"There are things worse than little white lies." Tiá's dark eyes sparkled.

"Don't let him go when the dismissal bell rings. I'll come in with regrets and tell him we had a drunk on the playground who needed to be shooed off. Since I'm so late, he might as well go home on his own. Just this one time."

Tiá's smile enveloped her entire face. "It's too bad about all the emergencies that will come up this afternoon. But some days are like that. Must be a full moon."

That was the last time Allister Matthew MacKenzie broke his contract for foul language. And the last time Kate Mahoney put him on contract for anything.

In the Retreat...

The creek trail led through silver-trunked sycamores shedding their leaves of gold and yellow. Though thirty nuns lined the trail and sides of the creek, the only sounds heard by Sister Katherine were the gurgling of water and the swishing of serge against dry leaves.

The nuns' skirts hung down in the chapel mode, and their hands, thrust into voluminous sleeves that hung gracefully over their scapulars, were invisible. Here and there, black rosaries dangled at the meeting of the sleeves.

The nuns kept their eyes cast down, focusing all energy inward. The annual nine-day retreat as prescribed by the Rules of the Congregation were days of silent prayer interspersed with religious exercises led by a priest, in this case a Jesuit conducting the spiritual exercises of Saint Ignatius of Loyola.

They'd just finished Saint Ignatius's meditation on death that had placed each nun on her own deathbed, examining her life in the light of its final hours. This meditation forced Sister Katherine to face the lie she was living. Though she knew she didn't belong as a religious, there was no way out.

"You don't feel their peace, do you, sister?"

Startled, Sister Katherine pushed aside the mahogany branch of a manzanita bush to find Mother Philippa Manning. Not a person with whom she wanted to share these thoughts. She held the branch for the emerging superior. Mother Provincial tugged at the young novice's sleeve and nudged her into a side ravine away from her sisters.

"Mother, I need to get back to the others." Sister Katherine pulled a pocket watch out from under her scapular. "It's almost time for the next exercise."

"Sit." The Provincial used her large man's handkerchief to brush off a fallen log, then sat and patted the space beside her. Sister Katherine remained standing. "You can relax, sister. Remember, this is only a dream. You've already made your decision and left us." Though the elder nun was breaking Great Silence, her face was calm, without guilt.

It was the novice's spirit that was troubled. "That decision haunts me. As a third grader, I promised God I would become a nun if my dad came home safe from World War II. I had no choice." Her voice sounded foreign to her after days of silence. "I had to be a nun, but I always felt wicked because I didn't want to be what God wanted me to be." Her lips quivered.

"Few are called to this life." Mother pressed the novice's hand. "And God doesn't lay decisions like that on the backs of third graders. Later, if you didn't want it, then God wasn't calling you. You were right to leave."

Sister Katherine drew a white handkerchief from the folds of serge and dabbed at her eyes. "This is a dream I've had a hundred times. Always trying to make the decision with peace."

"*Requiescant in pace*. Rest in peace."

"Mother!" Sister bolted at the quote from the Latin funeral mass.

Mother Provincial smiled. "I'm celebrating your freedom, not your funeral. Be at peace." Mother looked directly into the young nun's eyes. "But, sister, your eternal rest will begin soon if you continue to expose yourself to your enemies. Theo is right to be worried about you. Please reconsider my invitation to find sanctuary in the Mother House on Innis Mor."

Sister Katherine changed the subject. "Have you any information about the murder?"

"Were there any business dealings that would render her death profitable? And don't assume all her dealings were legal." A worldly-wise look settled in the Provincial's eyes. "Were there any unusually large money outlays that went across her desk in the previous months?"

"You sound like a businesswoman, Mother."

"I was. A very shrewd one. Surely, you didn't think I got this position because of my saintliness." She chuckled. "Now, go in peace. And watch your back or you will *requiescant in pace* before your time."

7

Unsettled by the dream, Kate took her warm milk to the front balcony, where the city lights diminished the stars. Twenty years since she'd left the Congregation, but the dream kept returning. She searched the stars and the moon for a promise of something bigger, vaster than her own problems. The chill of the night air was a respite from the scorching heat of a desert summer. The autumn leaves stirred gently, falling even as she watched.

Kate had turned to reenter the townhouse when a familiar sound, followed by a whiff of incense, floated through the crisp night air. Ralph always chanted the same Japanese words, Nam-Moyoho-Renge-Kyo, over and over. She'd heard him on his balcony many times before, but this time his voice seemed to pulsate like an ocean wave in rhythm with the universe…as low and powerful as a temple gong. She gave herself to the sound and let it throb in time with her heartbeat.

Kate didn't know how long she stayed there, humming and swaying to the chant, but it softened and soothed her, so she slept "in pace" when she made it back to bed.

The mirrors on the health club walls caught Kate's reflection as she stretched her back muscles and twisted her torso. Like the Tin Man in the Wizard of Oz, her muscles groaned when she climbed on the exercise bike, set the controls at Level 1 and pumped away at 25 MPH. She checked out the bikers on either side of her. Level 3! Level 4! They were all doing more than 25 MPH! Damn! Why had she neglected her workouts? Level 2 brought stronger complaints from her thighs, heart, and lungs. Sweat assured her that something was happening to her body. Her sweat mixed with the other gym odors.

Seeking distraction from her pumping heart and gasping lungs, she used the mirrors to scan beautiful trim bodies and self-consciously flexed muscles. When she spotted herself, sweating and puffing, she looked away. Into the amused gaze of Wallace Talbot.

"So you use the Desert Springs body factory, too." His eyes suggested a depth of interest that startled her. She smiled back and kept pumping. As long as she had pumps left in her, she wasn't going to stop for anybody. He'd have to wait until she'd tortured herself to the max.

Wait he did, his eyes wandering slowly across the mirrors, and then coming back to her. Kate kept on going for another two minutes. When she climbed off the bike with a loud sigh of relief, Wallace put a towel around her shoulders and invited her to the juice bar for a cool down.

"The best thing about that exercise bike is getting off it." She mopped her face with the towel and ordered a tall orange cooler. The smell of hard-earned sweat wafted through the bar. "So how long have you been coming here?"

"For a couple of years. I usually get my workouts in the afternoon, after I've had a chance to make the rounds of the construction sites." He looked her over, eyes never lingering, but registering approval.

"I haven't seen you around Saguaro for a couple of weeks. How are you coming with the design of the bus drop-off for the new high school?" The orange cooler must have reduced the temperature in Kate's brain, allowing her to think more clearly despite Wallace Talbot's gaze.

What were the large money outlays that went across her desk in the previous months? The construction of the new high school was the most expensive bond project going, and who knew it better than the president of the contracting company? "I'm amazed you've had the time to handle details like the design of the bus area when you're responsible for...how many building sites?" Kate peered with big innocent eyes over the rim of the frosted glass.

"We have seven projects going right now, but the high school is definitely the largest." Wallace played with the water spot made by the sweating glass. "I take a little piece of the design action occasionally and run it through to completion to keep my skills up. I'm a designer by training."

His glance left Kate wondering about the nature of his designs.

"You subcontract out much of the work, I imagine."

He positioned his glass precisely on the water spot he'd created. "Actually, we're a pretty big outfit. We have our own plumbers, electricians, roofers, and so on, but we do contract out the landscaping." He leaned over the glass into Kate's space. "Would you like to take a look at the progress on the high school? I could show you around some late afternoon, and then we could toast the project at dinner."

"I'd enjoy that."

"Next Thursday at five?"

"Sorry." Kate felt a pang of regret. "I have to make a presentation at the Board of Education meeting that night. Friday?"

Wallace's eyes settled on her face, measuring the truth of her words. Well, let him wonder. He could check out the Oasis School Board agenda, if he was that interested.

"Friday won't do for me. I'll be out of town that weekend."

Kate could guess who'd be with him. Sexy Flora. Thinking of her own upcoming weekend filled with teacher evaluations to be written, student test results to be analyzed, and the budget to be balanced, she suppressed a twinge of jealousy and smiled. "Monday?"

Wallace looked genuinely pleased. "Okay, Monday at five. Another cooler?"

Kate nodded.

"I'll get it. Our waitress seems to be busy."

She watched him move to the juice bar, tall but graceful as a cat. His movement touched a nerve, and she shivered, feeling momentarily fearful. A feeling of déjà vu. She smiled when she realized his jaguar-like grace reminded her of a stalker she'd seen last week on late night TV. The mind plays strange tricks with the nerves.

Kate's nerves felt a different twinge when he brought the cooler, fingers touching a fraction of a second as he brushed against her hand. She felt a blush move up her neck into her face. No déjà vu there. Just the nervous system of a celibate. Wallace looked pleased.

Look at the big money transactions. A long slow drink gave Kate time to phrase the next question. "I've been working for a couple of weeks on my school budget. Definitely not my favorite activity. I can't imagine the procedure you must go through to prepare a bid for the construction of a high school. Twenty-two million dollars, wasn't that your bid—the low bid?"

Wallace mimicked Kate's tactic, a long slow drink. Was he mocking her? Or was he stalling while he thought? Why? Her question couldn't have been that taxing. He could just say his accountants handled such manners and let it go at that. But then Kate would know he was lying. No contractor would hand a school district a bid without calculating the level of profit involved.

Wallace coughed and shifted his chair so he could look out the glass enclosure at the parade of bodies going to and from the exercise area. "I wonder if people can gauge the amount of time they spend here by the amount of flab they continue to carry," he said with a grin.

Kate sucked in her tummy; glad she'd spent the extra bucks to buy workouts with built-in control. Though self-conscious, she wasn't going to let him evade the question.

"It must have taken a team of accountants to prepare such a large bid."

He glanced at his watermark. "We broke the project into small components and had the site supervisors submit their bids. For example, the head carpenter estimated the cost of man-hours and materials for all the cabinetry and finishing work, the chief plumber did the same for plumbing supplies and installation. Then my management team and I met with our accountants and prepared a bid, factoring in an acceptable profit margin that would still allow us to underbid our competition. It was a long process that began as soon as we got the architect's blueprints. The high school contract took months."

With a Desert Springs cocktail napkin, he wiped away the water spot left by his drink and placed the second icy drink in exactly the same spot. "This town is littered with the bones of contractors whose companies went bankrupt because they cut their profit margin too short in order to underbid their rivals. But enough of this budget talk."

He turned on the smile that probably helped him become president of the company. "If you're like me, you're here to work budget worries out of your system, not wallow in them."

Kate smiled in a way calculated to convince Wallace Talbot she was just making industry small talk. Was he buying it?

Having been principal while a new building was planned and constructed at Saguaro Elementary, she hadn't learned anything new from Wallace. What had interested her were his reticence and his thinly disguised irritation. Preparing a successful bid on a major project was an enormous undertaking. Why didn't he want to talk about it?

When she bade him goodbye outside the women's locker rooms, Kate had already begun to form a list of questions for the following Monday. Questions she'd carefully disguise as small talk. It would be so much easier if the president of Icarus Construction weren't so smart.

Kate was coming out of the showers when she spotted Flora strutting into a shower, naked as Venus and just as blessed. There was something phony about Flora. Why hadn't she joined them at the juice bar? She didn't seem the type to accompany Wallace to the gym, and then forget about him. Especially if he were giving attention to another woman. Something was phony there—but it certainly wasn't her figure!

His office was driving Theo crazy. He'd taken down the smiley face posters Officer Keith had sworn were good for the students' self-images. Well, they were bad for Theo's self-image. How could he, Theo Buloski, one of the best, though underappreciated officers on the Tucson force, keep his self-respect with Barney the purple dinosaur spouting pious platitudes over his shoulder? He'd replaced Barney with the Statue of Liberty.

Asking for "your huddled masses, yearning to be free," the Lady of Liberty promised a life of opportunity to immigrants. The teachers here made good on that promise. They worked their buns off to help the kids succeed. In return, the kids loved the teachers and the principal and even him, Theo, the cop. Officer Buloski to them. None of this Officer First Name stuff. The teachers were Mr. and Ms. Last Name. He was Officer Last Name. Buloski wasn't that hard to learn.

He knew about half the kids' names by now. He was good with names, necessary for a cop. The kids loved it when he remembered. All this love going on made him nervous. Smiley faces and loving "take my hand" kids were closing in on him like the walls of this small office. Loving was something he wasn't good at. Didn't he have his failed marriage to prove that? Ancient history. Fifteen years ago. He hadn't changed. Loving was not his thing.

Sex, he understood. Simple and to the point, so to speak. But love? It annoyed him that Kate Mahoney came to mind when he got on the sex/love wavelength. He snorted and took out a cigar. Looked at it. Gave it a second glance and stuck it in his mouth, unlit.

What these kids needed were good dads. What *his* kid had needed was a good dad. Hell, he'd tried to get custody after the divorce. No way. Courts used to go with the mom even if his ex, Lorraine, wasn't the responsible parent. If his son, Doug, had lived long enough, Dad might've mattered. He turned his thoughts away from the broken body and twisted bike of his eight-year-old son. Never knew what hit him, the doctors said. Theo had worked for years to find out *who* hit him. It was still an unsolved case of hit and run, still open only because the dad was a cop.

So, if he couldn't be a dad to one kid, how could he satisfy hundreds? If he weren't careful, the boys, especially, would attach themselves to him like little leeches. He kind of liked the kids, but, geez, they drained him. He could never give them enough of what they needed.

The teachers were getting used to him, sort of. He gathered from conversations in the teachers' lounge that they had the same problem. Their caring was never enough to fill up empty hearts. But they consoled themselves that they made a difference in their kids' lives. Blooming saints! He chewed on his cigar, then slipped it into his shirt pocket when he heard a knock on the office door.

"Come in."

Louie Castillo slid in through a partially opened door, and then shut it immediately behind him. Probably didn't want the other kids to know he was in here. Dark brown eyes peeked out through long brown lashes, looking first at the officer, then abruptly shifting to the Statue of

Liberty poster. He stood staring at Lady Liberty for the two minutes of intimidating silence that Officer Buloski deemed appropriate.

"Why do you have her in here?" Louie demanded. "The little kids like Barney better."

Not according to plan. It was Officer Buloski who was supposed to mercifully break the silence. Still, this kid was the first one who even noticed the Lady's presence.

"When it's time to talk, I'll tell you, Louie."

Louie beamed. Mistake. He shouldn't have let the kid know he remembered his name. He should have called him "kid." They lapsed into silence for another two minutes.

"Isn't my silence time up?"

"What?" Theo knew he should've followed up on his demand for silence. Teachers say, "Consistency's the thing," but his cop's curiosity got the best of him. "What do you mean 'silent time'?"

"The kids say when you get called in here because you're in trouble, you always start with silent time. About two minutes. How come I got more than two minutes?" The eyes under the lashes looked at his captor and began to moisten. "Am I in big trouble?"

"I'd say so. Come here."

The kid approached the desk, holding both hands over his jeans pockets. His eyes were guilty as sin.

"Empty out your pockets on my desk."

"Do I have to? Do I need a lawyer?" His eyes scanned at warp speed. Probably recalling cop shows on TV. "You can't make me do this without a search warrant. Are you going to read me my rights?"

"Listen, kid—"

"Louie."

"Listen, Louie—" Theo was amazed at the skill with which this fifth grader moved to control the situation. Bet he controlled his mom, too. "Since you're into the law and all of that, you should know here at school we operate 'in loco parentis'."

Louie nodded. With the Latin, his eyes widened.

"You know what 'in loco parentis' means, don't you?"

Louie nodded, looked guilty, then shook his head. "No."

If only crooks were this transparent. "Well, Louie…" Theo let the name slip because he liked the kid. The boy wouldn't make a good crook. Not yet, anyway. "'In loco parentis' is Latin for 'in place of the parent.' In other words, school officials, of whom I am one, can treat you as if we were your parents. So when your dad tells you to empty your pockets, you do so. Now."

Louie sidled up to the desk. "I don't have a dad."

What else is new? "Loco parentis" should have guessed.

Louie gingerly pulled the contents of his left pocket out one by one. Rubber band. Bubble gum wrapper. Pencil with the point broken off. Smooth gray rock with black streaks in it.

When the pocket was empty, Theo ordered, "Turn it inside out." No school official would turn the pocket inside out for a kid. Too close to the private parts and a sexual abuse charge.

As Theo had expected, the contraband merchandise, a pack of Virginia Slims, was in the second pocket. Kids' evidence always turned up in the last pocket to be searched.

Louie shuffled his feet and looked around. Seeking an escape route? Then, abandoning flight as a bad idea, he glanced at Theo, blinked and looked away.

"Stand here, Louie." The police officer indicated a spot on the carpet directly in front of him. Louie centered himself on that spot. "Now look at me."

The young lad tried but his eyes kept wandering off. Theo took the boy's chin in his big hand and moved in close so Louie's eyes had nowhere else to look.

"You smoke cigars." Louie wrinkled his nose. "I can tell by your breath. Cigarettes are bad for your health, but cigars are worse."

Damn, this kid was good! He ought to be a police interrogator. It took an effort for Theo to control his admiration. But control he did.

"We're not talking cigars here, Louie. We're talking Virginia Slims. Before I ask you where you got them, I want you to reflect on why I called you in here. Why did I want to know what was in your pocket? Somebody tipped me off. Just chew on that before you give me some cock and bull answer."

"You're not supposed to talk to me that way."

"What way?"

"Cock—you know."

Theo scowled and shook his head. "A cock is a rooster…among other things." What was he, the cop, doing on the defensive? Gonna sign this kid up for the Police Academy! "The cigarettes, my lad. The cigarettes."

Louie heaved a sigh and tried to look sideways, but Theo's eyes were there, blocking. "You already know. I took them from the Circle K, but they're not for me. They're for my mom." Louie returned Theo's glare. "She's sick. Got the flu, and she needs cigarettes. Addiction, you know. And we don't have any money, so I thought the Circle K wouldn't miss them much. They're rich. They can afford to lose a pack of cigarettes." Truth told, his attitude shifted from defensive to offensive. "Who was the snitch who told you?"

Theo heard, but ignored. "Did your mother send you out to steal them?"

"No!" Louie's voice squeaked. "She'd be mad."

"How were you going to explain where they came from?"

"I'd think of something."

Theo didn't doubt it. "Your mom's at home sick?"

Louie nodded, tears welling to the brim. "Are you going to put me in jail?"

"I'm going to take you home, and you're going to tell your mom what happened. As far as jail goes. This first offense—it is the first time you've been in trouble with the police, isn't it?"

Louie nodded vehemently.

"Yeah, well, I could make this a paper arrest. That means I document it and turn you over to your mother's custody, providing—"

"Providing what?"

"Providing you can give me worthwhile information about Tamoni. If you can tell me something valuable I don't already know, I'll make this a paper arrest. Of course, if you ever shoplift again, this documentation will be pulled out, and both cases will go against you."

Louie curled his upper lip and glared through eyes suddenly turned old. "So you're cutting me a deal."

Theo was glad the kid understood, but he was getting a bad taste in his mouth. He'd have preferred to cut a deal with anyone but school kids, but he had to play the hand he was dealt. Two murders and Kate's life in danger.

"If you've got something worth hearing, I'm keeping you out of juvenile court, but I'm riding your tail 'in loco parentis' from now on." That was part of what was eating Theo. He needed information, but he was uncomfortable being too close to this kid. He didn't want to be playing daddy.

"Don't worry about me getting punished. My mom'll give me hell. Probably grounded and no TV for a month. Okay, this is what I know—"

"You what?" Kate's response wasn't the high-pitched squeal of a hysterical female. More like the low deadly growl of a mama grizzly encountering the male who'd do damage to her young. Her tone made even a seasoned cop wish he hadn't been so candid. But it was too late. Louie's revelations had made Theo euphoric and, for some lame-brained reason that for the moment escaped him, he'd been anxious to share the news with Kate. The same Kate who now leaned over her desk, deciding which part of his anatomy to mutilate first.

"You copped a plea with an innocent fifth grader!" Again, the low tone. She slowly edged toward him. Theo resisted the urge to leave his chair and move back. Instinctively, he scanned for a weapon. The only thing handy was a brass letter opener. He could handle that.

"Don't get dramatic. I made a paper referral on the shoplifting, a perfectly legal move, in exchange for information that's going to be useful."

"Damn." She picked up the letter opener and ran a finger over an edge. It had to be wishful thinking on her part, but Theo instinctively put both hands in his lap. She stood two feet away from him, hovering.

"He'll be punished. His mom was furious when I took him home. Yes, she was sick. Yes, she needed the cigarettes, but she doesn't want to raise a crook. She brought out a belt and asked whether I wanted to witness the impression she'd make."

The boss lady rolled her eyes and threw the letter opener at his feet. It stuck up straight in the carpet. He bet she'd practiced that move and done it before; it was too slick for the first try. He suppressed a chuckle.

"I told her not to make the impression too strong. We didn't want to see any bruises on him in school tomorrow, and then I got the hell out of there." He picked up the letter opener and placed it near his chair.

The low growl concluded. "Don't you ever again exchange leniency for information from one of my students."

"They're my students, too!" Theo couldn't believe he said that. The impact of it shut him up.

"If you do, I'll go to the chief of police and our acting superintendent or whoever it takes to get you off this campus."

Theo wanted to say, "Promises, promises." Instead, he kept quiet.

They sat in silence for a couple of minutes, just like he'd done with Louie. Enough! He had his hand on the doorknob, when she asked, "Well, what did you learn?"

Theo thought he was hearing things. "What did you say?"

Kate didn't blink. "I said, what did you learn from Louie?"

"You on your high horse, lecturing me about corrupting your little dearie. But you want the spoils of that corruption? Now I'm damn well not going to tell you!"

"Since the deed is done, and you've learned something, you need to tell me. We're working on this case together." There wasn't a hint of apology in her voice, but the low growl was gone. "Please. We need to put our differences aside and see what we've got."

"I don't give a damn what *we* need to do. I know what *I'm* going to do. Work on the information I've got and to hell with sanctimonious dames. You're so used to calling the shots! A first class ball buster!"

He stomped out of the office, slamming the door so hard he hoped the glass would break. It didn't. It was the damned unbreakable kind.

Valley View High School was a skeleton being unevenly fleshed out. Nothing was finished. The library was rising, concrete block on concrete block, rebar sticking up like silent steel antennas to reinforce the walls. The administration building was already roofed, its window holes gaping like empty eye sockets. The two-story classroom wing was a walled fortress enclosing steel beams that would support the floor of the second story. A seventy-foot crane stood silent, its cab abandoned. The air smelled of wet concrete.

Kate noticed how much the end of a construction day resembled a school after dismissal. During the workday, both vibrated with the activity of hundreds, but when the whistle blew the workers disappeared within minutes, leaving only the leaders to jaw over the day's work.

A few job bosses wearing yellow hard hats were milling around the construction trailer when Kate and Wallace approached. They exchanged the gruff comments of men making something important happen. Wallace's presence as company president was taken for granted, the sign of an administrator who gets out in the field and grubs along with his workers. Kate liked that.

A couple of supervisors telling a joke lowered their voices when she came within earshot. A petite brunette in the construction trailer was bent over a set of blueprints that must have weighed fifteen pounds. A table of rough lumber that filled the end of the trailer supported them. It was high because the bosses were always standing when using it. Underneath the table, other blueprints lay flat on shelves. One, Kate guessed, for each building. The rest of the trailer was filled with unruly desks, computers, and a coffee pot that hadn't been washed in ages flanked by twenty cups, each hanging on its own nail. Nothing fancy, everything functional. Not a woman's world.

Wallace's introductions followed the no-nonsense pattern. "Kate Mahoney, principal at Saguaro Elementary—Priscilla McDaniels, one of the architects. You remember Flora."

Kate nodded. She hadn't seen the blonde seated at a desk behind the trailer door, working with what looked like paychecks. Flora raised an eyebrow, stared, and then returned to her paperwork.

Ms. McDaniels peered over half glasses. "You know, Wallace, split face rock exterior wouldn't cost much more than the concrete block called for in the building specs, and it would sure look a lot better."

"That extra expense isn't included in the bid, and Icarus Construction sure as hell isn't going to eat it."

"Approach the district superintendent—"

"She's dead."

"Oh, yeah, that's right. Well…talk to whoever's taking her place and get this extra expense approved. It may not be large enough to require board action."

Kate was amazed at how the two business people sailed right over the fact that the district superintendent was dead. A human being is dead. Who cares? Detour around the corpse and solve your problem with the new chain of command. Then she remembered how she'd forgotten to count Dr. Mason along with Elijah and Juan as losses at her own faculty meeting. *Mortal flesh is passing, a la St. Ignatius.*

She compared the exterior sketches being touted by the architect, who had taken to nervously patting the bun at the nape of her neck. The concrete block looked a little like a prison despite some mitigating design features. The split-face resembled the exterior of Loews Ventana Canyon Resort in the foothills. The difference in cost would be substantial.

"Well, then, I'll take it to the Faculty Building Advisory Committee, let them make the choice and put on the pressure." The architect closed the blueprints with a bang. "It should have come from you!" She thudded her hard hat on the blueprints.

"You go ahead and get the teachers' committee riled up over this exterior change." Wallace's face reddened. "It was your responsibility to have those plans complete before they went out to bid. You damn females! Playing macho in a man's world! And then you go whining to the faculty committee to cover your asses."

He picked up the hard hat and held it in midair. For an instant Kate had the feeling he was going to hit the architect with it. Instead, he handed it to Kate, gripped her elbow and guided her out the door. When Flora grabbed a hard hat and followed down the trailer steps, Wallace abruptly turned to her and said, "No." Her lips turned pouty, and she retraced her steps back into the trailer.

Wallace's grip tightened. Kate wondered whether she'd have a black and blue elbow, but she was relieved to get out in the fresh air away from the hostility. She let him lead. They walked in silence, stepping over short pieces of lumber and around hardened cement drips. He lifted the yellow hazard tape, and they ducked under to enter the classroom wing. The empty shell was enormous.

"Looks big, Kate, but it has to house thirty-eight classrooms, a thousand square feet each. There's a lot more work to be done before we can partition the space. There will be movable walls between each set of classrooms to provide flexibility in room use." He again took her arm and guided her around a pile of steel supports. "First the roof. Today the men used that seventy-foot crane outside to place the steel ridge beam that'll support the roof. It's something to see—that baby being swung into place." He looked up at the "baby" with pride. "That main beam is about two feet wide and thirty feet up. Tomorrow, hod carriers will be scooting across it carrying their bricks and mortar as if it were two feet off the ground."

"You're really proud of your men, aren't you, Wallace?"

"Damn right."

"But not of your women."

Wallace blanched.

A vision of Flora in her mint green silk suit flashed before Kate's eyes, and she hastened to amend her statement. "I mean, the women who work for you."

"Kate, I don't have women working on my construction sites. It's no place for women. You can see how out of touch that architect was."

Kate sensed she was working at cross-purposes. She was not winning his trust this way, but she had to say it. "What about equal opportunity employment?"

"There's ways to get around that. And all of my secretaries are women." He flashed a charming smile that left no doubt about his management skills in gender specific areas. "Building is man's work, just like your work with children is what women do well." Another smile. "You can't improve on nature."

Kate swallowed the argument that some of her best teachers were men. She had to stay focused on getting financial information about this building project. How did Wallace feel about women school superintendents? Dr. Mason had invaded a man's field.

"Let's take this cherry picker up to the top. It'll give us a view of the whole layout."

They rode the hydraulic lift up in silence. Wallace's eyes flicked over the work site that fell beneath them as if mentally making notes for his site bosses. Watching the cement mixers and wheelbarrows diminish until they seemed the size of children's toys, Kate had the strange feeling that she should have stayed below, way outside the yellow danger tape.

The company president stepped lightly out of the lift and onto the steel ridge beam. He turned to help Kate up beside him. "Don't look down. It's like walking along a sidewalk. Just a little narrower."

Kate looked down. It was a long way to the concrete floor below. Two stories and their crawl spaces made it at least a thirty-foot drop. Why was she scared? She'd walked ledges this narrow when hiking along cliffs. Yet something told her to stay in the lift.

"Here's a rope we'll put around your waist, so if you slip I'll haul you back up on the beam." Wallace was amused. Kate was tempted to walk along that ridge, with or without a rope, just to show him!

She resisted the temptation. Something in this picture was out of focus. Chief administrators are famous for their fear of accidents and lawsuits. Why was he pushing her to take a risk? Probably, he was so confident he didn't consider it a risk. He'd be in control. Kate wasn't ready to hand her life over to his keeping, so she lied.

"I should have told you, I'm afraid of heights." Kate hated the fake fear in her voice. "I'm okay as long as I'm inside an enclosed space like the cherry picker, but I'd be scared to death walking along that beam."

Wallace's lifted eyebrow indicated that was what he'd expect of a woman. He walked part way out on the beam without a rope, looked around as if inspecting his kingdom, and then came back—satisfied.

Show off! Next time Kate had to go to Allister's home, she'd take him along.

Dusk was setting in by the time they reached ground level. As they exited under the yellow caution tape, Kate had the strange feeling she'd visited the building site with Wallace at one elbow and Mother Provincial at the other.

In the Parlor...

The cloister furnishings in the Celtic Cross Novitiate and Retreat House were Shaker simple. A professed sister's cell contained a twin bed with a simple, white metal headboard, a straight back chair, a plain desk, a closet for her habits, and a washstand supporting a white pottery basin.

Novices and postulants slept in dorms, their spaces separated by white muslin curtains that were pulled open during the day. Their furnishings were the same as the professed, but without the chair and desk.

Ornamentation was reserved for the chapel with its Gothic arches, rich Celtic design, tabernacle, and candlesticks of gold. The only other room decorated with a compromise to comfort was the parlor.

Two Queen Anne-style wing chairs flanked the fireplace. The walnut coffee table received fresh flowers each morning, a joyful contrast to the portrait of Mother Bridget O'Leary, foundress of the Congregation, who frowned from above the mantel. For an Irish congregation, the parlor had a decidedly English look, perhaps to emphasize its distance from the daily cloistered life.

Postulants and novices could see their family members once every other month. Other visitors were allowed only with express permission of the Mother Mistress. Male visitors who weren't family members were never allowed.

Standing in the far corner of the main parlor, Sister Katherine heard the crackle of the oak log in the fireplace, but felt no warmth. She reached to touch the wing chair, but her hand was stopped, as if by glass. She tried the other hand. It met the same barrier. She tapped the invisible wall. Her tap made no sound. She could see and hear, but she was enclosed in a dream, unable to act.

Down the hall, a young man's loud voice mingled with the kind tones of Sister Laura, the ninety-two-year-old convent porter. The novice thought she recognized the male voice. Could it be?

Sister Laura explained with exaggerated patience, "You may wait in here, young man, but Sister Katherine O'Brien's in the strict year of seclusion required by canon law, Rome's own law. Are you a Catholic?"

A tall blonde sailor in navy blues, white hat in hand, appeared in the doorway. "Yes."

"Then you must understand why we can't allow Sister Katherine to break cloister." She directed him to a wing chair.

He remained standing. "I don't understand, sister. And I want her to explain it herself."

"I'll go right up to Mother Mistress's office, but I don't travel very fast." The old nun shuffled across the room to the door. "And she might be busy, but I'll present your request. If you get tired of waiting, you know the way out."

Sister Katherine could hardly breathe. The sailor looked through her as if she weren't there. He shook his head, lips tight together the way she knew so well.

"Eliot. It's me. Kate."

He didn't hear, but began pacing the parlor, twirling his white sailor hat between his fingers. Sister Katherine tried to move. The barrier allowed no passage.

They'd gone through all of grade school together at Saint Finian's. In the sixth grade, Sister Mary James had complained that Eliot wasn't a proper name for an Irish Catholic boy. "Who ever heard of Saint Eliot? There must be English Protestants somewhere in the family tree."

His eyes had an impudent twinkle as he'd agreed. "Probably so. Probably so. I feel a little Protestant in my blood every so often." No, Eliot was not one to be intimidated by the nuns.

At Catholic Central High School, they'd been soul mates. Celibate, as expected of Catholic kids. But the memory of steamy kisses at drive-in movies made her smile even now. When he'd left for the Korean War, his last words had been, "Do any crazy thing you want, Kate, but promise me you won't be a nun. You're not cut out for that life."

That was the one thing she couldn't promise. The last letter she'd written enroute to the convent had been to Eliot in Korea.

The commanding presence of Mother Philippa Manning appeared in the doorway, while a worried Sister Laura hovered near. "Mother Mistress is busy in class, Sister Laura. So I will attend to the young gentleman."

The Mother Provincial moved to one wing chair. She instructed the young man to sit in the other. He sat on the arm, a mute compromise.

"Mr. Eliot Redding, you must realize that Sister Katherine O'Brien entered this house of Our Lord of her own free will, and she has agreed to obey all of the rules of the Congregation. The rules don't allow male visitors who aren't family."

Elliot shot Mother Provincial the same impudent look he'd used on the nuns at Catholic Central. Kate loved it then, and Sister Katherine loved it now. "Mother, all due respect, but if you don't let me see Kate, I'll bring the police in to see that she's not being detained against her will." His raised voice shocked the halls of silence.

Sister Katherine cheered him on.

Mother nodded to Sister Laura, who disappeared through the door.

The sailor looked up from the white cap he'd been turning in his hands. "Thank you, Mother, I appreciate your cooperation."

Mother raised an eyebrow and waited, silent, tall, and motionless for a full ten minutes until Sister Laura again appeared, followed by a red-faced Irish policeman.

"Good day, Mother Philippa. And is this the cheeky young man who's disturbing your peace?" The robust cop moved to the side of the startled sailor, patting his baton. "And sure, sister says you're a Catholic, too. You ought a be ashamed of yourself. Come along, or I'll call your buddies in the Shore Patrol."

Eliot protested that he wasn't disturbing the peace.

"You have to understand, my man. In a place like this, it doesn't take much to disturb the peace." He took the sailor by the arm. "Sure, and you're on your way."

Mother Philippa approached the policeman. “Thank you, Officer Murphy. There won’t be any need to press charges as long as Mr. Redding doesn’t return.”

“At least, tell Kate I was here. That I wanted to see her.”

Mother Provincial looked at him, her face expressionless. She nodded to Sister Laura and floated gracefully out the door.

Behind her barrier, Sister Katherine was flooded with a deep sadness. Numb, she slumped into the corner chair until startled by the touch of Mother Provincial.

“Tell me this didn’t really happen.”

“It happened years ago, when you were a novice.” The Provincial tucked her hands under her scapular and shrugged her shoulders. “Now I’m sorry I sent Eliot away. If your vocation had been strong enough, it would’ve survived an ardent suitor.”

“You like playing God!”

“I play the role the Church expects of me.” Mother Provincial perked up. “Anyway, he wasn’t your type. I could tell. Neither, for that matter, is Wallace.”

“Mother, you‘d be the last person to know!” Curiosity niggled, nevertheless. “Don’t you trust Wallace?”

“It’s just a feeling I have, my daughter.” Mother Philippa sobered. “Don’t be around Wallace alone.” The older nun stooped to rearrange an iris in the coffee table bouquet. “You can come out now. The dream’s over.”

8

"Mrs. Mahoney, would ya cash my check for me?" Ebony, a second grader all eyes and glasses, made her plea over the office counter.

"So you've a check that needs to be cashed. We're not usually in the check cashing business, Ebony, but let me take a look at it." Life in Saguaro's front office zoomed in the fast lane. Kate liked being here. The speed dulled her worries.

The child proudly produced a check for "one hundrid dollers" signed by Ebony Walters on the line where the date should be. The blank check belonged to "Ms. Barbara Shoen," the parent of a first grader.

"Where did you get this, Ebony?"

Innocent eyes looked over the girl's glasses. "Patty's handing 'em out to everybody." She paused, measuring the principal's reaction. "Everybody's excited 'cause we're going to get rich. I only made mine out for one hundred dollars 'cause I didn't want to push my luck. You know what I mean?"

"I know what you mean, Ebony, but you can't do this." Kate softened the disappointment with a sympathetic smile. "The money in the bank belongs to Patty's mother, and Patty shouldn't be giving out her checks. Do you know what I mean?"

Ebony paused, then nodded, bobbing tight black braids. "I guess it was too good to be true. A first grader handing out checks. They're such babies. I should've known they don't know about money."

Kate rounded the counter and took the child's hand. "Let's go talk to Patty and try to track down the other checks she's given away."

Half an hour later, a fistful of checks in hand, Kate was back in the crowded office. Twenty minutes before the dismissal bell, too many bodies crammed into so small a space made the place seem muggy. Parents who picked up their kids usually did their business at this time. Kate tried to be available for parents and to help the secretaries handle the end of the day.

There was room for four chairs. In one, a third grader with a toothache cradled his jaw while staring off into space, wondering if home would bring any relief. The nurse had talked a dentist into caring for him free. Would his mom be willing to take him on the bus to keep the appointment?

A heavy mom sat on the second chair with her dress pulled up above the knee to expose a nasty black and blue bruise. She wanted to get the Resource Officer to put her kid in jail for parent abuse. Kate hadn't been able to change her mind. Theo was out, but she'd wait.

Toddlers left on the other two chairs were crying and fighting, while their dad explained in Spanish to Tiá that he had another son, a second grader, coming from Mexico, whom he wanted to attend Saguaro Elementary. So he didn't live in this school district. What the hell?

Two other kids sat on the floor, waiting their turn with the secretaries. In fifteen minutes, the bell would ring, and kids would flood in wanting to use the phone, or sobbing that they'd missed the day care bus, or looking for a lost backpack, or complaining some kids were going to beat them up on the way home. In other words, it was a normal dismissal time, a time when the secretaries needed Kate's help.

Kate sensed testosterone in overdrive the moment the two cops came through the office door. She'd never seen them before, but one look at their set jaws and mean eyes told Kate to drop everything and deal with them. The blue-eyed blonde was about six feet two with a neck that would've made an NFL linebacker proud. The Hispanic, a couple of inches shorter, had a mustache that drooped. The corners of his mouth followed the same downward trend.

She introduced herself and asked to see their shields. Officer Jose Valles rolled his eyes as she recorded their names and shield numbers. With each passing minute, their tension went up a notch, so she hustled them into her office and closed the door. They weren't interested in taking a seat.

"We're here to pick up Hassan Mahem for assault and battery. Is he here?" The blonde, Officer Speed Heath, blocked the door as if he expected her to bolt.

"Yes, he's one of our evening custodians. But it would be out of character for him to beat somebody up."

"He's big, and he's black."

It was hard to tell whose tempers were rising faster, theirs or Kate's.

"Yes, he's both. But he's a gentle giant. The kids like him. They're usually pretty good judges of character."

Officer Heath moved forward and stuck his face into Kate's. She could smell the cigarette smoke and secondhand onion. "You tell that to the little girlfriend he left battered. We're not asking you for a character reference. We're telling you to call him on the intercom *now*!"

"Did you actually see that she'd been battered, or is this hearsay?"

"Look, Mahoney, we know who you are." His mouth twisted in a sneer. "And we expect trouble from you. But if you don't get on that intercom and call Hassan Mahem to the office, we're going around the school till we find him!"

"I'll call him in, but please don't take him into custody until the school buses are gone and the campus is cleared. Fifteen minutes is all I'm asking for." They weren't hearing her. "Fifteen minutes, please."

"We're busy too, Mahoney." Officer Valles had taken over Heath's position at the door. Intimidation. "What's the response time when you call cops here for help?"

"Three minutes."

Heath barked the threat. "You keep stalling, and it's going to get a whole lot longer. Now get on that intercom."

All eyes in the main office followed her as she crossed the room and called for Hassan. The nurse's door didn't have a window, so Kate asked Ziona to vacate for a few minutes, and she put the police in there.

In a couple of minutes, Hassan sashayed in, gave the high sign to the kid with the toothache, winked and held his own jaw in mock sympathy.

"Hassan, I need you in the nurse's office."

"What's the matter, Ms. Mahoney? You look kind of worried."

When he saw the officers, his eyes widened, and his hands went up in submission. "Oh, no, this is Lulu Belle's doing!"

Hassan's face thudded against the wall as the officers shoved him into spread-eagle position. Valles shoved Kate out the door and slammed it. She opened it a crack to watch the cops beat Hassan's head against the wall and knee him in his butt while they searched for weapons. Finding none, Heath snapped handcuffs on, read him his rights, and dragged him out through the office.

Kate walked alongside them, trying to shield what was happening from the eyes of the children. The police had parked next to the bus-loading zone, where dozens of kids were lined up under the watchful eye of Mr. Nelson. Before the officers put Hassan in the police car, they made him spread-eagle and patted him down again for show.

"Let the kids see," snarled Valles. "They need to see what happens if they break the law." The excitement of his conquest smelled like sweat. Kate tried to control her queasy stomach as she kept between the cop car and the children.

A kindergartner cried and ran to her. "Why are they hurting Hassan? He's my friend."

Kate took her hand. "He'll be back to school soon. He'll be all right." She hoped it was the truth.

The kids waiting for their buses spoke not a word. Their eyes wide with shock mirrored the opinions being formed within. This wasn't the kind of police action Kate wanted them to see.

Jacqueline Stanley wasn't sympathetic with Kate's account of Hassan and the police. In fact, she wasn't responsive to anything. Kate chalked it up to her peer's fondness for reading through the night, then sleeping until one or two on weekends. Still, high tea time at Tohono Chul Tearoom was way past the wake-up hour.

The two principals met for Sunday tea every month or so. It gave them a chance to air gripes, laugh away worries, and exchange information about the nomad families that moved between Saguaro and

Mesquite Elementaries. These families, who routinely moved during the night when their rent was due, sent their children to either of the two schools, depending on convenience. Children from these unstable homes brought the most troubles to school, so shared information was useful.

Jacqueline yawned and glanced toward the arched Mexican entrance. Was she expecting someone more interesting than present company to appear in the archway? With her red and white checked shirt and dangling blue earrings, the Mesquite principal's style was somewhere between Italian tablecloth and American flag. She didn't care about style. A face leathered by years of Arizona sun revealed the true Jacqueline, a seasoned horsewoman. She spent her precious free time in the saddle.

It was when Kate fell into silence, listening to the gurgling of the nearby Mexican tile fountain, that her companion commented dryly, "We all have our problems, Kate. Try this one on. Thursday, a red pickup drove past the kids on the playground in the after-school sports program and fired two shots. Or so said some of the kids. And Trina, the director, backed them up." She took a long sip of her martini, pushing the olive to the side.

"Of course, the police were called, but there were no bullet holes nor any proof." She took a deep breath. This incident was exhausting even in the telling. "By Friday morning, the office phones were abuzz with parents calling to let me know they had seen the red pickup." She waved her hand to flick away the memory. "Do you know how many red pickups there are in Tucson, Kate?"

Kate declined to guess.

"Thousands!" Jacqueline continued. "And they all went near my school on Friday!" She leaned on her elbow again, looking vacantly at the arch. "And I can't tell you how many parents accused me of a cover-up. They claimed I should know which red pickup fired the shots, and I should do something about it!"

"It could've been a backfire." Kate's attempt to help earned her a scorching glance.

"Even my dull brain figured that out," Jacqueline retorted, then sighed. "I'm getting too old for this job!"

"Too old! I can't believe you said that."

Jacqueline looked around the room. "Where is that waitress?"

The high tea continued with the stability of English codified tradition. First, scones and clotted cream; then, finger sandwiches. A welcome constant in the changing world of red pickups and shots fired.

Still, Kate wasn't going to be distracted by a cucumber sandwich. She wanted to check rumors that her colleague was having fits with her new construction "punch list" for Mesquite Elementary. Having finished two years of construction at Saguaro, Kate was all too familiar with "punch lists," which enumerated building glitches that needed correcting after the construction was officially finished. In Oasis District, the school principals had the job of nagging the contractors until corrections were made. Since contractors often dragged their feet until building warranties were up, the list made principals want to do the punching.

Kate proceeded cautiously. "I'm seeing a strange pattern in the new construction. Last summer, when I got back from vacation, I found that swamp coolers had been installed in the new classroom wing. District policy calls for air conditioning in all new buildings, and I'm sure they were included in the building specifications." She took a sip of her merlot.

"Mistakes happen." Jacqueline wasn't interested.

"Yes, but this is the strange part." Kate tapped the glass table for emphasis. "When I complained to Julie, she had the district physical resource guys install new air conditioners in two weeks. Two weeks! Nothing ever happens in two weeks!"

Jacqueline caught the waitress's eye and pointed to her glass. "Two more—"

Kate put her hand over her half-filled wine glass. "No, I'm good."

"One, then..." She turned to Kate. "Don't you ever live it up, Kate? Always wine. Never a martini. No wonder you let the little things bug you."

Feeling pushed, Kate sat back. "Little things! Having air conditioning makes for decent learning in hot months here in the desert. Kids get sleepy in the heat. So you've never had trouble with your building specs being ignored?"

"Never." Jacqueline helped herself to a chocolate-dipped strawberry. "Don't worry about it. It's a one-time deal. A mistake, and it got corrected."

"Rumor has it that the same thing happened with Mesquite's new library. The contractor, so they say, put regular glass in the windows, and the district guys replaced it with the unbreakable type within the week. Is this some sort of a pattern?"

Jacqueline's answer was low and tense. "I hate the way these false rumors flit around the district. It never happened. We had unbreakable glass as required in the building specs." She took a generous swig from the newly arrived martini. "I'm surprised you listen to that gossip. You'd better check your specs. Your architect probably left air conditioning out."

Kate could feel her social patina wearing thin. Why was Jacqueline lying? Manny, the district carpenter, had put the glass replacements in himself. She slowly twirled the wine in her glass and soldiered on.

"Possibly, our superintendent had modified the building specs after our staff building committee had seen them and before she took them to the governing board. Sneaky, but within her right. It's hard to tell how strongly the board feels about the staff's input into this planning. Still, I doubt they'd want her to slip it by us like that."

The smell of freshly baked pastries floating in the wake of the waitress distracted her momentarily. "Swamp coolers would save money, but if air conditioners had been in the bid the cost to the district would've been more accurately portrayed. Maybe Julie wanted to minimize the true cost of the project. But why? There's money in the district bonds budget for large projects, but we never have enough funds in capital improvements for maintenance. Why would she have maintenance fix these mistakes?"

"I'm not going to listen to this nonsense. It's like the red pickup. You're making a big thing out of one simple mistake. Besides, she's dead now. If she made mistakes—it's all over."

Why was Jacqueline so defensive? And so personal about it? The only good thing about this high tea was the food. Certainly, not the company.

The waitress circled back, her cart displaying the dessert choices: chocolate covered cherries, petit fours, an almond marzipan, or sorbet parfait. This was Kate's favorite part of high tea, calories be damned. Jacqueline selected the parfait and ordered another martini. Kate settled on the marzipan.

Though she tried not to be defensive, Kate couldn't help it. "For years, we principals have tried to get a full-time construction manager on board. But neither Julie nor the former superintendents would go along with it. Since Larry died in that horrible auto accident this spring, only the principals are checking the construction work. We're not trained for that."

Jacqueline's eyes glazed over. "I still can't believe he's gone."

Larry Denton, the former manager of Physical Resources had been Jacqueline's lover. Kate reached over and touched her hand. Jacqueline pulled it back, but the lines on her face softened. The principal and manager had groused about being too busy to tie the knot. Kate suspected they both liked their independence.

"He was officially responsible, but he used to complain that it was impossible for him to stay on top of all the construction and also manage the district's physical resources. The district is growing so fast, there are too many projects going on at once." Jacqueline shrugged. "It's been five months since his death, and still Central Admin hasn't found anyone to replace him. Neither have I." Mist came to her eyes.

The two colleagues sat in silence for a couple of minutes.

Kate changed the subject by echoing a pet gripe. "I'm responsible for my six hundred and fifty kids. I start questioning the financial practices of Central Office and all of a sudden discretionary funds headed for Saguaro will get rerouted to other schools. You've seen it happen."

Another large gulp of martini. If Jacqueline ordered another drink, Kate would offer to drive her the twenty miles to her ranch house. Maybe it was because she was still dwelling on Larry, but the Mesquite principal leaned over the table with a look in her eye as mean as a weasel's. "Yes, I've seen it happen. I've seen federal funds—Chapter One funds, Headstart funds—go to Saguaro Elementary, while my school took the leavings. Discretionary funding is always available for the bright young principal with her school's splashy new programs, while the old hack who makes waves for Central Admin gets zilch!"

Kate couldn't have been more shocked if Jacqueline had thrown the martini in her face. Competition for dollars had always been a divisive factor among Oasis District principals, but this? It must be the booze talking. She felt a chill run through her. Sometimes, martini talk is the most honest.

"But we've always cooperated, Jacqueline."

There was no mistaking the edge in the other woman's voice. "You've called it cooperation because you've always gotten the better end of the deals." Jacqueline put her glass down with a thud that slopped liquid over the rim. "I've kept quiet because I've had too many other worries. But this latest is beyond all endurance."

"What are you talking about?" Kate's cheeks flushed.

"The arrogance of youth! Didn't it occur to you that our teachers talk to each other? The nerve, sending out a memo asking for persons whose first name is Jacqueline in connection with Julie Mason's death." As her shrill voice rose the ladies seated at the adjacent table looked her way.

So that was the burr under Jacqueline's saddle.

"Jacqueline, that had nothing to do with you! It was in response to a lead we'd been given, and I got several names back. No one sent yours in." Kate suddenly felt warm.

The tipsy colleague rose and towered over Kate.

"Do you need a ride home?"

"That's the final insult!"

When Jacqueline picked up her glass, Kate prepared to duck. Instead, Jacqueline gulped the contents and turned to stride through the arch, martini glass in hand. Leaving Kate to pay the check.

The next morning, as she fought rush hour traffic, Kate was still smarting over Jacqueline's words. Maybe there was some truth there. Probably so. She'd always been ambitious for her kids and pulled out all stops to get funding for them. Some of Saguaro's grants were splashy, but they helped the children.

Was it all for the kids or was it about her own personal drive? God knows, she liked to win—she always intended to win. The accusations niggled at her. Of one thing she was certain: Jacqueline Stanley was a different woman when she had too many drinks. Was she capable of murder?

Before she left home, Kate had called Terri to say she was stopping at Central Administration to dig the Saguaro classroom building specs out of the files in Physical Resources. Curiosity or penance?

The breakfast hour had come and gone, so the employees' cafeteria in Central Admin was empty except for two secretaries and a lone, disheveled figure slouched over a pile of files at a corner table. Kate, seeking a cup of coffee before heading to the files, breathed in the homey smell of bacon. While pouring her coffee, she spotted freshly baked cake donuts.

She was about to choose one swathed in chocolate, when her eye caught the nods of the two overweight secretaries, who were happily munching theirs. The principal returned the nod with a smile, letting her hand slide past the goodies and back to the styrofoam coffee cup.

Starting out the door, she took a second look at the occupant of the corner table. He reached for one of the two cups placed at arm's length away from the papers, took a sip, and replaced it, never taking his eyes from the manila file in front of him.

"What are you doing here, Theo?" They hadn't spoken since the row about Louie, and her nerves remembered the police brutality with Hassan. Still, she was curious.

Eyes that looked half asleep under droopy lids glanced in her direction. "Is that how you say good morning? I could ask the same of you."

"Yes, but I don't have to give you an answer. I'm the boss." Kate sat down and moved his cups closer to him to make room for hers.

"Not my boss. Thank God." His eyes went back to the file. He jotted down something in the three-by-five notebook he'd drawn from his breast pocket. "And I thought Rawlins was bad!"

Kate's ire rose like a switchblade, ready to spring open and strike. She got up, walked over to the tray of donuts, used a waxed paper square to pick up two of the chocolate-covered ones, changed her mind, put one back and selected a glazed donut in its place. The cafeteria lady ignored the violation of health regulations and rang up the sale.

Returning to Theo's table, she placed each donut on its own napkin. "Peace. Take your pick."

Theo looked up, the furrows over his heavy black eyebrows switching from one brow to the other. "Humph. I've always been a sucker for bribes." He chose the chocolate-covered one, pocketed his pen and tilted his chair back on two legs. The hint of amusement in his eye irritated Kate. She resisted the temptation to knock the chair out from under him.

"For the price of a donut, I'm supposed to tell you what Louie said about Tamoni. Right?" He pulled out his wallet and threw three quarters on the table. "That takes care of the donut."

The switchblade almost escaped from Kate's lips. She watched the two secretaries depart. Her buns would look like theirs if she kept eating donuts—the booby prize for having to put up with this infuriating male!

"I've got some information that might interest you." Without waiting for his offer to swap tales, and knowing full well her information had no bearing on the murder investigation, she elaborated on Jacqueline's response about paying for building expenses out of the capital budget. She exaggerated a bit to put frosting on the donut, to make him think she considered this valuable information.

"So I'm here to drop in on Physical Resources and check on those building specs."

The pen and notebook stayed in his pocket. The amusement in his eye grew to a twinkle. "I think I like you best when you're playing dumb. You play the part so poorly."

Kate kept her switchblade sheathed, but sat and glared at him.

"Okay, Kate. In the interest of our partnership, I'll play 'you show me yours, I'll show you mine.'"

The thinly veiled sexual reference produced the intended annoyance, but Kate kept silent. She intended to get the information even if the price was feigned humility.

Theo's eyes slipped into their working mode. "Pat Jackson was right about Louie and Tamoni being good friends. Since they both lived in the West Wind Apartments, they used to hang out at each other's place. Louie doesn't miss much."

Kate nodded. "He takes it all in."

"So he knew Elijah was around a lot. Sometimes, he was there when Elijah was teaching Tamoni how to use the drums. Said he learned a little about drums himself. But he was smart enough to keep quiet about Elijah's visitations."

The principal wished the cop would get to the point, but the professional look in his eyes meant he was on the right track. Patience.

"A couple of weeks ago, Louie heard Elijah complain to Jacqueline that Julie Mason was on his back—that she wanted something from him. Louie remembers it because he asked Tamoni who Julie Mason was. Tamoni said that Mason was Mrs. Mahoney's boss. Both boys worried that someone so powerful would be giving Elijah a bad time."

"What did Julie want of Elijah? "

Theo eased the chair down on its four legs and rubbed his bald head. "Louie says he doesn't know, and I believe him. That kid wouldn't make a good liar." He patted the open file in front of him. "So that's why I'm going over Elijah's personnel file again. What skill or connection in his background would make him valuable to the superintendent?"

"Elijah's a young teacher—good, but inexperienced." Kate didn't like puzzles she couldn't solve. "Anyway, if Julie wanted him to do professional work for the district, she'd probably have gone through me. Or, at least, let me know."

"Sexual favors?"

"They were both single, but Julie's not Elijah's type. Or vice versa. Besides, he was involved with Jacqueline."

The pen and notebook came out of Theo's pocket. Kate wondered whether he was recording the possibility of a sexual liaison. On a scale of one to ten, the chances of that were less than zero. She'd better stress that point. "Even Julie wouldn't dare be on his back over sexual matters. Sexual harassment is the politically correct object of litigation these days."

Theo thumbed through the pages in his notebook. "Remember when I told you Elijah worked for Icarus Construction for a couple of summers while he was in college? Seems he was a hod carrier for them."

Kate thought of the high main beam on the high school construction site and shook her head. "That's dangerous work, terribly hot during Tucson summers."

"He was a substitute hod carrier, so he must have replaced the regular guys who went on vacation." Theo shuffled through papers from the opened file. "One of his letters of recommendation is signed by Wallace Talbot. That's getting support right from the top. What brought him to Talbot's attention?"

"Wallace is out on job sites every day." Kate wondered why she felt protective. "He gets to know his men."

Theo gathered the papers and closed the file. "I'm going to visit Elijah and ask him about this connection. Icarus Construction's beginning to feel like an itch I need to scratch."

Kate picked up the empty styrofoam cups and dropped them in the wastebasket. Why had Theo needed two cups for coffee? Seemed like a waste. He could have gotten his refill in the first one. Strange man. She turned back to him. "Do you want to go with me to the Physical Resources office?"

"No. All due respect, but I doubt your findings there will shed any light on thc murder." The twinkle was back. "They might make you want to murder someone, but…too late. She's already dead." His eyes switched to serious. "If there's any connection, your looking over files with a cop at your elbow would tip your hand. Keep your cards hidden, Kate, until you're ready to play."

As it turned out, the classroom building specifications called for swamp coolers. She checked Mesquite Elementary's library specs. Regular glass for the windows. Why had Jacqueline lied? Why had the change been made before the specs went to the Board? Kate left the office thinking that Theo needn't have worried. There was no danger she'd tip her hand when she had no cards to play.

Theo caught up with her as she put the keys into the door of her district car. "Can I catch a ride with you back to school?" He slid into the passenger seat before she could answer. "My chariot's in the shop."

There was something rather satisfying about being in the driver's seat while traveling with Theo. She found herself telling him about the two cops who had pushed Hassan around.

"Valles and Heath are assholes." Kate had to admire the simplicity of Theo's psychological evaluations. "Ignore them, Kate," he advised. "They were a little bit of hell sent by Rawlins to make your day shitty."

"You know, Theo, I can put up with your language when there's just the two of us in the car, but be careful you don't use it around the kids. It's that kind of talk that sent Allister home on contract. You have to set an example. Our kids saw enough bad stuff about cops last Friday." Well, at least he wasn't lighting up his cigar.

"Geez! I don't talk like a frustrated school marm, so you're going to send me home on contract?" He looked like he might leap out at the next stop light. "How do you manage to breathe? The air up there in your strata must be too thin for oxygen, Mother Superior."

Kate wanted to remind him she could be down and dirty when the situation warranted, but she kept the switchblade closed. She needed him as a partner, dammit!

He continued, "Since you and I are involved—"

"Involved!" She jerked her head in his direction in time to see a red flush creep up his neck, into his face, and across where his hair should have been.

"Watch out!" he yelled.

Her foot hit the brake the instant her eyes snapped back to the road, stopping her car within an inch of the Peugeot convertible that had braked in front of her. The driver turned around and flipped a bejeweled middle finger at her, while his eyes took in the Oasis School district logo on her front license plate holder. The district would hear from him, Kate was pretty sure.

"Want me to drive?"

Kate didn't give him the benefit of a response.

"If I'm going to be involved with a partner *professionally*, I want to be fairly sure she's not going to kill me."

It was Kate's turn to blush. She threw him the nasty look she reserved for people who caught her being wrong.

"Patience, princess, patience." His cigar was in his left hand, but he hadn't lit it. At least, not yet. "Calm down, and we'll get through this relationship—this *professional* relationship—in one piece. Two pieces—you and me—individual and separate. Okay?"

Somehow, Kate liked him better when he swore.

After a day of P.E. classes, the gym smelled like kids, tennis shoes, and dusty backpacks. The area by the stage was piled high with library books, loose-leaf notebooks, lunch pails, and a few windbreakers and sweaters. Tucson's weather in early November was warm enough that most kids preferred to endure a few minutes of morning chill rather than lug a sweater around all day. Mothers sweatered their kindergartners if there was any nip in the air. By first grade, after they'd lost many sweaters, most moms went along with their kids' thinking, unless it was a real cold day.

It was break time in the City Parks and Recreation After-School Program, so the little kids sat in a circle, some pulling apart the Velcro straps on their tennies to hear the sound, while they waited for free juice packets to be passed out. Older kids hung in groups; a fifth grade blonde twirled her sunglasses in her fingers. Louie was making his yo-yo "walk the dog" to the amazement of his admirers, who included the blonde. Some sixth graders were playing a half court pick-up basketball game on the kitchen end of the court.

Things had been mellow while making a Thanksgiving mural the first hour after school was out. Using sponges, the primary kids filled the background with poster paint leaves of scarlet and yellow. Never mind the absence of maples in Tucson. The teacher said the Pilgrims had them in Massachusetts.

The older kids were less enthusiastic about their Pilgrims and Indians. True, Thanksgiving was coming up in a couple of weeks, but you could only make so many Pilgrims and list only so many things you were thankful for. Ho hum. By snack time, boredom had settled over the room like a fog.

But the minute the principal walked in, there was a stir. What's she here for? What's going to happen? Every eye followed her as she walked up to Bonnie McGee, the After-School Coordinator. Every eye except that of the blonde, who was still watching Louie, his yo-yo now limp at his side.

Kate was in the gym to escape from the unending problems in the office. Every few hours, she had to get out with the kids to remember why she put up with all the stress. A teacher-to-the-bone, she sensed the malaise. She caught a stray basketball. The kids howled in delight as she shot a basket, missed, then challenged Bonnie to shoot. Suddenly wide-eyed, the children cheered. Soon, all the adults were testing their skills against the sixth graders, and the kids were winning handily.

The gym was jumping when Hassan, back on the job without missing a day of work, came up behind Kate and tapped her on the shoulder. Her first impulse was to get him into the game, but one look at his enormous eyes that stood out white against his ebony face told her something was wrong. He looked as if he'd seen a ghost. She nodded toward the kitchen.

Hassan was physically trembling, so she pulled up a kitchen stool for him. He wouldn't take it, just kept moving around, agitated from head to foot.

"What's the matter? Are the cops here again?"

Hassan had grown up in Louisiana and never learned how to read. But he was an expert at reading people, especially the ladies. He did special little favors for all the lady teachers, whether they be sixty or twenty-one. Be they pretty or fading, they'd get a flower on their desk every so often. So what if the flowers were pilfered from the schoolyard? On their birthdays, every teacher on his wing received a candy bar pasted on a construction paper butterfly. Not signed, but everyone knew who left it.

The Hassan shaking before Kate was not that confident, gallant gentleman custodian, not the big, strong athlete whom the kids loved to challenge to touch football. At this moment, he was as scared as a first grader who'd lost his way home.

"What could possibly be so bad, Hassan?"

"Miss Kate, you gotta save me." With shaking finger, he pointed toward the gymnasium entrance. "It's Lulu Belle. She's going to come right in here and get me, and then tell the cops I was hurting her, and they're going to be dragging me away again." The fear in his eyes was real. "It's real bad—real bad—when the cops get you. And she's going to get me into trouble—and this time they'll keep me." He put his head down on the stainless steel dishwashing counter and began to cry.

Kate went over and touched him on the shoulder. "No, no. She can't come in here and start trouble. I'll call the cops if she tries." Kate put on her stern principal voice. "If you knocked her around, you can't blame her for being mad."

"I didn't hit her. She's not mad about that. She's mad because—" Hassan rolled his eyes and looked up at the ceiling. "She's mad because I got another girl. Lulu Belle—she can be a sweet little thing—but she knocked me for a loop more than once. Nearly took my head off the other night. I've had enough of it. I got myself another girl."

Reality check. Kate tried to picture this "sweet little thing" who was capable of manhandling Hassan. "Where is she?"

"Right out there. Right outside the gym door, waiting for me to come out, so she can lay into me and call the cops when I try to defend myself. Help me, Miss Kate. She'll get me for sure."

"Hassan, I can keep her off this campus, but other than that you're on your own." Kate opened the kitchen door and moved through the gym, where the free-throw competition was still going strong. She had a niggling curiosity about this "little thing" who had gotten Hassan into so much trouble. A "little thing" could get awfully mad if she saw her man going in another direction.

When she stepped out of the gym into the crisp November air, the only woman she saw was an African American who must have weighed three hundred pounds and had bulging muscles that would make a blacksmith cringe. The woman, hands firmly planted on ample hips, her feet spread wide, looked at Kate from the top of her eyes.

"Have you seen a little lady named Lulu Belle?"

"Lulu Belle's my name, and you got my man, Hassan, in there, and I want him out. He's got business with me."

"Well, my name's Kate Mahoney, and I'm principal here." Kate's rage fueled by the police and the woman's size blew up in Lulu Belle's face. "You've got your nerve. You come to this school—my school—and try to get him into more trouble. Out! Immediately. Or I'll call the police and have you arrested for disturbing the peace on a school site. And, believe me, you *will* spend the night in jail!"

It never occurred to Kate that Lulu Belle might deck her. The woman moved forward swiftly, graceful and powerful as a sumo wrestler, then she paused and turned away, her nose in the air. "That boy better watch his back when he gets out in the real world. I'll get him."

"I'll let the cops know you made that threat."

Lulu Belle was halfway across the courtyard when she turned and yelled at Kate, "Nigger lover!"

Kate couldn't help laughing.

Back in the kitchen, she gave an abbreviated report to Hassan, omitting the name she'd been called. When she suggested he be a little more careful about his choice of women, his smile spread to the corners of his eyes. "I'm truly working on that, Miss Kate. I'm working on it. But, you know, the ladies just seem to love me."

Kate walked away, chuckling at the ladies' man with a gift for manipulating the fairer sex, including his boss. Her hand was on the doorknob when she heard a serious, subdued Hassan call, "Miss Kate, you and I gotta talk. I don't want to tell you this, but you helped me, and I need to help you."

Surprised, Kate returned to his side. Talk had never been his strong point.

"What I say I hate to tell, but I gotta." He brought the stool Kate had offered to him earlier. "You just sit right there and—" He shook his head and looked away.

Kate waited.

"Well, see this here bruise?" He fingered the mark on his forehead gingerly. "The cops let me go last night after they got a look at Lulu Belle and found out I was the one with the marks from our fight. I was pretty worked up, so I stopped off at The Thirsty Saguaro for a drink. I go there sometimes—well, pretty often—and I needed something for my nerves." He measured Kate's reaction out of the corner of his eye.

Kate smiled. "I'm not your mama, Hassan. You don't have to apologize to me." She recognized The Thirsty Saguaro as a tough watering hole on the other side of town.

"Well, I don't want you to think bad of me," he said, activating devilish dimples. "Anyway, Jim, the bartender there, knows me." A worried look flashed across his eyes. "Don't worry, Miss Kate, he and nobody there knows I work here in your school. I keep my mouth shut. Don't want no guys and no gals to know my business. I got careless in a moment of weakness..." he looked away, embarrassed "...and I bragged to Lulu Belle about where I worked and look at all the trouble. Anyway, I told Jim about being roughed up by the cops and, boom, a double shot of tequila with a beer chaser appeared on the bar in front of me."

Kate nodded her appreciation of the kick of a boilermaker.

"I told Jim I was okay, he didn't have to do that, and Jim says, 'It wasn't me that set you up. Those guys at the pool table say they got a soft spot for anybody gets roughed up by the cops.' So I went over, friendly-like, to thank them, and the big guy kinda gets me playing pool and keeps the boilermakers coming. These guys—rough and white. There's no way they're buying me drinks and sweet-talking me for nothing. But I was kinda curious, so I keep drinking the beer and pretending to down the tequila, but getting rid of it other ways."

Kate was tempted to ask how, but thought better of it.

"Well, this goes on for a couple of hours. I don't talk none, and I'm getting boozy, but not drunk. Meanwhile, these guys are getting drunk, and they don't think I hear stuff, I guess. People are like that. If you don't talk, they think you don't hear. I hear just fine.

"The big guy gets in the face of this little weasel, complaining about why did he have to get rid of Juan. Said Juan could hold his liquor better than the weasel. Better man in every way. Little weasel guy got uppity, saying the big guy blew it with the broad. Little Chickie got away, not once, but twice."

The little chickie!

Kate grabbed the stainless steel sink and steadied herself.

Hassan took her by the elbow. "You okay, Miss Kate? You look real, real white. I wouldn't be tough talking like this, but I'm wondering. Could it be *our Juan*?"

"Tell me, Hassan, this big guy—was he wearing hiking boots?"

"As a matter of fact, he was. How'd you know, Miss Kate?"

Theo was off campus. While Kate was on the cafeteria phone trying to reach Officer McNary, the custodian slipped out. When she and McNary visited his trailer that night, all signs of Hassan had vanished. The police lost a witness, and Saguaro, a gentle giant. Hassan knew telling his story would mean he'd have to leave town. There was no way he was going to work with the police.

That night, a new customer began frequenting The Thirsty Saguaro. A tattooed black man with a rap sheet as long as his arm and an inability to hold his liquor, he kinda liked playing pool. The police could only hope Hiking Boots and the weasel would feel an urge to drop in and shoot a few balls with their undercover agent.

In Mother Provincial's Office...

Why had she been summoned to Mother Provincial's office? Sister Katherine tapped on the open door and entered the empty room. As a canonical novice, she was forbidden to leave the Novitiate wing except for a grave reason, yet Mother Provincial had called for her. Why?

Mother Bridget O'Leary and Bishop Francis Murphy, stern founders of the Congregation of the Celtic Cross, peered down from the oval portraits that flanked the crucifix behind Mother's desk. Founding a new Congregation was serious business. They looked up to the task.

While she waited, Sister Katherine checked the bookshelves and found the nine volumes of *The History of the Congregation of the Celtic Cross*. Next to the history books stood *The Roster of Celtic Congregation Saints* that listed all deceased Celtic Sisters recorded by the day they died—2,378 dead sisters to date. On the anniversary of their deaths, their names will be read at evening meal in every convent, reminding the 1,834 living nuns to pray for their departed souls and to remember their time will come.

The sound of Mother Provincial's beads preceded her entrance from the inner office. "Come." Mother Philippa nodded in response to the novice's bow.

Entering the back office, they moved to a high table that extended along the west side of the room. It was like the one Kate had seen in the construction trailer. Similar, but different. This one was custom made with mitered corners.

The novice ran her fingers over the smooth dark finish. "Walnut?"

"Mahogany. A piece left over from the sacristy remodeling."

"Sister Colette's work?" The precision and simplicity of design suggested the work of the nun who managed the woodworking shop.

Mother stroked the wood lovingly. "Yes, she's more than a carpenter. She's an artist. The open shelves underneath hold blueprints for the province's construction projects." She touched each blueprint, starting with the one on top and working her way down, shelf by shelf, to the floor. "The Cancer Center at St. Bridget's Hospital…the Fine Arts Building at Celtic College…the new gymnasium at Saint Finian's Elementary…the parking garage at St. Brendan's Hospital…the library at Saint Patrick High School."

She straightened, put her hands back in her sleeves, and beamed.

"You like it. You really love building, don't you, Mother?"

"It's my duty to like it. With thirty-two million dollars worth of building projects in the province, it's my duty to represent the Congregation's interests."

The superior's defensive tone made Sister Katherine push harder.

"It really exhilarates you, spending thirty-two million dollars, doesn't it, Mother? What about this detachment we've been studying in the Novitiate?"

"I didn't call you here, my impudent daughter, to conduct my examination of conscience." The Provincial looked over half moon reading glasses. "And the last I've heard, you're not my confessor!"

Sister Katherine had gotten under the superior's skin. She wouldn't have thought it possible.

"Now, I've called you here to go through some building specifications." Mother moved to a matching mahogany bookcase, where dozens of plastic-bound papers were stored. She pulled out a couple.

"Mother, I know what building specs are. Remember, in my real world a new classroom wing was built on our campus. I represented my school district's interests there, as well." Her voice betrayed the satisfaction that she was much more than Mother Provincial's "daughter" in the real world.

The Provincial, equilibrium restored, ignored the novice's tone as she moved to the straight-backed bench near the fireplace. She patted the bench, inviting the novice to join her. Sister Katherine remained standing.

The Provincial studied the novice. "I understand you were unhappy because building specs were altered after your faculty saw them."

"How do you know about our conversation at the Tohono Chul Tearoom? Are you allowed to eavesdrop on my daily affairs?" Sister Katherine, her arms folded, backed up to the hearth, seeking warmth from the unlit fire.

"This conversation must have been important because I was allowed to overhear it. I can only eavesdrop if the subject matter is relevant, and not always even then."

"Who decides?"

Mother Philippa feigned deafness. Sister Katherine repeated her question and the older nun sighed with exasperation. "For heaven's sake, whom do you think?"

"I don't know. I've never been dead, Mother!"

"Well, you must wait and see. Being dead has its limitations. Enough of this! Back to the problem at hand—the altered building specifications."

"Yes, Mother, we did have some problems, but just as you have the last word in the province, the governing board calls the shots in the district." She flicked a dust spot off her habit. "The superintendent made changes after I saw them, and Icarus Construction bid on the altered specs. All legal and proper."

Mother Philippa stared into the hearth where the wood lay unlit. She leaned forward, resting both forearms on serge-shrouded knees, the way Shawn used to study a piece of equipment he needed to repair. The novice saw only wood laid for a fire. What had caught Mother's eye? Why the uncharacteristically common pose?

Mother straightened. "So the district building specs matched those that Icarus Construction bid on."

"Of course, Mother."

"Did you compare the district specs sent to Icarus with the specs sent to the other contractors who bid?"

The novice's mouth shot open. "They wouldn't dare!"

Mother Philippa leaned back, her hands fingering the beads that hung at her side. “Why not? Who’s the keeper of the store?”

“Store?”

“Who bears legal responsibility for the integrity of the bidding process?”

The novice, struggling to follow the path they were treading, saw only the calm elegance that was Mother’s modus operandi. “The manager of Physical Resources supervises the building projects. But there’s no one in that position right now, so I guess the superintendent would mind that store.”

Mother suddenly sat up. “Why no Physical Resource Manager?”

“The manager, Larry Denton, was killed in an automobile accident five months ago, and they’re still looking for a replacement.”

The Provincial’s eyes returned to the unlit hearth. “Killed? Very interesting.”

“You don’t think—”

“Yes, I do. That’s why I have this job—and I want you to think, too. The two people responsible for the bidding process are both dead. Coincidence? Maybe.”

Sister Katherine took a deep breath. “So…I need to compare the district specs with those sent out to the contractors who lost the bid.”

“Not you. Let Theo do it.” Mother rose and placed both hands on the novice’s shoulders. “You’re too trusting. He’ll watch his back.”

“Mother, you…a chauvinist?” She removed the superior’s grip.

“Chauvinist? What do you think I am under this habit?” A smile crossed the face that had been solemn a moment before. “Certainly, not an *it*. This has nothing to do with gender, my dear. It’s about temperament. You’re not devious enough for this kind of task. You’d never make a Mother Provincial.”

Mother slipped through her office door with only the movement of her beads breaking the silence, leaving a still novice to mull over her words.

9

Kate had been trying all day to get in touch with Theo. His office at school remained closed; items in his mailbox in the teachers' lounge were left unclaimed. Nobody'd seen him since the weekend, and she'd left a couple of messages with the Homicide Division secretary at police headquarters. This afternoon, after asking, "You again?" the secretary said he'd be back in a few minutes. "Probably off on a coffee break."

Or a cigar break, Kate would've bet. Even the den of homicide detectives had to obey the no smoking ordinance the Tucson City Council had imposed. Ignoring her overflowing "In" basket, she grabbed her car keys and took off, leaving Terri with the vague promise to be back soon.

She needed to talk with Theo about the best way to check the building specifications sent to the seven contractors who lost the high school bid. What if Icarus had been able to bid low because their building specifications were less costly than those sent to the competition? The spilling of those beans would expose the district to lawsuits. The exposure might not provide answers, but it certainly would get her into deep, deep shit with Central Admin.

If she were going to help Elijah and lessen her guilt about Juan, she needed to solve those murders. Let someone else expose a fraud. But if the bids had been rigged, and the two overseers of the bidding process were dead, the finger of guilt might shift away from Elijah.

Even if she were connected to construction fraud, why would Julie be killed? If—and it was a big if—there was fraud in the bidding process, the death of the superintendent would end their game. Why kill the superintendent who laid the golden egg?

The word *laid* triggered her second worry. How about Coach Holman, who wanted Julie Mason dead for a very personal reason? His affair with Julie was short-lived; he broke it off when his wife became pregnant and the Board had approved his administrative hire. He claimed Julie was furious and appointed him as principal to the most difficult school in the district. She'd threatened to tell his wife, and he was afraid the murder investigation would dig up this dirt.

That lead needed to be followed, but when she called Coach's office the secretary always claimed he wasn't in. "Not in" for her, anyway. Coach had confided in her in a weak moment, and he probably wanted her to forget what he'd said. Theo couldn't be told since the information had been given in confidence. Strange, Mother Provincial had never mentioned the Coach.

Kate's nose twitched, a signal that she was working at cross-purposes. Maybe Theo could unravel this Gordian knot, but would he be willing to delay the fraud charges to get to the murderer? Or perhaps they were two completely separate issues. Reality check. The fraud existed only in her imagination, placed there by a dream.

Kate hit the signal to make a right turn into the visitor's lot at the main police station on Stone Avenue, and then something made her continue straight ahead. The Ford pickup behind her honked its disapproval. She hadn't been in the station since Shawn died. Now, it had a new facade, a stucco facelift to blend in with the surrounding Spanish architecture. A good idea. Saint Augustine's Cathedral rose white, saintly, and Spanish just two blocks north.

She must force herself to put one foot in front of the other and walk into the Homicide Division to find Theo. She circled the block again, this time not bothering to touch her turn signal. She shot by the parking entrance.

It was Shawn. She couldn't go back to that room where she used to visit him. Shawn never had an office; those were for the captains and lieutenants. If he had lived, he'd have one by now.

She could imagine Theo's desk, shoved up against another cop's. The physical closeness made for bonding and communication for the same reason her teachers shared offices. Cops were part of a team, a brotherhood that cut both ways. Bonded for justice. Bonded to cover up? Probably the paint on the Homicide Division walls was still a bland beige on beige. She could imagine the entrance door with the small glass windows through which she used to look to see if Shawn was at his desk. The door probably still creaked as it swung open. But Shawn wouldn't be there. No, she wasn't going in.

She used the phone at a corner Circle K, and this time got Theo at his desk. Yes, he understood that she wasn't crazy about coming into the station. As a matter of fact, he didn't want her dropping by his desk, anyway. She wasn't exactly the Patron Saint of the Department. He'd meet her at the back entrance, where the squad cars were parked. She could park on the street and walk in, and he'd be waiting for her.

Most of the squad cars were out on the day shift, leaving their numbered spaces empty except for oil spots. The few that remained were scattered throughout the parking area like black and white hound dogs, asleep but ready to move with the pack at an instant's notice. The smell of motor oil brought a wave of déjà vu as she crossed the lot. She brushed nostalgia aside and focused her attention on finding Theo.

He was waiting for her in the shadow of the porch by the handicapped ramp. Hands in his pockets, his fedora shoved back to expose part of his bald head, he had an unlit cigar in his mouth. "So what're you coming here for?" He took her by the arm and moved her inside as a squad car rolled into the lot and parked in an area reserved for lieutenants. Theo cracked the door enough to see the driver.

"Oh, damn, it's Rawlins!" He scowled at Kate as if it were her fault. "What am I going to do with you?" His hold on her arm tightened as he pulled her down the hall.

"Stop manhandling me!" She struggled to get free. "What's the matter with you? Ouch, you're hurting me!"

His grip loosened for a moment, then tightened again. "In here!" He pushed open a door marked MEN, poked his head inside. "Anyone here?" Getting no response, he pulled his captive inside, shut the door, and locked it.

Kate's mouth flew open. Theo covered it with his hand, and she nipped him. He jerked it away for a second, and then replaced it with a firmer hold. Putting his mouth on her ear, he whispered, "Be quiet, or Rawlins will hear you. Trust me. Be quiet. I'm not going to hurt you."

If Kate had been able to move her jaw, she'd have bitten again. Theo had secured her waist so tight, she couldn't kick or wiggle. She could only move her eyes to verify that this was indeed a men's room. One toilet and a urinal. She looked away from the urinal and into Theo's image in the mirror. His face and bald head were beet red. She'd never seen him so embarrassed. Good! That made two of them! The smell of his aftershave was too intense…too close. She started to struggle when she heard someone try the door; then the irritated voice of Lieutenant Rawlins.

"Unlock this door. There's room for two in there." Another loud bang. "I need in now. My back teeth're floating."

"Go find yourself another john." Theo's hand tightened across her mouth. Kate was sure she'd have a black and blue lip, but she stopped struggling. Between Rawlins and Buloski, she'd take the latter any day. "I've gotten sick in this one. Too many prunes."

Kate glanced into the mirror. Theo's red had deepened to vermilion. Another loud bang on the door. "I've always said you're full of shit, Buloski. This proves it." Rawlins guffawed at his cleverness. Then the sound of his footsteps diminished.

They waited. When the footsteps were gone, Kate jerked and pulled to be free. Theo continued to hold her tight. "Now, listen, Kate. I know you're mad, but we had to hide. Rawlins couldn't see us. He's gotten wind that we're helping each other on this case. He's trying to get me transferred out of Saguaro, and I'm here doing some favors, kissin' ass with the Captain so I can stay."

Kate's flashing eyes in the mirror were saying, "*Let go of me! Get out of my life! I don't want you to stay!*"

Theo's response was sad and low. "Lady, I'm staying at your school whether you want it or not." His mirrored eyes were somber beneath heavy lids. "You're going to get killed if I'm not there to keep things in line. Besides, there's just a chance—a very remote chance—we might be able to solve this case." He was relaxing his grip when someone tried the door, pounded, swore and walked away. As the sound of footsteps disappeared, Theo released her but kept his hand on her mouth.

"I'm keeping you quiet because I want you to listen." His voice became low and gentle. "Kate, I'm sorry to manhandle you this way, but we couldn't be seen together. When I let you go, you can hit me if you want. Better yet, let me take you out to dinner tonight at the Metro Grill. I promise I'll explain everything."

She sprang from his grip like a cork out of a champagne bottle. He didn't defend himself from the punch she threw. It left a red mark on his cheek below his left eye. Her right hand stung from the blow, and she shook it out, then nursed it with her left. Tears welled in her eyes. Why did life have to be so difficult? Mother Philippe never had to be held captive in a men's room. Maybe the Provincial had chosen the better part. Maybe Kate should have stayed and been a good nun and avoided this entire trauma. She couldn't help it. She started to sob.

Theo looked miserable as he moved to the john to get her a piece of toilet tissue. She blew her nose and made an awkward gesture indicating she'd be all right.

"I'm really sorry, Kate. Er…I mean…" Theo stammered, and the bright red returned.

Kate's mouth fell open. This was too much. She headed for the door. Theo got there first, raised a hand, then peered out.

"Coast clear." He held the door for her. "Six tonight at Metro Grill."

"Six thirty?"

"Six thirty."

She shot by him and ran across the parking lot. Why had she agreed to meet him? The answer was as clear as the fresh air that hit her face when she stepped into the breeze. They had two murders to solve. She needed his help.

Today's pile of papers spilled out of the "In" basket onto her blotter, disheveling the piles she'd assembled last weekend for dispatch. Kate visualized herself buried in a paper avalanche, her moans for help unheeded. When the office cleared at five o'clock, she clicked the door's dead bolt with a sigh and kicked off her heels, determined to diminish the paperwork before her six-thirty dinner with Theo.

The computer lab schedule had to be readied before tomorrow's faculty meeting. Primary teachers wanted more lab time since their students, now three months in school, were better able to concentrate.

The intermediate teachers had settled into a workable schedule and didn't want to budge. How to compromise?

Somebody began banging low on the outside office door. Probably a primary student wanting to visit. Not right now.

Kate was on course when the banging began on her window. It was little Maribel Ferguson, a second grader with corn rows that stuck out in all directions. The white of the child's terrified eyes emphasized her cinnamon skin as tears coursed down her cheeks. To hell with the paperwork. Kate let the wailing child in. The child's thin body bobbed as though she had the hiccups.

"M...m...my mama's hurting awful." Kate cradled the little girl in her arms, gently rocking her. "M...m...my mama's having a b...b... baby, and it hurts her awful." A piercing wail and then, "Sh...sh...she's gonna die. You gotta come."

"I'll come, honey. I'll come." Kate knew Maribel lived across the street from the school. The memory of another night when she'd gone out into the neighborhood alone sent prickles up her spine.

Maribel's sorrow, mitigated by a handful of jelly beans and the promise of help, trailed to a sniffle while the principal called the night custodians on the intercom to tell them where she was going. The child held the outside office door open. Kate plucked Maribel's card out of the emergency file on the front counter and glanced at the mother's name.

"Does your mother go by Isabelle?"

A quick nod.

"Wait there a minute." Backtracking, Kate opened her bottom desk drawer and took out the revolver, then thought of the little girl. No bullets with Maribel along. She removed them and dropped them into her dress pocket. Forcing down images of black ski masks and hiking boots, she put the empty gun into her tote.

Together, they jogged across the street, squeezed through the stuck gate in a chain link fence, and zigzagged around dog poop.

"Got a dog?"

"Yeah, Terminator. He's out looking for a girlfriend...a doggy girlfriend."

From the looks of things, Terminator was big and had been in residence quite a while. Good thing he was out roaming. The small girl expertly guided her past an adobe duplex with "For Rent" signs in both front windows and around the back to a small adobe dwelling that had probably been a guest house when this part of town was enjoying better times.

Isabelle's screams made them quicken their pace. When they burst through the front door, Maribel froze, connecting to her mother with huge, questioning eyes.

Kate wasn't surprised at the bareness of the room. Living room, kitchen, and bedroom all in one. Maribel and her mother were in and out of Saguaro and Mesquite Elementary Schools. They'd live for a couple of weeks out of the beat-up 1989 Ford Fairlane that was parked out front; then get the welfare check and move into another low rent dwelling. All the moving didn't seem to bother Maribel, who'd never known anything else, but it raised havoc with the continuity of her schooling.

A gas stove and a workbench with a stained sink defined one corner as the kitchen, where the smell of cooked cabbage and mildew hung in the air. The sink was piled with dishes that needed scraping before they could be soaked. A battered Coleman ice chest was pushed up against the refrigerator door, whch was tied shut with the sash of a dress. Stacks of books with the Tucson Public Library logo on the spine supported a wood plank that provided a makeshift table where Maribel and her mother probably ate. An uneven table: the books weren't of matching widths. At least, they weren't from the Saguaro Library, Kate thought automatically. Then she felt guilty. Being petty in the face of such need.

Kitty-corner from the kitchen, the omnipresent TV blared forth the "Wheel of Fortune" in living color. Vanna White in designer gown was the only human contact in Ms. Ferguson's time of pain. Isabelle lay on an old sleeping bag that had been washed at the laundromat one time too many.

Having relinquished responsibility, a calmer Maribel sat cross-legged on her own sleeping bag, examining with renewed interest the jelly beans left sticky in her hands.

Kate knelt beside the mother, an ebony woman weighing probably over two hundred pounds. Large-boned and muscular, Isabelle was an Amazon made larger by the child now determined to enter this world. And Maribel was so small! What had daddy looked like?

"What you doin' here? No time for you to be botherin' me about little Maribel's grades. Got no time for you—" Mama's words were punctuated with a loud scream.

The second grader dropped a jellybean and scowled. Ms. Mahoney wasn't supposed to let the pain go on.

"Maribel, have you got a phone?"

A vigorous shaking of the head. The mother took a couple of deep breaths, her eyes wide with the apprehension of the next knife of pain.

"How long between contractions, Isabelle?"

"'Bout two spins of the Wheel of Fortune. Only don't call no ambulance. Last time I was in one, Maribel's daddy died."

Kate knew a gunshot had killed Bob Ferguson, not the ambulance.

Since there wasn't time to go back to school for a 911 call, and she didn't want to deliver a baby while waiting for the ambulance, Kate went along with the mother's request. She couldn't bring herself to look under the woman's floral dress to see whether the baby was coming. All of her instincts cried for professional help.

"Time to get to the hospital, Isabelle. Where are your car keys?"

Maribel climbed on top of the ice chest, felt around the top of the refrigerator, and produced the keys. With the child leading the way, Isabelle, with the principal bearing some of the weight, negotiated the dog poop and got into the Ford that started with a growl. Kate belted Maribel in the front seat, but as soon as she started to drive, the second grader released her belt and stood on her seat looking down at her mother curled in a fetal position on the back seat.

Despite Kate's disregard for speed limits, rush hour traffic stretched the ten-minute drive to University Medical Center into a twenty-minute trip pierced by screams that occurred at ever-shorter intervals. They were within sight of the hospital when Isabelle cried, "It's coming. I can feel the blood gushing."

The Ford lurched up a driveway and continued on the sidewalk for a block to get around traffic, then bounced off the curb and sped up the ramp into the hospital emergency entrance.

"Maribel, go get the nurse."

"Don't be a wimp!" the mother commanded. "Get under my skirt and help the baby out. I think it's coming." Then she screamed.

"Push, mother, push!"

Kate saw the top of the baby's black head in the entrance of the vagina. Instinctively, she placed her hands to stabilize the neck should the next push thrust it out. At that moment, two nurses and an orderly took her place to transfer the mother to their gurney. The larger of the nurses took one look at Kate's bloody hands, "Lady, haven't you ever heard of using gloves?"

Stunned, she looked first at her hands, and then at Maribel's shocked face. "Your mom's going to be just fine. Come on, let's go find a bathroom and clean up." Silently, they walked down the hall, the youngster opening doors.

Washed, Kate noted the emergency card and called Maribel's aunt.

"Be right over. That Isabelle, she don't tell me nothing." Something about that voice brushed Kate's nervous system. Where had she heard it before?

Since they weren't allowed in the delivery room, the principal and child went to the cafeteria to get Maribel a chocolate ice cream cone. Sitting in the delivery waiting room, they wondered whether the new baby would be a boy or a girl.

"If it's a girl, she's Rosabel. Maribel, Isabelle, Rosabel—get it?" The little girl took a couple of chocolate licks. "But we'll keep him if it's a boy, and we'll call him Mahdi." Large brown eyes tested Kate's reaction. "That name means 'Ruler.' Mamma likes it because this boy'll be special, but I don't. I'll be the ruler of the kids, not the new baby."

For all of their sakes, Kate hoped Bob Ferguson, who'd been a drug user, was free of HIV. She went to scrub her hands a second time. When she returned, Maribel was greeting Isabelle's sister, another Amazon. The second grader made the introductions.

"This is Auntie Lulu Belle. See, even she has a Belle name."

The large woman's full red lips curled to a sneer. "Well, well. If it isn't Hassan's mama!"

Why, with all the possible Lulu Belles in Tucson, did Maribel have this one as an aunt? Kate updated her on her sister's birthing, then the two settled into a stony silence. Maribel sensed something was wrong.

"Don't you like Mrs. Mahoney?"

Auntie Lulu Bell motioned for the child and began to whisper in her ear.

Kate whisked a dollar bill out of her purse and interrupted. "It's been a long day for you, Maribel. Why don't you get something out of the vending machine in the hall?" Magical words for the hungry girl. She took the money and ran.

Kate moved to the plastic chair beside Lulu Belle. "Maribel came to my office because she trusted me to help her. Don't say anything to change that trust," she stage whispered.

Lulu Belle's lips opened, showing large white teeth clamped tight together, then they shut as quickly.

Kate made her point. "Simply said, Maribel needs me a lot more than I need her. It won't hurt me, but it will hurt her, if you break that trust."

The large woman shifted her weight, trying to get comfortable in the cramped plastic chair. "I knew it was Hassan's mama when I heard your voice on the phone." Clearly, she wasn't comfortable with the present company. "Why do you think I came here? To watch your fat white ass sashaying around the room? Telling everybody what to do? I came to help Maribel." Her eyes softened as she saw the child, Butterfingers in hand, reenter the room. "Now hush up." She grabbed the top magazine on the pile and turned her full attention to *International Golf.*

They sat in silence until the doctor entered to announce that Maribel had an 8-pound, 2-ounce brother. Maribel assured him, "It's okay." To Kate, she confided, "It wasn't his fault, you know. Doctors don't make baby boys and girls. I know how it's done."

Lulu Belle picked up the exhausted child, and Maribel snuggled into her ample bosom. Giving a nod that wasn't returned, Kate made her exit.

What time was it? Seven-thirty! Only then did she remember Theo waiting at the Metro Grill. She phoned the receptionist, who remembered a bald gentleman waiting at a table for two. He'd left just a few minutes ago, after attending to the bottle of 1982 Mouton-Rothschild Cabernet Sauvignon that he'd ordered when he first arrived. Kate brushed off a momentary pang of guilt. Theo was so independent, he'd hardly miss her absence. Still, a bottle of Mouton-Rothschild would cost a bundle. How unlike him. Indubitably, a peace offering for this morning's abduction.

Kate tried his home and left a message on his answering machine. She needed to tell him that the two persons responsible for the district bidding process had died within the last few months. Coincidence? Had the police made the connection or were they so sure of Elijah's guilt they'd missed other possibilities?

The silver dollars bordering the ceiling of the Silver Dollar Bar were like those sealed under the glass bar top—unreachable. At the moment, Theo found them also unpredictable, shifting ever so slightly right before his eyes.

Joshua, the bartender, also seemed a little flaky tonight, his face blurring when he approached. Theo put on his reading glasses and struggled with the focus. Things should be stable in a bar. It's the one place a man can go and be his plain, uninspiring self. No knight in shining armor. No defender of the oppressed. Just plain old Theo, warts and all.

The Silver Dollar used to be a place a man could count on. Currently, it was failing him. Getting a little wobbly. Hell, he'd been coming to the Silver Dollar for thirty years. A lot longer than he'd been married to Ramona.

Ramona. He could see her face in his beer. Young and slim face. Young and slim everything. Breasts as perky as puppies and just as cuddly and tender. Mainly, he remembered her eyes, green with flecks of gold. He'd bought her a pair of green, gold-flecked, jade earrings once. They'd matched just fine, but he remembered how his wife had hinted that she preferred diamonds.

Still, those eyes promised love. Promises kept in those days. He remembered how those eyes sought him out in the campus diner, where she waited tables to help pay her way through school. The way they looked up at him after they'd made love, relishing his maleness and protection and desire. Desire—with Ramona, it was love. They'd been in love when they got married. Not just him. She, too. Married for a year and a half, and the baby came fast. Doug...a real strong little kid. He'd grab Dad's little finger and pull himself up to a sitting position. Dead at eight. He shouldn't have let Ramona get custody. He'd have taught the kid bike safety.

Then all hell broke out in Korea, and Theo's National Guard chits had been called in.

He remembered the cold Korean winter when his bed was sometimes a snow bank. On patrol. Staring into the damn cold night, bazooka at the ready, waiting for the skinny boys from the north to cross the line. The memory made him shiver, and he downed a jigger of Chivas Regal for warmth. There were nights his fingers and toes had gotten so cold, he was sure they'd fall off when they defrosted.

Then North Koreans did cross the line, and his buddy, Smiley, caught a bullet in the ear. Died right next to him—in the same foxhole. Two or three feet to the left, and it would've been Theo's ear. He felt guilty about that. Guilty and lucky.

Lucky, until mail call and the letter from Ramona. He still remembered the words, "It's not working out." He wrote her back, saying their marriage shouldn't be expected to "work out" when her husband's halfway around the world. Now was a time of waiting, and what they had was worth waiting for.

"My friend, Joshua—another." Theo tapped the shot glass.

Joshua looked like an undertaker, his small head perched precariously atop the thinnest neck Theo'd ever seen. The years had reduced his hairline to a few wisps that he kept plastered down. He claimed those black strands were proof he wasn't bald. At the moment, Joshua was gazing through thick glasses at Theo.

"I swear, Joshua, you look like you're conducting a funeral service, and I'm the corpse."

Leaning forward like a giraffe straining for a leaf, Joshua moved into Theo's face, talking real low and personal. "Don't you think you've had enough, Theo?"

"No! I want to drink to the gal who stood me up tonight. Here's to Ramona, the raven-headed beauty who stood me up. Good. Permanently." Jabbing a hole in the air, he gestured toward the bottle of Chivas Regal on the mirrored shelf behind the bar.

Joshua ignored the gesture, forcing Theo to toast with his empty shot glass.

"Who got pregnant with her boss, while I was freezing my ass off in Korea. She got her diamonds, all right. And they're still married, damn them." He leaned forward and whispered. "Now that, Joshua, is getting stood up! Stood up in a grand style! And she stood me up again tonight! Damn her!"

The bartender fished a wine glass out of sudsy water, rinsed it, and held it up to the light, scrutinizing with eyes that never lost their chronic sadness. "Ramona hasn't been in your life for thirty years, Theo. It must have been someone else. It's almost one o'clock. Closing time. Want me to call you a cab? Your car will be safe here tonight."

The undertaker was getting downright annoying. "Joshua!" Theo articulated his words with painstaking care. "You're not listening to me. It was Ramona who stood me up. Don't I know that woman inside and out? And you're telling me I don't know her."

Joshua shrugged and dunked another glass into the suds.

"You're sure wobbly tonight, Joshua. How can you handle glass when you're so fidgety? It's you who needs a cab. Not me."

As the bartender moved to the far end of the bar to serve a customer, Theo raised his voice to accommodate the distance. "Or maybe it was my mother who stood me up tonight. My mother died when I was ten, you know. She stood me up, too." Theo stared into space, searching for his mother's face. It was out of focus. "Naw, it wasn't her fault. She didn't wanna die. She didn't stand me up. What am I saying?"

Joshua gave Theo a melancholy glance, dried his hands on the towel that hung at his waist, and moved toward the phone.

"Don't call that cab!" Theo slammed a handful of bills on the bar and eased off the stool. "I'm outta here."

Like everything else tonight, his car key was flaky. Theo had a heck of a time getting it to fit in the ignition. "They don't make cars like they used to," he grumbled, took another try, and finally wiggled it into place. "Too damn complicated."

It was less than a mile to his apartment, but the night was fuzzy, so Theo drove nice and slow. He was aiming for the apartment parking entrance when he saw the red and blue lights flashing in his rear-view mirror. They made him feel right at home, and he was downright cordial when he rolled the driver's window down and stared into the grinning, yellow teeth of Officer Heath.

"Oh, shit, it's Officer Asshole!"

The ride to the police station sobered Theo. Being slammed spread-eagle against the cop car, handcuffed, and kneed in the groin brought him back to reality. By the time he got handed over to Pete McMahon, the booking officer, he was back in the ball game.

"Heath! Valles! Why'd you have to bring him in? How far was he from his home?" McMahon was disgusted. This could've been handled in a more brotherly way.

"It was really sad. Buloski was practically on his doorstep, but we had to do our duty." A grin flashed between the two arresting officers. "Buloski always goes by the book. The book turned around and nipped his drunken ass. Put him in with the bad guys, who've got a special love of cops."

They were still chuckling as they headed out.

"Theo, I can't believe you're doing this. A DUI—Internal Affairs'll have you for breakfast!"

Sheepish, Theo surrendered his fingers for printing.

"I didn't even know you drank, not like this." Pete McMahon consulted his computer. "First offense. First DUI. That's all you've got going for you. You know a night in jail is mandatory." McMahon handed him a cup of black coffee.

Theo took a sip. His thoughts began to coagulate. Jail, he'd been there before, years ago for the CIA. He wasn't afraid of jail. Jail. Something clicked. He searched through the fog in his head for the elusive thought. "Do me a favor, Pete." His tongue was six inches thick and made of cotton. The coffee had brought his stomach to the edge of revolt. "Get an extra cot and put me in the cell with Elijah Jackson."

"Elijah Jackson, the murderer? He's over in the west wing, and you're supposed to go into the holding tank." McMahon hit the computer keys hard. "I'll arrange to put you in a cell by yourself, that's my best offer."

With difficulty, Theo focused his eyes on the booking officer. "That's not good enough, Pete. I gotta go in with Jackson. Do me this one favor, and I'll owe you."

"I put a cop in with a murderer, and he ends up dead, so am I!"

Theo scratched his bald head, remembering the most stubborn officers were chosen for booking. They didn't let anybody talk them out of anything. But Pete and he'd worked the same shift a few years back. He knew Pete's wife and kids, had attended his daughter's wedding. Theo'd pulled him out of many a scrape. He'd try again.

"I'm sober enough to know what I'm doing, Pete. I need to get in that cell with Elijah. Big favor. Do it!"

Officer McMahon shook his head and shut down his computer. Then he walked Theo through the security gate and out to the west wing.

In Mother Mistress's Class...

By 9 a.m. a good chunk of the novice's day had already happened. After greeting the 5:30 bell with "Let us rejoice on this day which the Lord has made," they spent the next three and a half hours in Great Silence.

Quiet as cats, they assembled in the novitiate chapel at 6:00 for morning chants and meditation. At 7:00, Mass was followed by breakfast and silent morning duties. This schedule, followed strictly in the forty-eight Celtic Cross missions in Ireland and America, kept all 1,834 nuns on the same page. Tradition.

Mother Alfreda Bennett, known to the novices and postulants as Mother Mistress, molded undisciplined American women to fit that tradition. Insofar as was humanly possible, she was considered a perfect example of the Holy Rule. And she had the compulsion to control. A perfect match? Not in the eyes of Mother Provincial. The uneasy truce between the two was a miraculous manifestation of obedience to Mother General.

At exactly 8:59, Mother Mistress, her hands hidden in large choir sleeves, stood ramrod straight outside the novices' classroom, observing the decorum of her charges as they arrived from morning duties. Without speaking and never glancing up, they changed into choir sleeves and flowed to assigned desks from which they withdrew the Holy Rule Book and black loose-leaf notebooks.

Mother Mistress assigned the most spirited novices to the farthest duty stations, allowing them to practice religious decorum under the stress of rushing. And she'd be there to observe the degree of their success. Testing. Always testing.

When the last novice had taken her seat, Mother Mistress closed the door and floated to her desk at the front of the classroom. She was satisfied. The young nuns had been calibrated against her norm of perfection, and none had been found wanting.

"Good morning, Daughters."

With her words, Great Silence was lifted and, for the first time since prayer the previous evening, the novices looked into the face of another human being. Modesty of the Eyes was still in effect, so they weren't allowed to look at each other—just at their teacher. Sister Katherine kept her eyes down on her notebook, running her hand over its smooth blackness.

"Sister Katherine, do I have your attention?"

"Yes, Mother."

"Daughters..." Mother Mistress's eyes, gray and penitential as ash, completed their scan, "...for the last year you've been studying the Holy Rule of The Congregation of the Celtic Cross. By order of Rome, it's modeled on the rule of Saint Vincent de Paul, written in 1624, as are the rules of all religious women's congregations.

"Until 1624, all religious women were cloistered. The notion of women with vows working outside the cloister was scandalous. So Saint Vincent didn't call his sisters, who nursed in the slums of Paris, nuns. He called them 'Daughters of Charity, Servants of the Poor' and wrote the Holy Rule that allowed them to work among the poor, but remain cloistered in their hearts."

Mother Mistress had the young nuns' total attention. Every eye was on her face. Not a twitch. Not a sigh. Not even a cough. Mother Mistress's pleasure with total conformity turned to irritation as the classroom door slowly opened.

Mother Provincial padded in. The novices began to rise, but the Provincial signaled them to remain seated. "Don't let me interrupt, Mother Mistress." Without a sound, Mother Philippa slipped around the back of the class, up the aisle, and laid a hand on Sister Katherine's shoulder. From within her sleeve, she drew out a note and placed it in the novice's hand. She then retraced her steps and was gone.

Mother Mistress cleared her throat. "Sister Katherine, bring me that note." She ignored the collective gasp of disbelief. Sister Katherine stood and opened the note. "Bring it to me now, before you read it! You know all communications from professed nuns are subject to my censorship."

The young novice took her time to scan the contents. When she approached her superior, her eyes were filled, not with defiance, but with concern. Mother Mistress saw there were only a few words on the legal size sheet of lined yellow paper. A violation of poverty! Little messages required little slips of paper, preferably paper already used on the other side.

She read, "Theo got drunk and is in jail with Elijah. Go to him."

Mother Mistress let out a little squeak and swooned dead away.

10

Elijah eyed the wreck of a man on the cot next to his. When the cellmate had moved in last night, Elijah's objections had fallen on deaf ears. When he'd asked to call his lawyer, the jailer eyed him as if he were speaking another language. Theo was the cellmate from hell. During the night, he got sick, then fell into a deep sleep, snoring nonstop.

Elijah lay awake, wondering why the cops would plant an officer in his cell. Were they building a false case against him? Would Theo plant false evidence in his cell? Elijah didn't trust cops, and now he was rooming with one. He slept fitfully, awakening easily when the morning lights were turned on.

"O-o-o, turn off the light!" The wreck groaned and rolled over. The metallic ring of cell doors closing and the swish of Lysol-laced mops slapped around by the morning cleaning crew didn't rouse him.

Seeking strength to jump-start his day, Elijah usually read a chapter from Kahlil Gibran's *The Prophet* while sipping his morning coffee.

Yet, you cannot lay remorse upon the innocent nor lift it from the heart of the guilty.

He found consolation there. He wasn't guilty, so he felt no remorse. Just anger. A hot burning anger that Jacqueline hadn't gotten in touch with him. He shouldn't expect her to expose herself for his sake, but part of him wanted her to sacrifice as he was sacrificing. He tried to remember the smell of her perfume. Tried to replace his cellmate's stench of last night's booze and vomit with thoughts of her. It didn't work.

Also angry with Julie Mason! She'd paid with her life. Still, she had no right to pull him into this. He wasn't sure who murdered her and couldn't tell what he did know without involving Jacqueline and her family. Being innocent was the booby prize.

The cop rolled over on his back, painfully opened his eyes, and then shot straight up, his stocking feet hitting the cement floor with a thud. The jolt sent Theo's hands to his head, and he moaned. Slowly, he stood up and inched his way to the bars. A hangover or damn good acting.

Steadying himself at the bars, Theo turned and stared at Elijah with eyes like red coals in deep sockets. "You? You?"

Elijah snapped back at the cop, "Who else? I didn't ask to have you here."

Theo banged on the bars with his shoe, then winced as the sound waves slammed against his head. He stood gritting his teeth and looking as sociable as a wounded grizzly bear. Hearing no footsteps, he raised the shoe to bang again, then thought better of it.

"You heaved last night, otherwise it'd be worse."

Theo moved slowly back to the cot and slumped down, his head in his hands.

"You wouldn't happen to have some aspirin, would you, Elijah?" Every word took effort.

The tall black giant couldn't help chuckling. "You know better than that, Theo." He studied the miserable creature, trying to figure out his intentions. "They stripped me just like they did you. They're not going to leave any kind of medication on us jail boys. So why are you here?"

"Pretty obvious. DUI."

"I see the DUI part. But why here, with me?"

The burning eyes that looked up at Elijah had a strange innocence about them, like a schoolboy who's been caught zipping up his fly. Even dissipated, there was honesty in those eyes.

"Last night, when I was thrown in jail, I wasn't thinking real straight." He looked down at his unwashed hands. "I had the idea, maybe, if I could get in with you, you might tell me something." He rubbed his hands together. Wanting to clean up.

The eyes that bored into Elijah's were intelligent and decent. For the first time, Elijah saw the man behind the cop. He looked away as Theo continued, slowly and with effort. "We know for a fact Julie Mason was leaning on you."

"You want me to provide a motivation for murder. My lawyer says to keep my mouth shut. That's exactly what I'm doing."

"Maybe if you told us why she was interested in you, it'd be a piece of the puzzle that could get you out of here." The cop's gaze emanating from a blanched face fixed on Elijah. "My problems are real, Elijah, and so are yours. After last night, I'll be lucky to keep my badge and, with your silence, you'll be lucky to get your freedom back. Can't we help each other out?"

Elijah's eyes measured Theo's. Why should he trust this guy? Because misery likes company? Because this cop has feet of clay? Who doesn't?

"So nobody knows you're in here."

"Nobody except the arresting and booking officers."

"Then you're not working for the cops."

"No, I'm here on my own. After last night, I'm not sure I'll be working for the cops ever again." The reply was matter-of-fact, but tinged with poignancy. Elijah almost believed him.

Theo winced at the sound of a metal door slamming at the end of the corridor. A silver-haired guard with cold, calculating eyes stopped at the cell door.

"Well, well. Look who we have here."

"Your hospitality is overwhelming, McDonald. Make it perfect by getting me some aspirin."

"You want to wash up?" The jailer handed a towel and soap through the bars. His hard-edged voice continued, "You've got a pretty lady visitor. Kate Mahoney. Hope she's got a good attorney. You're going to need one this time, Buloski."

Elijah came to the bars and looked down on Theo. "What was that you were saying? Nobody knew you were here. I've got to hand it to you, Buloski. You're a bullshitter with the eyes of a choirboy. Even when you're hung over, you lie good."

Theo shrugged. "I don't know how she found out."

Kate Mahoney was the last person he wanted to see him like this, but curiosity overcame his chagrin, so he washed up and headed out with Officer McDonald. Did the arresting officers call her to gloat that her sidekick was in the cooler? She wouldn't have believed them if they had. No way McMahon would've contacted her. So who told her? His curiosity made him forget his headache. Almost.

"McDonald, how about that aspirin?"

"So I'm going to leave you alone with that babe while I go hunt up some painkillers for a guy who deserves to suffer?" Officer McDonald unlocked the door to the west wing and kept his hand near his nightstick as the two moved into the visitor's section. "I can see the headlines now. COP HELPS COP ESCAPE."

"What the hell, McDonald. I'm not in on murder."

Officer McDonald looked straight ahead. "If you'd hit somebody while drunk, it would've been murder in my book."

Theo couldn't argue with that. He turned his thoughts to Kate, who had always leveled with him. So she wouldn't go out to dinner with a guy who manhandled her in the men's room—his temples pounded without mercy—but she'd always been honest with him.

The smell of disinfectant in the visiting room was so strong, Theo wondered what kind of germs the jailers were trying to kill. Trying to protect the public? Or the prisoners? Probably the guards.

Kate's eyes widened as she rose from a chair on the visitor's side of the table that ran the full length of the room. "What happened to you? You look like hell!" Her hand slowly slid down her throat as she lowered herself to the chair across from him. "Are you all right?"

All of a sudden, Theo really didn't want to talk about it. He scanned the bland room. Nothing homey about the institutional beige, the red floor worn to the gray concrete by nervous feet. Feet that belonged to inmates who were on the spot, their nerves twitching because of what their jailing was doing to their loved ones. Feet that moved while lips lied, professing innocence.

Theo changed the subject. "How'd you know I was here?"

"I just had a premonition. I just knew it. I knew I had to come."

The last time Theo had seen her so pale was the night of her near kidnapping.

Her voice cracked around the edges. "What happened to you? For God's sake, Theo, how could you get in such a mess? Jail! My God!"

"You don't need to use the Lord's name in vain." His altar boy past kicked in, bringing color to his neck and cheeks. He didn't have God on his side, despite the sanctimonious tone. With things the way they were, it wouldn't be easy to put her on the defensive. Still, he could try.

"I wasn't swearing. I was praying." Kate looked across the room at Officer McDonald, who was standing, hands behind his back, taking it all in. She leaned as close to Theo as the wide table permitted. "Does he have to be here?"

Theo nodded.

"What have you done? Why are you in here?" Her tone bordered on frantic, a tone he'd never heard from this tough lady. Somehow, it made him feel good. He'd tell her all. Just as soon as she revealed her source.

"Do you need a lawyer?"

"I've got one in mind. What happened to you last night? I waited over an hour at the Metro Grill."

"Yes, drinking a bottle of 1982 Mouton-Rothschild Cabernet Sauvignon all by yourself," Kate whispered, watching Officer McDonald out of the corner of her eye. The officer moved closer. "What's going on? Expensive wine? Jail? Are you well?"

Theo leaned back. "So you did show up after all." He tried to shake his head but it hurt. "All that drinking for nothing."

"All that drinking— You're in here for a DUI?" Kate closed her lips tight and stared, "How could you be..."

Theo finished the sentence. "...so stupid." Her schoolmarm look made him want to retreat to the more welcome company of common criminals. He looked down at his hands. They still didn't look clean. He'd give his soul for a shower.

"Well, what's done is done. I hope they won't take your badge."

He shrugged. "What held you up last night? Why didn't you call?" Put *her* on the spot.

Kate started the saga about Maribel and her mother's birthing, but Theo interrupted her. "After almost getting kidnapped, I can't believe you went back into that neighborhood alone. Maribel could have been a setup. You're a target as long as the killer thinks you're a witness." He was annoyed at the distraught tone in his voice, but he had to go on. " How could *you* be so stupid. At least I'm still alive!"

McDonald cleared his throat as if he wanted to join in the conversation. Theo shot him a look he ignored.

"Take a good look, Theo. So am I! I knew Maribel had a genuine problem. I can tell when a child's conning." When he didn't respond she continued. "Besides, I took my .38 revolver."

"Empty—because of the little kid, I'll bet. A lot of good that would do you." Despite his pounding temples, he softened as Kate recounted the events of the previous evening. So he hadn't been stood up, after all. Kate wasn't Ramona. The relief that flooded over him was too comforting. Why did he care? He looked up at McDonald, then turned away from the jailer's smirk.

"When are you getting out? There are some coincidences about Julie Mason's murder I need to discuss with you." She glanced at McDonald. "But not here."

"No. No." Theo's rapid head shake unleashed demons that hammered away at the inside of his skull. He rose. "I'll be in touch when I get out. Hopefully, tomorrow. No more going into that neighborhood, understand?" He received no answer. "And, Kate, don't go nosing around until we can work together. Coincidences call for backup."

Still no answer. Damn her. He'd be gray worrying about her if he had any hair. She was like a cut on the top of his mouth that he couldn't stop tonguing. It wasn't till he was following McDonald back to his cell that he realized he still didn't know how Kate had learned about his arrest. *Premonition*? What the hell did that mean?

Kate had left three messages on Jacqueline Stanley's answering machine, but didn't receive a call back until eight o'clock Sunday morning. Jacqueline's tone betrayed no sign of the anger that had seeped out at the Tohono Chul lunch, but that didn't mean things were hunky-dory. Kate knew how well principals learn to hide their feelings. Jacqueline said she planned to work at school later in the day, but Kate could come over right away.

Hoping to get a reading on the principal, who was drinking too much and turning mean, Kate wanted to see Jacqueline in her home. Was she was still mourning Larry? They'd been lovers for nearly a decade, and it was understandable that anger would be a stage in her mourning.

But what if Larry had learned something about the bidding process that caused his death? Jacqueline was an incredibly smart maverick, who wasn't afraid to work on the fringes of the law. Did she suspect Larry was murdered? Would she be willing to avenge Larry's death with Julie's murder?

Impossible. Kate forced her thoughts back to the murder scene and the tall man who left through the fifth grade classroom while she and Winnie hid. That shape wasn't Jacqueline's. But she could have hired someone to do the job. Not Elijah. That wouldn't make sense.

Last year, Jacqueline had moved to Catalina, a growing village north of Tucson populated by Arizonans who often disliked big city living and were willing to commute. Increasingly, the open spaces between Tucson and rural living were being blurred by the expansion of developers.

This was the first time Kate had been out to Jacqueline's new home. Keeping one eye on the road, she consulted the directions she'd been given. Her Corolla rolled through the business district that stretched along Highway 89, and then Kate made a right-hand turn at Claire's Restaurant. The side road continued through a neighborhood that was a patchwork of trailers guarded by chain link fences and snarling dogs. Every so often, there was a ranch-style house, usually with a corral or barn out back.

She turned left where three middle-class homes huddled in a row under some cottonwood trees, then moved onto Calle Fortuno. When the paving gave way to a dirt road, Kate rolled up her windows and slowed to avoid potholes. The cloud of dust would announce her presence. Her fingers drummed the steering wheel. Funny, she'd never felt this nervous around Jacqueline before.

The road ended at Jacqueline's large ranch house with its wide verandahs wrapping around three sides of the brick building, verandahs that protected the living quarters from the Arizona sun. The patina of age graced this hacienda. The barn with a corral and another structure, perhaps a guesthouse that had once been a bunkhouse, were shaded by huge cottonwoods. An oasis in the desert. Nothing shabby here. Nothing cheap, either.

As Kate silenced the engine, a whiff of hay and horse manure breezed by. Mild, not offensive, the smell of a well-maintained ranch.

Kate walked across the large front yard, where cow pies bore evidence of its use as a pasture. Evidently, Jacqueline had the rancher attitude that any grass not eaten by their cows was a "gosh darn waste." Kate had never guessed that the Mesquite principal had ranching in her blood. But then Jacqueline was a private person.

The mistress of the oasis, wearing jeans, cowboy boots, and a long-sleeved, plaid cotton shirt with damp circles under the arms, met her on the front steps. She pushed her Stetson back and beckoned Kate inside.

"Don't mind my looks, girl. I've just come back from riding Horace. Do you ride?"

"It's been a while."

The living room's central focus was a fireplace that stretched its full width, the stonework forming an interior wall. The head of a large elk dominated the space above the mantel. An enormous iron caddy held short sections of logs, two feet in diameter. Kachina dolls in glass cases supported by clear Lucite ledges gave the room an otherworldly, yet earthy appearance, blessing the room with spirits from the Hopi mesas. A large red, gray, and black Navajo rug covered the hardwood floor in the seating area, where three leather couches converged in front of the fireplace.

Jacqueline caught Kate eyeing the magnificent elk head. "Twelve points—that's a royal. Very few hunters make a royal kill."

"Larry must have been some hunter," Kate said without enthusiasm.

"Not Larry. I shot that elk." From the tiled bar at the far end of the room, Jacqueline picked up a tray that held a tall frosty pitcher with matching Mexican blue glasses with lime slices on the rims. "You'll like my gin gimlets."

Ten o'clock in the morning? Still, Kate intended to get Jacqueline to talk, and the gimlets might help. She sipped the cooling lime drink as she turned to the breathtaking view of Pusch Ridge seen through a plate glass window that formed the entire east side of the room. An elaborate telescope pointed toward craggy granite peaks that reached to the sky, daring mortals to scale their vertical rise. Desert bighorn sheep made their home on these forbidden ledges. The steep rise and limited access made this ridge in the Catalina Mountains the closest Wilderness Area to any large city.

Kate nodded toward the telescope. "Do you see the bighorns often?"

"Rarely. Old timers say they used to be abundant, but the foothills weren't included in the Wilderness Area, so their grazing habitat has been cut back and, with it, the size of the sheep population."

So Jacqueline had an interest in the outdoors that she'd never mentioned. The wealth evidenced in her home was also a surprise. Kate stepped toward the mantel to admire an exquisite Fabergé egg, purple with gold overlay, showcased in a transparent Lucite cube. A green jewel was set in its crown like the centerpiece of a queen's tiara.

"Not an authentic Fabergé, but a very real emerald," Jacqueline volunteered.

"Breathtaking! But is it safe out in plain sight?"

"We haven't had problems with burglaries. Women wear diamonds all the time without a worry. Wealth is to enjoy, not hide." Jacqueline gave Kate a superior look, then smiled coyly. "Besides, it's insured—for thousands."

Jacqueline went on about her two horses, Horace and Mann, and the fifty-acre spread she and Larry had bought jointly. Fifty acres at twenty thousand an acre, the going rate around Catalina. Kate calculated a cool million. From the clothing and jewelry Jacqueline wore, Kate had suspected her family came from money. A spread like this couldn't be bought on a school principal's salary.

"I didn't realize you were interested in ranching. You run cows on these acres."

Jacqueline smiled. "My grandparents ranched near Winkleman. I loved going there as a kid, so I jumped at the chance to buy here with Larry. Actually, the cows belong to a neighboring spread." She chuckled. "I'm not into milking. But they can graze where they want. No sense in letting good grass go to waste."

"Aha." Kate suppressed a smile.

"The last year of his life, Larry lived here on the ranch. Actually, Mann was his horse. He left the horse and his half of the ranch to me when he died." A shiny film came over Jacqueline's eyes, and she lifted the gimlet to her lips.

Mourning was the problem, Kate decided. Kate remembered how she'd felt when Shawn died. How she missed him even now. She reached for Jacqueline's hand.

Jacqueline waved her away and took another sip of the drink. Kate sensed an anger building and decided she'd better get right to the point. Too much drinking and the mean Jacqueline might return to the older woman's eyes.

"This week, trying to finish my 'punch list,' I've been looking over the building specs, and something kind of strange stood out. Did Larry ever talk to you about irregularities in the bidding process when he was preparing bids for—"

Jacqueline dropped her glass. It shattered across the Navajo rug, spraying lime gimlet over her cowboy boots and Kate's running shoes. As Kate helped her soak up the wet with cocktail napkins, she saw a flash of anger in her friend's eyes. Who wouldn't be upset about spilling liquid on the precious rug? Calm had returned by the time Kate took the dustpan and brush from her hostess' hands and swept up the crystal pieces. Once more the gracious hostess, Jacqueline poured herself another gimlet and suggested, "Why don't we go for a ride?"

Kate agreed. "It's been a long time, but Shawn and I used to ride in the back country." If she got Jacqueline away from the booze, she might be more relaxed.

"Good, I'll fill some canteens and meet you out in the corral."

Savoring the beauty of the most rugged stretch of the Santa Catalina Mountains, Kate headed across the pasture to the corral. Against the innocent blue sky, it looked as if a giant down pillow had been torn open, spilling white fluff clouds across the horizon. To the east, a dust devil turned the desert stillness into sudden motion like a miniature tornado, and then silently passed. The November sun caressed the air. A perfect day for a ride. Shawn used to praise her for her horsemanship. When he was killed, she'd stopped riding, stopped doing many things that brought back memories.

The bay ambled over to the lodge pole pine fence that formed the corral. Kate stroked his sweaty head, moving her hand gently over his nose. She reached into a fifty-pound burlap sack stashed outside the gate and found two carrots. The bay accepted his with gusto and tossed its head, inviting her to continue the feeding. Mann, the Appaloosa, hung back in the shade of the barn and watched. The scent from the corral was good, clean animal smell.

Jacqueline placed two canteens on the feed trough. Kate, wanting to get rid of the citrus taste, unscrewed a lid and raised it to her lips. The smell of gin and lime stopped her midair. Quickly, she replaced that canteen with the second one, filled with water and obviously intended for her. Jacqueline was in deep trouble; the day suddenly lost its innocence.

Kicking up corral dust, Jacqueline expertly lured the two horses, Horace and Mann, into their bridles. They accepted the bits, but Kate noted the look in the Appaloosa's eyes. She eyed her buff walking shoes. Her chinos were okay for riding, but these shoes? The big heels of cowboy boots hook neatly into stirrups, while her shoes could slip and get caught, causing her to be dragged if she were bucked off.

"Mann's your horse. Much gentler than Horace." Jacqueline slung the saddle on the Appaloosa, then tightened the cinch that reached under the horse's belly and kept the saddle in place. A loose cinch could cause the saddle to slide, sending the rider under the animal into galloping hoofs. A cinch too tight would annoy the animal.

As Mann tossed his head and pawed the ground, stirring dust and dried manure, Kate fed him a carrot and patted his spotted rump, sweet-talking him into settling down. She tied her handkerchief on the reins. Helpful to have it handy to wipe away the sweat. Taking the reins, she put one foot in the stirrup and began to swing her other leg over the saddle. It didn't feel right. She backtracked and checked Mann's cinch. It was much too loose. Pushing her foot against Mann's belly, she got him to suck in, and she tightened the cinch.

Jacqueline tossed her a cowboy hat brimmed with salt and sweat. The two riders headed across the meadow and down into an arroyo. Now dry, the arroyo was marked with signs of last summer's monsoons. Debris, caught among the cottonwoods, junipers, and mesquites that lined its sandy banks, marked the height of last season's flash floods.

Any thought of relaxed conversation evaporated as Kate focused her energy on controlling Mann. He tossed his head and strained to gallop.

For no apparent reason, he reared, and Kate leaned forward to keep her seat.

Jacqueline guided her steed effortlessly. Though she was a more experienced horsewoman, she rode a more manageable horse. Why had Jacqueline given her a difficult horse and failed to cinch him tight? That question niggled at the back of Kate's mind as she worked her whole body to control the beast under her. Her legs ached from imposing her direction, and she could feel dampness between her shoulders and in her armpits. Half an hour into the arroyo, her ride got a little smoother, but she had to remain constantly alert, unsure of what Mann might do next. No way to carry on an interrogation.

Horace led down the arroyo, his rider ignoring Kate. As long as the other horse kept the lead, Mann would follow. Even if Kate could have broken away and headed Mann back to the ranch, she didn't want to be riding him alone.

Abruptly, Jacqueline turned Horace around and circled behind Mann. Relieved they'd be heading back, Kate wiped her forehead with a shirtsleeve and started to turn her horse. As he fought the turn, Kate heard the crack of a gunshot. Mann went crazy. Rearing first, he then fled from the sound. Kate gripped the horse with her thighs, leaned forward over his neck, and hung on.

Another shot, and Mann sped like a demon out of hell. Deadly! Kate glanced back and saw Jacqueline aiming the revolver *at her!*

As Kate leaned in close to her mount, thoughts raced through her mind as fast as the horse galloped. "*Let Theo do it. You're too trusting. He'll watch his back better.*" And "*Kate, don't go acting on your coincidences until we can work together. Coincidences require back up.*"

Another shot whizzed by. The animal's terror made them a fast-moving target, hard to hit. Kate ducked to avoid overhead branches. Why hadn't she questioned Jacqueline and Larry's sudden wealth? Why had she dismissed Jacqueline's hostility? And Jacqueline's dropping of the gimlet glass when she mentioned the bidding process?

The answer sped on the wings of Mann. It had been so much easier to trust. She had accepted her own cozy Pollyanna reality. Lazy thinking! Dammit!

Her fear turned to anger. Anger at herself. At Jacqueline. At Theo and Mother Provincial for being right. Anger fueled a gigantic burst of strength. She wanted to hit someone, knock 'em out cold. Instead, she urged Mann to fly. The spooked horse didn't need any encouragement.

Kate's mind worked furiously. Jacqueline hadn't expected to miss. At the very least, Mann should have dumped his rider. On the ground, she'd have been an easy target. Ironically, it was Mann's erratic moves and speed that helped her elude the deadly bullets. Horace couldn't keep up with the fleeing animal. He and his rider were soon out of sight and shooting range.

Kate turned her attention to calming her mount. It was impossible. Afraid of being dragged, she kicked her feet out of the stirrups and pressed her legs against the horse with all her might. Without stirrups, she was practically riding bareback. Couldn't manage it for long. Her chance came when she saw an overhead branch in Mann's path. Her one chance! With both hands, she grabbed the branch, praying it would hold. It did. The galloping horse sped out from under her, and she hung on for a moment to be sure she was clear, then released her hold and dropped to the ground.

She stayed there, curled up in a ball, trembling like a frightened child. Finally, her brain kicked in, and she rose to walk out. If Jacqueline came after her to finish the job, Kate would kill her. She didn't know how, but she was certain she'd do it. The canteen was still on her belt, and she had the cowboy hat to keep the sun at bay. Good! She'd make it out.

As she trudged along, keeping an eye out for her mounted enemy, her thoughts began to make sense. Jacqueline was capable of murder. That didn't mean she had killed Julie Mason. But she sure could have!

The bidding for contracts was the touchstone that had set Jacqueline off. Something had been going on, and Larry was involved in some way. And the sudden wealth. Kate couldn't prove any of this, but she'd acquired new knowledge. The ugly corollary was that Jacqueline would have to come after her. Kate now knew too much.

She quickened her pace, wishing she'd retrieved her handkerchief from the reins to keep the sun off her neck. She needed to get out of the desert alive to tell Theo. The thought of her head mounted alongside that of the royal elk created a flash of black humor that made her shudder. She covered her tracks and kept to the undergrowth as she moved in a wide circle around Jacqueline's spread.

Oh, God! Help me never to be so trusting again!

"Tackle 'em, Louie. Get 'em now! Now!"

The red of Theo's bald head flooded into his face as he waved his clenched fists in the air and yelled at the Saguaro fifth and sixth graders he was coaching in touch football. The whistle blew, and referee Frank Fredericks stood with both hands on his hips, his Arizona Wildcat baseball cap pushed back from his brow, his dark and angry eyes glaring at Theo.

"You two coaches. Over here. *Now*."

As Theo approached the hostile authority, Louie ran alongside him, stage whispering, "You don't tackle in flag football, Officer Buloski. It pisses off the referee." He tossed the ball to his coach and backed off.

The muscles in Frank's neck bulged as he strained to be patient. He folded his arms, shooed the kids back, and eyed Theo as if he were an errant schoolboy.

"This is *flag* football, Officer Theo—"

"Buloski. Call me Buloski."

"These kids aren't suited up for tackle football. They're young kids. Tackling will break them, they'll get injured, and we'll get lawsuits." He sighed and reached for the football that Theo held in both hands, fingers spread wide. Theo didn't release it. "We're here to be sure they *don't* tackle, Officer Buloski. Clear?"

"I got it." The cop threw the ball to the players.

When the judge had sentenced him to 200 hours of community service to accompany his $850 fine, Saguaro seemed the natural place to work. The dad who'd been coaching after-school sports had gotten a job at Albertsons and had to abandon the teams. Theo fit in fine. After his workday, a couple hours working with the kids seemed like a good idea, and he owed Louie, after strong-arming him. He liked the kid, and this seemed a good way to make it up to him.

But this Frank Fredericks was something else. Used to bossing a room full of kids, he treated everybody else like they were preadolescents. Preadolescents with IQs of 60.

Still, Theo knew he had it coming. For forty-five years he'd been either tackling or yelling for someone else to tackle. What kind of football can you have without tackling? The cry to tackle had slipped out automatically. He could handle it. He'd have to remember this wasn't football; it was something else he was coaching. Not football. All his players had to do was snatch the flag from the quarterback's belt. No tackling. He'd better get used to it.

He returned to the sidelines, noting that Kate had joined the cheering section, a worried look in her eye. That woman was always worried. He wouldn't let these kids get hurt.

The referee blew his whistle, and the players fell into their former positions.

As Louie Castillo rushed by to get on the field, he whispered, "You can handle it, Officer Buloski. You can handle it."

It occurred to Theo he might learn more than he'd teach. And the kids needed him. They were pretty good at throwing, but catching was the problem. An interception was a miracle. Still, he had to hand it to these fifth and sixth graders. Boys and girls alike could really move.

A panting chubby sixth grader on the opponents' team thrust out his hands for a pass. When he caught it, he was so surprised, he stood, a stunned brown Doughboy, and stared at it a second before beginning to run. Breathing heavily, he ran in the wrong direction.

This confused both teams. Some of his teammates supported him in his quest to score a goal for the opposition. Others figured out what was going on and tried to stop him. A few stopped playing in disgust.

Theo's team came apart. Most of them were unwilling to help Chubby, even if he was going to make a touchdown for their side. It was Louie who was running interference for Chubby, pushing aside players of both teams to assist as he made the touchdown for the Saguaro Mustangs.

A quick thinker! "Go, Louie, go!"

Chubby's touchdown ended the game with him in tears, his teammates ready for a brawl, and Theo's team slaphappy, gloating over the stupidity of the opposition. With a rebellion threatening, the referee declared the game over. Saguaro's win.

Yep, Theo's kids had a lot to learn. He got his team into a huddle, and the first thing they learned was how to win gracefully. He was still feeling pretty good when, half an hour later, Kate dropped into his office.

"You sure look cheery for somebody who's spent two nights in jail. Evidently, your headache's gone." She pulled up a chair and flopped into it.

"You sure look miserable for somebody who never gets into trouble, Mother Superior. Where'd you get that sunburn?"

She took a deep breath. "It's a long story, Theo. Are you still a cop?"

"Yep, you're stuck with me. On probation, but still in the game. They just let me out this morning."

"That's a relief." She allowed a grin. "You've still got your police car?"

"They slapped my hands, but didn't take away my toys." He put his .38 revolver on the desk. "Is this idle curiosity on your part? Sympathy? What?"

"Well, I do have a practical application for your police skills." Smile lines began to play around her eyes and lips. "All right, I do need your help, but I'm relieved they didn't kick you out."

Theo took a cigar from his breast pocket and bit off the end. "Help in what way?" He lit the cigar.

Kate ignored the slight. "I need a police car to take me to pick up my Corolla in Catalina."

Interest sparked in the officer's eyes. He raised his eyebrows and took a puff on his cigar. "And what might your Corolla be doing in Catalina?"

"It's a long story." She took a deep breath and nervously pushed up her three-quarter length sleeves. "My car's at Jacqueline's house, and I'm afraid to go get it alone."

He noticed the scratches on her arms.

"You two have a cat fight?"

Kate rolled her eyes. "You're not making this easy, are you?"

He let cigar smoke escape from his mouth, not blowing it at her, but not blowing it away.

She turned away from him. "I told you about the emergency. If you don't want to help—" She rose and moved toward the door.

Theo put on his shoulder holster and slipped in the .38, grabbed his Phoenix Cardinals jacket, and stubbed out the cigar in a Pepsi can. Circling his desk, he followed her out the door.

"There could be gunfire. I have Shawn's .30-06 with a scope in my office. I'll bring it. Probably won't need it, but maybe—"

"Must have been some cat fight. Will I need backup?"

A smile flicked across Kate's lips. "I'm your backup."

Theo let out a "Humph" and looked worried.

By the time they arrived in Catalina, Kate had told Theo about her escape from Jacqueline and the long, hot walk out. Because he was driving, she could speak to him without having to look him in the eye.

When she told of the gunshots and Mann's breaking away, he turned toward her. "Why haven't you gone to the police? It's attempted murder! What the hell!" The heavy traffic on Oracle Road forced his eyes back to the highway.

Kate changed the subject. "Jail must have made a law-abiding citizen out of you. You're keeping to the speed limit."

Theo upped the speed five miles an hour. "Stick to the question. Why didn't you report this?"

"Maybe I can blackmail her. Get her to talk in exchange for not divulging it."

"Good luck. But as a cop I have to report it."

"She doesn't know that." Kate did not like the way this conversation was going, and was glad the heavy traffic slowed them down.

"You'd make a good crook. Murder's okay if one of your teachers does it. Lying's okay. That knocks out two of the Big Ten."

Kate tightened her lips and looked away.

"Okay, I'll play along. But, from now on, no more sermons. Cigar smoking isn't against the ten commandments."

Silence from the passenger side. She was tempted to counter that smoking violated "Thou shalt not kill," but decided against it.

"Why would she want to harm you?" He glanced sideward. "It doesn't make sense. You've worked together for years."

"Because she was living with Larry Denton, who handled the contractor bids. He's dead. So is Julie Mason, who took over the bidding process after him."

"So?"

Kate explained Mother Provincial's idea. Maybe a different set of building specifications were sent for bid to Icarus Construction. Building specifications that weren't nearly as expensive as those sent to the competing contractors. That way Icarus was always the low bidder.

"Even with the lowest bid, Wallace and his company could make inflated profits if they cut corners. At the new High School, the exterior was concrete block instead of split face facade—easily tens of thousands difference. At Mesquite Elementary, plain glass had been installed instead of unbreakable glass, another difference worth thousands. At Saguaro, swamp cooling rather than air conditioning."

"It's a crazy theory, Kate. Contractors make mistakes on three different building projects—hell, contractors make mistakes all the time. If they didn't make mistakes, it'd be so out of character, I'd worry."

"I'll tell you what's out of character. When each principal complained, Julie Mason quickly dispatched the district personnel to correct the situation. *Quickly* is out of character."

"For the sake of argument, let's say this little fraud—"

"Big fraud."

"Let's say they were actually pulling off this fraud. Julie Mason was a key player—without her, it wouldn't work. The last thing they'd want is her death." He turned on the car lights, then peered at her. "Is this idea another of your premonitions?"

She looked out the window. The crags of Pusch Ridge were casting dark shadows as the sun lowered in the western sky. Why was nature predictably breathtaking, so beautiful, while the work of man was convoluted and often ugly? "So what if it is?" she replied. "The last premonition was correct. You were in jail."

"Where do we go from here?"

It took a moment for Kate to realize he was asking for driving directions as he turned off the highway and slowed past the restaurant and trailers. She guided him, then completed her thought. "Anyway, Jacqueline and Larry have gotten a whole lot richer these past couple of years. I believe she knows what's going on." She told about how Jacqueline dropped the crystal goblet when Kate mentioned the bidding process. "And she meant to kill me!"

Theo drove in silence until they reached the dirt road. "Does she know we're coming?" The police car plopped heavily into the ruts, its headlights on high, seeking out potholes.

"The secretary at Mesquite Elementary says she hasn't been in all day. And all I got was the answering machine. She's probably home, nursing a hangover. I hope she won't be waiting for us with a high-powered rifle across her lap."

In the dark, Kate saw some movement flash across the headlights as they pulled into the driveway next to her Corolla. Theo turned off the lights and was walking toward the porch when a sudden shape whisked toward him, then retreated as he drew the .38 from its holster.

"Mrs. Stanley. This is the police," he called. "Please come out, so we can talk about claiming Kate Mahoney's car."

Silence. He mounted the wooden steps of the darkened house, his revolver held at his side, and knocked on the door. The shape advanced across the lawn, creating a wind in its wake. Theo knocked again, and the shape retreated. He retraced his steps and showed Kate how to operate the floodlights on the police car.

"Something's out there. Maybe one of your damned premonitions. I'm going back to cover the door. When I say, 'Now,' turn on the floods and duck behind the car. We need to know what we're dealing with."

Avoiding the steps, he swung onto the porch and stood, revolver drawn, against the wall alongside the door jamb. "Now!"

The floods illuminated the pasture and picked up a riderless horse, fully saddled, that whinnied and pranced outside the corral gate.

"It's Mann. He's saddled the way I rode him yesterday, even to the handkerchief I left tied to his reins." Mann reared and pummeled the air with his front feet. Behind him in the corral Horace paced back and forth. "I don't think he's ever been unsaddled, Theo. Jacqueline would've removed my handkerchief."

Suddenly, she spotted something more alarming than the horse.

"My car! Theo, look at my car!"

Oblivious to danger, she dashed to the Corolla, now illuminated by the floods. Spider webs of broken glass crisscrossed all the windows, and the tires were flat.

"Get outta the light, Kate." Theo leapt off the porch and whipped around the back of the police car to snap off the floods.

Kate hardly heard him. "Did you see my car? That bitch! How dare she?"

Theo pulled her back from the Corolla, and together, breathing hard, they squatted behind the police car.

"First she tries to kill me, then she kills my car!"

"Easy does it. Easy does it." His patronizing tone increased Kate's ire. "I'm calling for backup. In the meantime, we're going to sit here nice and calm with a bulletproof car between us and that Jezebel, and wait for our buddies from the Catalina police."

Keeping low, he flicked on the radio and called, explaining, "The woman responsible for the damage is a crack shot with a hunting rifle. We want to be covered when we go in nice and—Kate!"

Kate had pulled out her .30-06 rifle and snapped off the safety. Before Theo could stop her, she slipped around the police car and zigzagged to the porch using bushes for cover. From the corral, Horace whinnied a warning.

She crouched on the porch under the living room window, waiting for Theo to join her. Which he did immediately, fuming under his breath. "Damn woman! How've you lived so long?"

"Shh, shh." She knew he'd come. Moving stealthily forward, she straightened alongside the doorframe, flattening her body against the brick wall. Leading with the rifle barrel, she tried the screen door. It was unlatched. Using the barrel, she probed at the massive wooden front door until it eased open.

Theo was holding her back, tugging at her belt as his lips brushed her ear. "Get back, you fool. With a sawed-off shotgun, Jacqueline could blast a hole in that frame. Make you look like one of your car windows."

Kate gave Theo's pull some slack until he lessened his grip. Then with all her might she thrust forward, jerked her arm around the doorframe and turned on the light switch inside the door.

Theo pulled her down with a force that brought both of them to their knees. Then he sprang up to peer over the edge of the window. "Oh, no." Again he intercepted Kate's forward thrust, this time without urgency. "You don't want to see this, Kate."

Shaking him loose, Kate moved through the doorway, following the lead of her rifle. What she saw made her lower her gun and stand as frozen as a statue.

Another crystal gimlet glass had spilled on the rug, but this time it wasn't the glass that was broken. It was the drinker. Jacqueline Stanley lay face down, her arms flung wide and her legs spread. The blood that had flowed from the massive gaping hole at the base of her neck had dried a shade darker than the red in the Navajo design.

While Theo moved to the corpse, Kate staggered out, leaned over the porch railing, and vomited. She was still shaking when he returned to her side.

"That makes three."

Retreating from the porch railing and the smell, Kate looked up at him. "Three bullet holes?"

"Only one—must have been a Magnum. Not much of her head left. She didn't know what hit her."

"Three what, then?"

"Three people dead who were privy to those contracts."

Kate limply gestured toward the side of the porch. "Sorry about this…my stomach won't…I…"

Theo took her arm, steadying her. "Don't worry about it. If you remember, that's the way we met."

Kate shuddered again. "She must have been killed yesterday before Mann got back to the corral."

"By someone she knew and felt comfortable drinking with."

They both looked toward the dirt road, where two police cars with lights blazing were negotiating the potholes. They weren't using their sirens, and they didn't seem to be in any great hurry. Theo called the Tucson Dispatcher and requested the Crime Lab Unit.

"It's out of their jurisdiction, Theo," Kate cautioned.

"Trust me, Catalina cops will be glad to have the unit. I'm going in with them to be sure no evidence is messed with. Our lab boys will dig to get the bullet. It went through her head, probably through a couple of walls. Let's hope they can find it." He started to move toward the blue and red beams of the cop cars, and then hesitated. "I'll be here for a long time, Kate. Do you want one of the Catalina cops to take you home?"

"I'll wait for you. In the meantime, I'm going to get Mann into the corral and feed the two horses. I wonder if she has—had—any more animals that need tending to?" She looked Theo square in the eye. "No, I don't want to see Jacqueline again. If any officer needs to talk to me, they can do it out here."

Theo nodded and moved toward the parked police cars.

In the Provincial Accountant's Office...

The office of the Provincial accountant, Gene Howard, was unlike any other room in the Provincial wing. The large crucifix wasn't behind the desk; rather, it was over the door. A required accessory relegated to an out-of-the-way site.

The walnut desk, kept highly polished by a postulant, resembled those in the other Provincial offices. The similarity stopped there. On this desk, an adding machine anchored copies of the *Wall Street Journal*. Some were open to the stock market pages. Others still had the rubber bands around them. Investing in stocks and bonds was considered too worldly for religious, hence Gene's position.

Sister Katherine studied the accountant, rationalizing that, since he wasn't looking up, she wasn't obliged by modesty of the eyes to look down. His skin wasn't so much black as dark brown, highly polished like the walnut desk. He almost shone where the rays of the afternoon sun touched his face and neck. It was hard to tell his age, though his chenille-like black hair was white at the temples. Probably he was forty or fifty. Although she'd never seen him before, he seemed strangely familiar.

"Sister, Mother Philippa requested your presence at this meeting. She's been delayed, but will be here shortly."

The novice glanced up to see his brown eyes rest on her. His heavy lips parted in a generous smile to expose even, white teeth. She couldn't help herself; she had to return the smile. Delicately. With control. Without undue enthusiasm.

Why was she called to this office? Novices never visited with men who weren't family members. What was Mother Provincial thinking?

Her gaze returned to her lap, where one hand held the other. She smoothed her habit over legs that rested tightly together, black oxfords, side by side, touching each other. How could the accountant work at such a cluttered desk? She stole another glance. To her chagrin, he was watching her with a gentle, almost sympathetic look. He smiled again and went back to the *Wall Street Journal* he was reading. Sister Katherine looked away and checked the door. It was open as prescribed by Rule when a nun would be in the presence of a man. She refused to look at him again. When kneeling before Mother Provincial's table in the refectory, nothing would be more embarrassing than having to confess to eyeing Mother's accountant.

Checking out his office, she was intrigued by an oriental screen that partially obstructed a window so it couldn't be seen from the door. A flash of dark appeared on the sill. A cat with fluffy black fur dropped behind the screen. A pause, then scratching, probably against cat litter. What was this? Religious were forbidden to have pets. Must be the accountant's cat.

"Sister Katherine, so sorry to keep you waiting."

Mother Provincial took the novice by the hand and guided her to the desk. "Sister Katherine Mahoney...Gene Howard, the Provincial accountant. Sister Katherine is very capable. One of these days, she could be a Mother Provincial herself." Her tone grew sad. "But we both know that's not going to happen, don't we, Sister Katherine?"

If Gene noticed anything peculiar about the comment, he gave no indication. His was the neutral demeanor of a servant who's expected to forget the privileged words or actions of the employing family.

"You may speak freely in front of her, Gene. She has discretion that is...ah...otherworldly."

The tall black man stood and moved to the Provincial's side. As he handed a letter to her, he spoke with an authority that Sister Katherine had never heard anyone use when addressing the woman. "Mother, all due respect, but do you really think Mother General is the one who should be advising us about the stock market?"

As if a heavy weight had been placed on her shoulders, Mother Provincial sank into one of the upholstered chairs. "She's the one responsible for the financial well-being of the entire Congregation. When she speaks of the risks we're taking, she's thinking of the future of the nuns." Mother sat tall, pulling away from the softness of the upholstery. "When we make decisions for our sisters, security must be a top priority."

"Whatever happened to 'God will provide'?"

Mother rose to her feet and moved directly in front of the accountant. They were almost the same height. "Gene, God has provided me with a boss. And her name is Mother General, and she's commanded—not advised, commanded—me to pull these funds out of the stock market. Commanded by virtue of my vow of obedience." Mother Provincial's face hardened as she raised her voice. "I trust you will execute the conditions of this letter immediately."

The nun went to the screen, picked up the black cat, and stroked him. His purr seemed loud in the silent room. When she turned around, her benevolent demeanor was restored. "Sister Katherine, meet Archangel." She crossed the room and placed the black cat on the novice's lap. The cat jumped down and began rubbing against Mother's black serge.

Gene was not to be distracted. "It was profits from the stock market that built the cancer wing at Saint Bridget's. I trust those who've been cured wouldn't share your Mother General's disdain for the world of finance!" He strode toward the door and looked over his shoulder, his hand on the knob. "And, Mother Philippa, you can find a new home for your cat. Archangel! Michael was the white archangel. The black archangel was Lucifer himself." He slammed the door and was gone.

Mother picked up Archangel and brushed him with hard, strong strokes. "He didn't have to take it out on you, Archangel. From now on, you'll stay in my bedroom." She reached out and patted the arm of the stunned novice.

"Mother, why did you want me here?"

"You needed to meet Gene. In time you'll understand why. Don't let him shock you, sister. He'll get over it. And it could be worse. In the outside world, I could be married to him." She placed the cat on the floor. "Archangel, stay there."

The black cat leaped to the sill and disappeared. "And people think Mother Provincials have too much power. Very little, my daughter… very little."

From the look in Mother's eyes, Sister Katherine knew the Provincial Superior didn't believe her own words for a single moment.

"And don't worry about the forbidden cat, sister. God's two-legged creatures can be far more dangerous than Archangel. Which brings us to the business at hand. So now there are four corpses. Think of how they died, sister. Julie Mason was bludgeoned. Juan Ramirez, executed gang style. Larry Denton in an automobile crash. And now Jacqueline Stanley, one .38 shot to the back of her neck. Did the same person kill them all? Or are there four motivations and four murderers? Someone was really angry with Julie! Why? Think about it. Elijah has been in jail for the last two deaths. Shouldn't the police catch on? No, logic rarely prevails."

Mother placed both hands on the novice's shoulders and touched her cheek to first one, then the other side of the sister's wimple, giving her the kiss of peace.

"Peace, my daughter. The person or persons who killed those four wouldn't hesitate to kill you. They've already tried. Won't you reconsider visiting Mother Casey Whitehall on Innis Mor?"

Sister Katherine shook her head. Sadness slipped like a fog across her superior's face.

The novice asked, "Do you know something I don't?"

The fog expanded, and the scene disappeared.

11

The next day, when school dismissed, the principal left the building with the students. The kids carried book bags and banged-up lunch pails, while her tote contained a .38 revolver and a miniature camera. She went out through the kitchen, so Theo, who was out on the playing field with his team, wouldn't see her go. After lunch, he'd come to her office and ranted about her safety. Might Theo be a reincarnation of Mother Provincial? Mother Theo! Kate snickered as she slid behind the wheel of the district car.

Her Corolla was still at the body shop, recuperating. In Jacqueline's kitchen, Theo had found slivers of glass embedded in a baseball bat next to a chain saw with rubber in its teeth. He harped that there were worse things than dead cars, and she might soon experience them. If she'd returned to Jacqueline's house after that horse ride, there would have been two corpses on that Navajo rug.

At 3:30 the rush hour traffic tried her patience. Without thinking, she flicked on the radio, then changed her mind and turned it off. After last night's discovery and the non-stop pace at school today, the silence was welcome.

Bone-tired because she hadn't slept much, she thought about her dream and the warning that ended it. Doggedly, she disciplined her fuzzy thoughts into a rational mode. Four murders. But the person who'd been violent toward her was dead. Guilt at her relief irritated her conscience. The teenage driver in the car ahead was more interested in his hamburger than the green light. She honked. He threw her a fist, the middle finger pointed skyward. Relieved at the death of a colleague? She deserved the bird.

Theo said they'd found the bullet in the exterior wall on the other side of Jacqueline's house. A professional contract killer would've traced it and dug it out of the brick, so he wouldn't have to discard the murder weapon. Bullets, even ones that go through barriers, leave markings—signatures that identify the gun from which they've been shot. So not a professional. Would the killer discard his weapon? Where?

How did Coach play into all of this? He had the motive and opportunity to kill Julie. She would have let him into Saguaro that night. But would Coach kill a fellow principal? And why? Yes, if he'd killed Julie, and Jacqueline knew about it. Maybe he'd also confided in Jacqueline about his affair with Julie. Would he have the same motivation to kill his confidant from Saguaro?

Kate's heart began to pound, and she strained to keep her attention on driving. Why had Jacqueline wanted her dead? It probably had nothing to do with Coach, and she wasn't going to damage his family unless she had some proof of murder. Why did her heart continue to pound? Was her body telling her something she didn't want to hear? Hadn't she learned while riding Mann that she was too trusting? Too slow to recognize evil.

She patted the miniature camera on the seat beside her and planned the task ahead. Theo wanted to compare building specifications sent to Icarus with those sent to the contractors who lost the bids. But how could they get the competitors' building specs without showing their hand? Theo wanted her to back off. He'd get copies of the losing bids. How?

She was headed to the Icarus high school site to photograph the building specs for the exterior of the new high school. The architect had been surprised it wasn't split face, which was expensive, but much more attractive. Kate wanted to be sure the specs used on site were the same as those filed in the District Resource Office. It would only take a few minutes to flip to the right pages and photograph them. Then she'd do the same with the specification book. Site supervisors referenced it daily, so it should be close to the blueprints.

Kate left the district car some distance from the pickups that lined the construction workers' parking lot, an area still marked with the wide treads of the backhoe that had cleared the desert. It was four o'clock, one hour's work left for the workers. A woman could walk through a construction site about as easily as a cat could wander through a dog show. She skirted the area where construction was active and approached the trailer from the back. She hoped the bosses would be out inspecting the day's work.

When no one answered her knock, she slipped inside and peeked behind the door to find Flora's desk empty. Stood to reason. Flora would be tagging behind Wallace. His BMW wasn't in the parking area.

The blueprints were on top of the stand, opened to the plumbing section. Kate slipped in an envelope to hold the place, and then checked the index on the front of the plans to locate exterior design. Sure enough, plans called for the building of a concrete block exterior. She took three photos of four pages in rapid succession, then returned the plans to the plumbing. All in less than four minutes.

Where was the spec book itself? A legal document, it would be far more important than the blueprints. It would be about an inch thick and bound with a clear plastic cover. Her eyes flew over the papers on the shelf to the rows of coffee mugs. No specs. After glancing out the trailer door, she quickly opened the filing cabinet and scanned the multicolored tabs. Flora kept neat files, but no building specs.

Kate was opening the second file drawer when she heard the tread of heavy construction boots on the graveled path near the trailer. She slipped into Flora's chair behind the trailer door and scooted it against the wall, so she'd be out of sight. As a cover, she fingered through a cosmetic catalog she found in a pile of unopened mail on the desk. From the postmarks on the mail, Flora had been neglecting it for a week or so.

Metal-toed construction boots kicked against the wooden step; their owners entered, slamming the screen door behind them. "He doesn't ask you to do overtime very often, George. Give him a break."

They were probably bosses, since they seemed to belong in the trailer. Kate heard a hard hat bang onto a peg. At least one of them was going off his shift. Then the sound of liquid pouring.

"Damn, this stuff's cold as shit."

"You wouldn't be worrying about coffee at this hour if you weren't working overtime. Hell, if we knew the boss wanted you to work late, we'd have made a fresh pot. Want me to make one?"

"Naw, I'll put a little kick in it to fire me up."

If they discovered her, Kate would tell them she was waiting for Wallace. She sat perfectly still, hoping her breathing wouldn't give her away. Her nose began to itch. Barely moving, she scratched it softly. Cigarette smoke and a strong smell of whiskey wafted her way. The itch threatened to turn into a sneeze. She held her nose with one hand, and the open catalog with the other.

The guy who sounded older had a deeper voice. "Wallace finds you carrying a flask, and you're history, George. Whiskey smells. If you have to drink on the job, drink vodka."

"This is an exception. Tonight I have a date with a gal who's a real looker, and Wallace comes up with this emergency. It doesn't make sense." Kate heard more liquid flow. "Why the hell does the concrete floor of a fuckin' tool shed have to be poured tonight? Using overtime!" A pause, then, "You know how fuckin' hard it is to get The Man to approve overtime when we need it. That tool shed can be put in anytime, and it won't make one fuckin' difference."

"Wallace is the boss; he can do what he damn well pleases. You should've known his old man. One son-of-a-bitch to work for. Wallace's a big improvement."

"You tell that to Ruby."

"Ruby?"

"My date. Ruby red lips, ruby red tits—"

"I get the picture. You'd better give her a call."

The only phone in the trailer was on the desk in front of Kate. An uncomfortable heat began to spread under her skin. She heard the sound of the large blueprint pages being turned, and then a pause.

"You won't find blueprints, it's only a tool shed."

More turning of pages.

"Guess you're right, but I'm still going to check the specs." A loud slap of the blueprints being closed. "It's hell to pay if we even install a fuckin' toilet without consulting Wallace's bible. It should be out here somewhere."

"It's probably in the bottom right-hand drawer of Flora's desk. She's taken to squirreling it away any time she sees it out."

"Why?"

"Who knows what makes that blonde tick?"

Kate was prepared when the younger boss stuck his head around the corner of the door.

"What the fuckin' hell are you doing here?"

George's blonde hair was slicked straight back in a way not common to construction workers. He was wearing a sleeveless denim shirt that stretched tight across his chest and showcased the bulging muscles of his upper arms. He worked with his men.

"I'm fuckin' waiting for your fuckin' boss, and since Wallace is late, I'm on my fuckin' way out."

George stood, arms crossed, between her and the door. He was not inclined to move, and she couldn't get around him.

"Don't worry, Big Boy, I didn't hear a fuckin' thing you said." She pulled her hand across her lips. "It's zippered." Their eyes met, and Kate knew immediately that he was good at bossing crews, a leader despite his limited vocabulary.

He stepped aside, and she took her time opening the screen door and going down the steps. Her visit hadn't been a complete bomb. At least, now she knew where the fuckin' building specifications were kept. She'd be back. Strange, though, Wallace wanting a concrete slab poured, all of a sudden. A concrete slab would be a great place to dump a body. Was there another corpse to be hidden? She shivered. Then it hit her like a kick in the stomach! What if that concrete bed was for her?

With the help of the district chalk-marking machine, the flattest part of the playground had been lined, turning it into a football field for the season. Volleyball standards joined by ropes became makeshift goal posts. Each player wore a new Saguaro tee shirt bought by Theo. Parents and buddies sat along the sidelines on blankets, on grass prickly to the touch, or on folding chairs with seats made of interwoven plastic strips.

Kate matched Theo step for step as he paced along the sidelines. He'd pace twenty feet, then stop and stare at the opposition team from Prickly Pear Elementary. Not the team itself, but its 230-pound running back, Jack Trudeau.

"How *old* is that kid?" Without waiting for an answer, he growled. "He must have failed three times to be that big."

"District policy allows only one failure."

"Thank you, Ms. Principal, for that valuable bit of information. Information that's not worth diddlysquat when he plows into our kids. He'll pulverize them! There'll be nothing left but mush."

Kate circled around the end zone nearest Pat Callahan, Prickly Pear's principal. She could've saved time by walking straight across the lined field, but nobody did that except players and coaches. When a game was about to begin, this little strip of playground was hallowed, every bit as important as the U of A stadium downtown that could hold forty thousand fans. Her conversation with Pat was animated with arms waving, fingers pointing, and voices raised. When she left to return to the side of her loyalties, a low hiss-s-s leaked out of the Prickly Pear cheering section. Callahan raised his hand, and the booing ceased.

Her report to Theo wasn't encouraging. "Jack's from Louisiana, from a parish school where they can fail the kids as many times as they like. So he's seventeen. Never been failed in Oasis District because he just got here."

Theo hit his head with the flat of his hand. "Our kids are twelve—thirteen, max."

"Please, Theo, a show of confidence." She waved to the Saguaro team, a big smile on her face as if all were hunky-dory. Ashen to a man, they weren't buying her perkiness. "Pat says Prickly Pear hasn't lost a game since Jack joined the team."

Theo reached for a cigar, then remembered, his hand in midair. "Yeah, you tell Pat his team's got a great plan. Let Jack Trudeau run the ball, and anybody on the our team who wants to commit suicide can try to stop him."

Kate left Theo's side and walked over to the Saguaro team, gathering them around her in a huddle. Their spirits were visibly lifted when they returned to their bench.

"What'd you tell them?"

"Just gave them a little plan." Kate's eyes twinkled, and she brushed the nervous coach aside.

"Dammit, Kate, you're meddling in my business. This is my team, and they take orders from me."

"I didn't give them orders. Just a philosophical suggestion."

The whistle blew, and Prickly Pear kicked off, with Saguaro taking possession on their 40-yard line. Saguaro held their own on the offense because Louie was fast, and he could maneuver around Jack Trudeau.

But once Prickly Pear got the ball, the Saguaro players avoided any contact with the 240-pound running back. They side-stepped out of his way with the agility of ballet dancers. The final score was posted, 94 to 14—Prickly Pear's win.

Kate realized she hadn't thought of Elijah or Jacqueline or Juan during the entire game. Her worry had been for the safety of the players. She ached to get back into that old familiar mode again. Would that ever happen? She went over to congratulate the players on a game wisely played.

A muscle strained in her back as she helped Theo put the volleyball standards back in the gym. His sweat and heavy breathing told her it was a load for him, too. After the game, the kids had swarmed around him, seeking solace, and he'd given it. Touching each child, he'd promised, "We'll win the next one."

Now, with the kids gone, he told the truth. "Damn, I hate to lose. I could've kicked Jack Trudeau off the field. What right does he have, mopping up the field with little kids? Murderers get away with it. Little kids don't have a chance."

So Sunday's corpse did get to him. Kate wasn't the only one having a hard time concentrating.

"Little kids! Don't let your team know you called them that. A lot of those little kids carry burdens that would crush big, middle-class adults." She was thinking of the "little kids" who tended younger brothers and sisters because their alcoholic or drug-addicted parent couldn't function. Little kids who tried to distract their brothers and sisters from the hunger that made them dread the weekends.

Theo threw the football flags and belts, smelly with sweat, inside the equipment cupboard. He shoved aside boxes of ping-pong balls and perched atop the P.E. teacher's desk. With his foot, he shoved the teacher's chair toward Kate. "Sit down."

Kate obliged, knowing what was coming, but not knowing how to handle it.

"What did you tell those kids in the huddle?"

"Did you ask them?"

"No, I'm asking you. Right now. And I want an answer."

Kate distracted herself by checking out the rows of volleyballs, footballs, tetherballs, and plain bouncing balls that lined the walls. The faculty building committee had worked with Bobby Peterson, the P.E. teacher, to plan the precise measurement of those shelves, so they were exactly the right depth for the different kinds of balls. The equipment was handy, but manageable. Like all the spaces in the new buildings that they'd shepherded through the contractor's painful birthing process, this room worked. Anger surged as she thought of the building details in other schools that wouldn't be right because Julie Mason had watered down the building specifications.

"Earth to Kate. Are you with me?"

"Let's go celebrate that the Prickly Pear game is over. At the Metropolitan Grill. My treat."

Theo shook his head, reached for his cigar, then just patted it in his pocket while chiding her. "You do that all the time, you know, and it gets damned annoying."

Kate knew what he meant, but she hoped it still might work. "Do what?" As soon as she'd widened her eyes, she knew she'd overplayed her innocent look.

"Change the subject when you don't want to answer a question. Bribe me with a dinner instead of answering."

Kate got up to go. Theo gently nudged her back into the chair. There was no way out, except the truth. "I told them, 'Don't get hurt. Stay away from Jack Trudeau and live to play another day.'" Truth brought relief. She turned to face the storm.

It never came. Theo dangled his legs, looked down at his hands clasped between them, and chuckled. "I told them exactly the same thing right before the game. Since you're so competitive, I was afraid you'd told them to go out there and die for Saguaro's honor, so I emphasized avoidance when faced with an impossible situation." He looked up. "I guess you've got good sense when protecting others. It's only yourself you expose to danger." He slipped off the desk, still grinning. "Let's go get something to eat. Nice you're buying."

Jail didn't frighten Elijah. The other cons kept their distance in the exercise yard, not wanting to mess with a strong, murdering giant. The cops had picked up on his friendship with Theo, so they didn't pull any shit that might get back to him. These two months, he'd even learned to tolerate his own company. Books helped, also TV and bodybuilding. He hated being locked up like a dog in a pound, but he wasn't afraid.

Not until now. As he followed the jailer down the concrete corridor, he could feel beads of sweat form on his neck and face. The two men stepped around a work crew chipping paint. The officer's hand automatically moved to his nightstick, then relaxed as they passed the workers. Elijah's heart beat so fast and loud, he wondered whether the officer could hear it.

"Relax, Elijah." The cop's tone had a sadistic edge. "The walk to the visitor's room is the longest hall in the prison. I've seen tough men break down and cry, begging to be taken back to their cells rather than face their women." The jailer snorted. "Jacqueline. Nice name. She says she's your cousin. It's amazing how many cousins come to call."

They stood before the double set of doors that led into the visiting room. The smell of fear lay heavy in the space between criminals and visitors.

"You can always go back. I'll tell her you don't want to see her," the cop taunted.

"Put me through."

The first gate clanged open. They moved into the holding area and waited for the door to bang shut. Elijah heard the click of the lock. Steel against steel. He could still turn back. Then the next gate slid open, and he was committed. Sweat plastered the orange jail garment to his skin.

A long table, separated every thirty inches by hard, transparent plastic dividers, stretched across the visiting room. In the first space, a grandmother, whimpering softly and dabbing her eyes, sat across from her grandson.

Brothers occupied the second space. They had to be twins; they looked so much alike. One free, the other caged.

At the end of the table, a woman rose. Elijah had traced her features in a thousand dreams, and there she was. Real. He hungered for her being. Her presence, tall and queen-like. He stood across from her, shaking his head slowly and feeling tears trickle down his cheeks.

"You're here."

"Yes." Her answer was barely audible. She wasn't allowed to touch him. Just stood without moving a muscle, the tips of her fingers touching the tabletop. Her eyes drank him in and clouded with a misty film.

They sat. Elijah's eyes absorbed her, tracing the ends of her curls, the wrinkle in her brow, the soft black skin of her cheek, her generous lips, the delicate line of her neck.

"You're beautiful."

Her eyes were large and worried, her lashes moist. "You look terrible."

"I'm doing all right. This is the best I've felt since the last time we were together."

Jacqueline took his big hand in both of hers and started to sob. She kept trying to still her grief, but it was useless. She covered her mouth with her right hand and pressed her lips to keep the sounds inside.

Elijah was no longer afraid. He ached to take her in his arms and caress her. To comfort her, he lied. "Everything's going to be all right, Jacqueline. How is Tamoni?"

"He misses you and Saguaro." Though her eyes denied his claim that "Everything's going to be all right," Jacqueline leaned closer.

"Why'd you do it, Elijah? Julie Mason was white trash." Her words shot like bullets from a silencer, quiet but loaded. "She wasn't worth a life behind bars!" Again, her hand flew to her lips. No cries escaped, but her eyes were full of pain.

Elijah's eyes widened, and his mouth shot open. He answered in a whisper, "You know who did it! You're protecting your brother, and that's okay for the cops, but you gotta be straight with me. We heard Hiram say he'd get rid of her. Remember, I said, 'No, I'll handle it my own way.' Why didn't he listen?"

Jacqueline was stunned. "But you left our bed in the middle of the night, left the apartment and didn't come back for over an hour. I couldn't sleep." She suddenly hunched forward in her chair, looking tired and drawn. "Then, when I heard you'd been arrested for that woman's death, I knew you couldn't take it anymore. Her being on your back, threatening to fire you if you wouldn't take that job as the District's Physical Resource Director. No, Elijah. It wasn't Hiram. I checked with Virginia first thing. He was in her bed all night. Hiram might lie to me, but Virginia wouldn't. Why was that woman killed in your schoolroom?"

Elijah shook his head. "I know nothing about that night in my room, Jacqueline. If Hiram didn't do it, then somebody else set it up so I'd take the fall." He saw the confusion in her eyes. "Like I told you: next morning, I couldn't sleep, so I went to the Circle K on the corner and picked up the *Arizona Daily Star*. Remember, I was reading it when you came and coaxed me back to bed."

A light clicked in Jacqueline's eyes. "Yes, I remember seeing you with the paper spread out on the table. In the mess that followed, I'd forgotten all about that newspaper." She spoke in hushed tones. "Why are you in here? You should be free."

"Too much circumstantial evidence. The victim was a big name in the community. They won't let me free until they find someone else to blame it on. Are you sure you can trust Virginia? Hiram sounded deadly serious when he threatened to 'off' Julie so I could go on teaching."

"No. No, Elijah." Jacqueline shook her head, making her gold loop earrings dance. "I'm sure of Virginia."

"He's killed for his gang before. I don't know how the two of you came from the same mother." Elijah's jaw twitched, and he looked away. Stupid! He was using this precious time to berate her brother. He shut his lips tight for a moment, then leaned over and whispered, "Don't worry, baby. I haven't told the cops about his threat. I never will. Not for him. For you."

"I stayed away for two reasons. I didn't want them to know about us. That you'd been with me and left my bed during the killing hour." She blushed. "And I was afraid you'd tell the police about Hiram's threat. When a man's in deep trouble and out of a woman's bed, he can forget about her. Men do."

"I don't." Hurt filmed Elijah's eyes. "Didn't you trust me?"

"I was afraid, Elijah. I don't trust men, and you kind of slipped through my defenses. When I heard you'd killed that woman, I was afraid you'd tell about Hiram. Then, when Mrs. Mahoney was almost taken, I was afraid you and Hiram had set it up because she was a witness."

"How could I have contacted Hiram? Did he have anything to do with the kidnap attempt? And the death of—Juan, was that his name?"

Jacqueline glanced at the officer in the corner, then back to Elijah. She held her breath for a moment, then plunged on, taking a giant leap of faith. "Hiram won't answer me when I ask about that kidnap attempt. He says he doesn't want to talk about it. Since he got out of prison, he's been running around with two ex-cons he met inside—A. J. and Buffo. Bad news. I worry about him."

"Would they be involved, if he tried to take out a witness? Is he going to try again?"

Jacqueline wouldn't meet his eyes.

"Tell him this, Jacqueline. Tell him Kate Mahoney never saw the killer. If she had, I'd be out of here. Tell him that and reassure him I won't implicate him—in anything. We're family. I don't like him, Jacqueline, but he's your brother, and I won't rat on him. But murder! That poor kid, Juan."

Jacqueline's eyes stopped his words. The jailer, who'd silently come up behind Elijah, touched his shoulder.

"Your time's almost up, man. Another five minutes." Like a sheepdog guarding a flock, he stepped back to the corner, never turning his back on the occupants of the room.

As if sensing the cold chill that slid down Elijah's spine, Jacqueline smiled. "He didn't hear anything. You stopped before he got within earshot. But Elijah—"

"Jacqueline, how could you still love me, thinking I'd murdered someone?" The words came quickly. There was so much to cover in five minutes.

"Thinking that, I still came. I knew you were being cornered. Horrible things happen when people are trapped. I can no more stop loving you than I can stop breathing." Tears welled. "The feeling I have for you isn't something I can turn on or off. It just is."

Elijah memorized the way she looked when she said those words. "Promise me, you'll come back. Soon. I can stand anything this jail can throw at me, but I can't stand losing you."

She glanced up to see the jailer look at her, and then turn away. "I'm afraid of what they might do to you in here."

"They can't destroy me as long as I know you love me and are waiting for me. When can you come back?"

"I'll have to assume a different identity. Maybe be your mother." She smiled. "With gray hair. If I come again as myself, there might be a detective waiting to question me." Jacqueline's manner turned solemn, "If neither you nor Hiram killed Julie Mason, then who did? Somebody set up that meeting."

"Kate's on my side right now, but if I told her how Julie Mason was pressuring me and threatening to fire me as a teacher, it would provide motive for murder. I've got to keep my mouth shut. I can't trust Kate the way I trust you."

As Elijah felt the presence of the jailer at his side, he gave Jacqueline a long look. Then he rose and turned away.

~

While they sat sipping their before dinner drinks, a margarita for her and a Bud Lite for Theo, Kate surveyed the other diners. They looked normal: a smile here, a haughty demeanor there, a burst of laughter from the far table in the corner. Normal. They weren't worrying about death threats, murdered acquaintances, dead bosses, accused coworkers. Sure, they had problems with teenage kids, household appliances, unpaid bills. But nothing deadly. Not murder as a daily diet, contaminating all thinking. Kate wondered whether she'd ever feel normal again.

"A penny for your thoughts. From the crease in your forehead, I imagine they're going to cost me more than that."

"Theo, how are we going to get copies of the bids sent to the losing contractors?"

Theo eyed the Peking duck placed before diners at an adjacent table. "Looks good."

"They're normal."

"Normal?"

"Normal people eating Peking duck. Not abnormal people like you and me, feasting on crow and memories of murder."

"Really?" Theo looked at her over the top of his beer mug. "The duck might consider himself murdered."

"Be serious."

"It's serious to the duck. Does that disgusted look in your eyes mean we're not going to feast on Peking duck for two?"

Kate closed the menu and unfolded her napkin. "It means, after this little discussion, I'm going to order something vegetarian." She noticed he'd evaded her question about bid records, but decided to let him feast on murdered Peking duck before having another go at it.

"You'd have made a good homicide detective. You're sour on murder now…" keeping a finger in one page, he lowered and closed his menu, "…because the persons killed and accused are so close to you. It's personal, so it eats at you. But regular, impersonal murder is really quite interesting. Challenging, a puzzle in which the stakes are enormous. This murdering business is a great life. I like it."

The startled waiter, who'd come up behind him in time to hear Theo's case for murder, dropped his pencil. Theo and the waiter both bent to retrieve it, and their eyes came within inches of each other. The waiter's were large and startled, Theo's amused.

Kate laughed. "Don't mind him. He's carrying on about the murdered Peking duck he's about to order. Ignore him."

The waiter bowed stiffly, defensively adjusted his bow tie, and cleared his throat. "About the duck. We don't consider it murder, ma'am."

As if on cue, Kate and Theo answered in unison, "But what does the duck think?"

The waiter stretched to his full height and glared at the two diners as if they were unruly teenagers. "Your order?"

Having dispatched the waiter with an order of Peking duck for the gentleman and alfredo fettucine for the lady, the two continued chuckling. It felt so good for Kate to laugh, to enjoy a normal feeling like other folks, she kept giggling, burying her mirth discreetly in her napkin.

While Theo was blaming her lightheartedness on the first margarita, she surprised him by ordering another. He watched her as he reopened an order of business.

"There's only one way to compare the losing contractors' bid specifications with Icarus's and those on file at Central Administration. The old-fashioned CIA way. I'll break into their offices and go through their files."

"What!" Kate glared at the offending margarita as if it had deprived her of her hearing. Then she bent over the table, touched his arm, looked into his eyes and, putting all her senses on full alert, whispered, "Will you repeat that please?"

What she got was a sexy look that sent her reeling. As if she'd received an electric shock, she retreated to her own space. *It must be the margarita!* "Please call the waiter over, Theo. I'm going to cancel that second margarita."

Theo's lips formed a crooked half smile, like the cat that had the canary within reach, dallying with the inevitable. It irritated Kate. No, she had enough troubles; she wasn't going to feel this way about him. She'd *will* the feelings away.

"A second margarita would be good for you. This is the most relaxed I've seen you in weeks. Normal, like other people. Relaxed—up until about thirty seconds ago." The half smile returned.

So did Kate's irritation and her next question, asked from a safe distance. "What's this about the CIA way of doing business?"

"You know I used to work for the CIA. After Korea." He watched her closely, judging the effect of the information. When he got no reaction, he pressed on. "Before I came to Tucson. That's one of the reasons the Tucson Police wanted me, because I'd learned unique skills in the CIA. My breaking and entering skills are top quality."

"If you think we're going to go picking locks—opening safes—"

"Not *we*. Me."

The waiter had connected with Theo's nod and stopped by the table. Theo sent Kate a questioning glance, and she decided to stay with the second margarita after all. With Theo as a partner, she needed something to blunt reality.

"Me," he repeated. "I know what I'm doing, Kate. I can get photos of those pages, and then we'll have the proof we need to obtain search warrants."

"Whatever happened to getting a subpoena or search warrant from a judge and obtaining the documents the old fashioned, legal way?"

Theo groaned audibly, took a cigar out of his pocket, bit off the end, and balanced it kitty-corner on the butter dish. Kate made a point not to notice. “Kate, we’ve got a hunch, that’s all. Yes, all three victims were connected to the bidding process. But they were connected by hundreds of other variables as well. Besides—” He blushed and looked toward his cigar. “Besides, I’m not suspended from the police, but that DUI put me mighty close to the edge. Nobody in the force is going to stick his neck out to help me with a judge right now. Sorry, it’s my own fault, but it’s a fact.” His bald head was as red as his face.

Seeing his vulnerability, Kate couldn’t help herself. “You do have certain James Bond qualities. Derring-do, breaking and entering, chasing women—”

“Chasing women!” Now Theo was irritated. The canary had taken a chunk out of the cat.

“And no judge is going to issue a search warrant with information acquired from a break-in.”

“They will if the information is provided gratis by an anonymous informant, a concerned citizen.”

“You!”

Theo smiled. “If it just shows up in the mail, they’ll act on it. Believe me, I know.”

Kate, sipping on her second margarita, deliberately sidestepped her legal inhibitions. She was weary from doing the right thing. It hadn’t helped Elijah. Virtue certainly hadn’t helped Juan.

“If you’re going to break in, then I’m going to help. We’re in this together.”

Theo shook his head. “I work alone.”

“If you don’t let me work with you, I’ll blow the whistle on you.”

“No, you won’t.” Theo’s eyes lit up like a boy’s, sure of himself, rushing towards adventure. Like a young man who thinks he’s immortal and doesn’t realize the danger till it’s too late. Kate had to save him.

“Yes, I will. Right now.” She touched the arm of a waiter passing their table. Vexed, he turned toward her. Kate guessed he considered the two of them undignified riffraff, not up to the standards of the house. “Young man, I need to tell you what this James Bond character is planning.”

The waiter’s annoyance turned to mild interest.

"Kate!" Theo kicked her shin under the table.

"Ouch!"

Theo apologized to the waiter. "Don't mind her, she's unusually high-spirited tonight. Normally she's rather…civilized, but…" he shrugged and nodded toward her margarita.

The waiter nodded knowingly and continued on his way.

"All right, you can go with me," Theo said with phony enthusiasm that made Kate know he was lying. "Now, let's enjoy our meal."

Theo spent all evening with the one beer he'd ordered upon their arrival. It amazed Kate that a man so sober could entertain such James Bond-like flights of fantasy.

In Saint Bridget's Academy...

The sister Provincial and novice entered Saint Bridget Academy's grounds and moved toward the back entrance, the one used by the high school girls.

Feeling homesick, the novice gazed at the leaded stained glass windows of the chapel. The Academy had been built in the early twentieth century, when the mines in Bisbee, sixty miles to the south, were going full swing. Mining magnates had contributed generously, encouraging this seed of gentility in the Wild West.

"You probably wonder why we're not using the front entrance."

"If you can't, Mother, who can?"

"If Sister Superior and the other nuns know I'm coming, they'll make a fuss over me. Such a bother. But there is someone I want you to see."

Silently, they climbed the wide wooden steps onto a deep back porch that ran the full length of the structure. They padded past the open windows of the piano practice rooms. Metronomes monitoring the pace of musical scales reminded Sister Katherine of the regularity of this establishment, where she'd gone to high school.

Near the middle of the porch, the nuns began the two-story climb up the fire escape. Mother Philippa held onto the railing with her right hand. With her left hand, she held her skirts and the giant rosary beads that hung from her waist, silencing the sound that might alert students.

At the top of the fire escape, they entered a small classroom through a gabled window.

A nun, her back to the window, was confronting a girl of sixteen, who wore the blue Academy uniform skirt, the regulation white blouse, and a red-letter sweater. Sister Katherine drew in her breath. "That's me!"

The provincial nodded as if bilocation were normal. "Watch what's happening."

Recall came in a flash! When writing an essay on democracy, the young Kate had thrown together platitudes that sounded both patriotic and Catholic. How could she miss getting an 'A'?

Sister Mary Victor, her English teacher, had pulled her aside and made her justify every line. The red-faced student had struggled to substitute a second level of platitudes for the first.

"No, Kate. Take your time. I'll wait."

Mother Provincial motioned toward the window. She climbed down a couple of steps on the fire escape and beckoned for the novice to sit next to her.

"Do you remember?"

"Do I remember? From that time on, I felt responsible for what I put down on paper. Are you going to explain how I can be in two places at one time?"

Mother Philippa rose to let the pleats in the back of her habit fall straight, and then sat back down. "These habits do bunch up, don't they? But, then, they weren't designed for fire escapes."

"You're ignoring my question."

Mother continued to ignore it. "What you saw back there was the making of a Mother Provincial."

Sister Katherine stared.

"You'd been with our nuns since kindergarten and talked about being a nun from an early age." Mother piled her beads on her lap. "In retrospect, much too early. You were bright. We couldn't resist it. We trained you in leadership from an early age."

"Isn't that self-serving? A conflict of interest...something against the teacher's code of ethics? I needed to be challenged because I was Kate O'Brien, not because of the Congregation!" Sister Katherine's cheeks warmed.

"We were preparing you for a life we thought God had destined for you. If you didn't choose to be a nun, you'd still have the benefit of privileged teaching over the years. But the scholarships were another matter."

"Scholarships?"

The provincial remained silent.

"Mother, look at me."

Mother Philippa's gaze focused on her beads while she spoke. "As salutatorian of your graduating class, there were three full scholarships available to you."

At first, Sister Katherine's eyes went blank. "But I was told by Sister Mary Elva, the principal, that only the valedictorian was awarded a scholarship."

"Sister Mary Elva lied. She was afraid scholarships would tempt you away from your vocation."

Sister Katherine rose and grabbed the railing of the fire escape with both hands. She started to run down the steps, but was stopped by a jerk on the back of her veil.

"Sit!"

From habit, Sister Katherine obeyed. "How could she have manipulated me like that? I was only a kid! I trusted you nuns."

"Never trust anyone who believes she thinks for God." The older nun took the novice's rigid hand. "We were wrong. If you'd stayed, you wouldn't be a Mother Provincial. You don't know how to face the dark side of human nature."

On the contrary, Sister Katherine now sat in touch with the dark side of her own nature, sorely tempted to push Mother Philippa Manning off the fire escape. She tried to rise, but Mother kept her anchored.

"Evil was close, and you chose to ignore it. You trusted Jacqueline, despite all the warning signs. She panicked and tried to kill you. Her killers knew the police would interrogate her. Jacqueline had to die. Four people dead. Maybe more than one killer. Be strong, Sister Katherine, and look unflinchingly into the dark side of those around you. You may know the killer, but not want to see."

"Who is he, Mother?"

"Or she. I don't know. Being dead is greatly overrated in the Catholic tradition. We all have to earn our own understandings, usually at a cost. I've learned something valuable myself today. Never give upsetting news on the top of a fire escape. Sit here and pray the rosary for a few minutes. These skirts can kill a body who tries to hurry down a fire escape with an upset soul."

The provincial's slow, penetrating look made Sister Katherine squirm. Had Mother realized the depth of her dark thoughts?

Mother placed Sister Katherine's hand on one of the large rosary beads in her lap and began, "Hail Mary, full of grace, the Lord is with thee..."

12

"Nam-myoho-renge-kyo..." Ralph's midnight Buddhist chant awakened Kate. The sound flowed from his balcony through the bedroom window she'd left open to catch cool autumn breezes. Half dozing, she let her mind sway with the repeating rhythm. Plaintive, like a Gregorian chant.

Never trust anyone who believes she thinks for God.

Kate sat up in her bed and reached for the lighted alarm. It was 2 a.m. She considered telling Ralph to knock off the liturgy at this hour. But the chant calmed fears that Mother Provincial's dreams always provoked. The rhythm promised, "It will be all right. It will be all right. Someone's watching over you."

Was Kate letting her irritation with Mother narrow possibilities? Strange. As she whispered the chant, it seemed to invite her to look inside herself. And be unafraid of what was there.

How well was she using Theo's skills? Theo? She had a funny feeling something was going on with him. But surely not at two o'clock in the morning.

The two snarling German Shepherds were a cinch. After gobbling hamburger laced with barbiturates, they snoozed like babes in a crib. In his CIA days, when he had an expense account, he'd used steaks to send guard dogs to slumber land. Now hamburger worked just fine. He knew the dosage to use, so the dogs would be just a little hung over. Later, the owners would have no idea their security had been breached.

He'd left his pickup in an empty lot halfway down the block from the Desert Construction Company office and walked on cat feet up the alley, dressed all in black. At 1:30 in the morning, who would spot him in this industrial park? Only the barking dogs he'd taken care of an hour earlier.

Dogs routinely protected the grounds of companies like Desert that specialized in large government projects with millions invested in the heavy equipment in their yards. In addition to the dogs, the six-foot fence surrounding the property would be alarm activated. It didn't take long for Theo to locate where the wires were hidden and make the necessary cuts.

He still felt his adrenaline pump as he worked in the dark by the penlight he held in his teeth. In the jobs he'd done in Russia, he would have been shot if he slipped up; he'd learned not to make mistakes. A sense of déjà vu reactivated nerves that stored memories of past risks. He got a rush when he snipped the right wires, and the alarm remained silent. On the way out, he'd splice the cut wires, so his visit would never be detected.

Over the fence and into the construction company office. There was no alarm system for the office proper. It was simply a matter of picking a dead bolt lock and slipping inside, with the whole night to go through files. He hadn't spent twelve years in the CIA for nothing.

Theo pulled down all the shades and settled himself on the office floor. This little break-in hadn't raised a sweat; maybe a grunt, when he climbed over the fence, but no fear. Was his talent for breaking and entering being wasted? Then he remembered what it was like, wondering which were the bad guys: the ones he was spying on or his bosses? He'd had enough.

Theo laid his tools neatly in a row and used the penlight to scrutinize the office. A worn-out tea bag and a half-full pack of Marlboros sat on the desk, which was piled high with blueprints. The computer station nearest the door was neat, with colored pens laid out in a precise row. A bud vase containing a solitary silk rose sat at the secretary's workspace. She'd notice if anything were left out of place. Nothing would be.

Well-kept files—it took him all of twenty minutes to locate the old unsuccessful bids. Three minutes to photograph the building specs for the new Oasis High School. Yes! They called for a split face exterior on all buildings. Much more expensive than Icarus's concrete blocks.

Instinctively, he reached for a congratulatory cigar, then patted its resting place and left it there. With this tidy secretary, cigar smell would set off an alarm faster than snipped wires.

After he'd spliced the alarm wires, he checked his watch. Less than an hour. If his luck held, he'd have time to visit two more construction offices tonight.

Now came the hard part. With three sets of photos in hand, Theo built up the courage to tell Kate the deed was done. He waited till she was in charge of the lunch cafeteria. She wouldn't blow her cool before three hundred excitable children.

Kate was wiping tables that first graders had just vacated in preparation for the second shift, the upper graders. "Here, Theo, would you finish this table?" She thrust wet rags smelling of disinfectant into his hand, picked up a dustpan and brush, and checked under a second grade table.

"Whoever threw a milk carton on the floor, please pick it up." The second graders all looked at Hootie. He dove under and retrieved the offending carton.

No table got dismissed until she'd checked everything. Kate had promised the primary kids that they'd eat in a clean cafeteria, but it was their job to leave it clean for the older grades. Sometimes, a newcomer would slip up, but their buddies would clue them into "the way we do things around here."

Theo wanted to put Kate in a good mood. "You've got a great way with the kids. A nice balance between respect and discipline."

Kate eyed him warily. "We have pride in the way we pull together, Officer Buloski. We're team players."

She knows! Geez, what is this? Mind reading? He started to wipe the sweat from his brow, but found his hands full of wet table rags. Throwing them down, he confessed. "Okay, so I went without you. But I'm trained in burglary, and you're not. Besides there was no reason for two—"

"You what?"

Theo's timing was off. The primary classes had gone out to the playground, and the upper grades hadn't come in yet. Only the Hearing Impaired kids were still eating. They could read lips, so Kate had turned her back to them.

"You already knew. That remark about teamwork and everything."

"Please turn your back to our kids."

Theo complied, wondering why he didn't throw the damn pictures on the table and walk out.

"You gave me a compliment. Of course, I was suspicious. What's this about a burglary? Last night?" Kate's tone frosted.

Theo chewed on his bottom lip and turned to face the class of Hearing Impaired. The kids read body language, so every eye was on the principal and school cop. He resisted when Kate nudged him to turn his back. Facing the children, he stated the facts. "I did three jobs like I've been trained to do. The results were consistent with what we'd expected. Any questions, see me after football practice."

There! The kids had nothing to chew on, and Kate had just enough. As he turned to leave, Mrs. Jackson's fifth grade class burst through the door, fast-walking toward the second shift food line.

He could face hardened criminals without a tremor, stand up to his bosses all too often, but this feisty principal made him sweat. Would it have been the same if the principal were a man? Why'd he come up with that question?

He headed for the P.E. room to pick up some footballs. His kids were generally smaller than their opponents, so he'd decided their wins would have to be in the air. Throw and catch on the run. Every noon they were at it. Throw and catch! And they were improving. It was crazy the way his murder investigations were sandwiched between football games and cafeteria fights, but, like Kate said, "The living come first." She wasn't going to let her kids down and, strangely enough, neither was he.

His gripes transferred from Kate to the size of his players. Why the hell didn't these kids' moms get the proper prenatal care? Why did so many of these kids go hungry before they started school? And were still going hungry, even now, on the weekends. Saguaro Elementary wasn't in a third world country. What the hell!

"Officer Buloski, everything okay?" Louie had gulped his lunch so he could help coach take out equipment.

"Fine. Fine." Loaded with equipment, they squeezed through the door that led to the playground.

"You should've seen what happened back there, Officer Buloski. Right behind me in the food line. Gladys tripped Desiree Burnheart, and then Desiree slapped the glasses off Gladys's nose and jumped up and down on them until they were nothing but little pieces. Mrs. Mahoney took both of them to the office with no lunch." Louie glanced sideways, checking for effect. "They'll get lunch later, after they've sweated it out. Mrs. Mahoney always sees they get lunch. I know. I've been there."

Theo smiled as they piled the footballs on the 50-yard line. "I'll bet you have been, Louie. I'll bet you have."

Standing outside the principal's door, Gladys and Desiree were a study in contrasts. Gladys, an ultra-proper blonde Barbie doll in a green velour jogging suit with hair tie and socks to match, was feigning innocence. Tall in her Nikes, nose in the air, she fingered her gold bracelet nervously, never deigning to lay her baby-blue eyes on her nemesis.

Desiree shot barbed looks through damp hazel eyes. A green rubber band held her long, brown hair, highlighted with henna, in a ponytail. Her ears had double studs, gold stars on the top, phony diamonds on the bottom. Her black tee shirt was drawn tight enough across her breast to reveal the lines of a training bra. Were the two little bumps on her chest nature's own or toilet paper stuffing? Hands thrust in the pockets of cutoff jeans, she stood with one hip thrown off to the side. When she stood up straight, she was still shorter than Gladys and much more angry.

Kate studied the two through the door's glass window. She'd let them stew while she contacted their parents. And there was the problem of Desiree paying for the broken glasses.

The principal knew Gladys Swenson well. A pampered only child, she had a sneaky way of drawing her classmates into conflicts, then ending up the innocent victim. Kate called her father at the downtown bank, where he was a teller, because she knew the mother would hold Gladys blameless. Her mother was the reason Gladys wasn't too upset; her father was why she was twisting her bracelet. Mr. Swenson promised to bring Gladys back to school after four o'clock, when he could get away.

Desiree Burnhart was an unknown quantity with an attitude. She'd been a student at Saguaro only two weeks, so her teacher, Mrs. Jackson, hoped the girl's surly snappiness would level off once she felt secure. She wasn't easy to like. Her teacher had to work at it, and the kids weren't convinced she was worth the effort. She sat at the end of the table at lunch and didn't try to make friends, not even among the African Americans, who usually went out of their way for one of their own. Curious. Kids don't become anti-social in a vacuum.

Desiree's home phone number replied primly, "This phone has been disconnected. " Grandmother's was also disconnected. The third number on the emergency card belonged to Danny. Just Danny. Kate hoped the mother knew Danny's full name by now.

This time, she was in luck. Mom was at Danny's house, but she didn't have a ride to get to school. Kate wanted her in at three so, Desiree's teacher could be included in the conference.

"Would you like me to pick you up at 2:30 and bring you to school?"

"No!"

In the background, Kate heard the coaching of a male, the voice sounding vaguely familiar. "Daphne, don't you be ascared of that high class cunt! Her shit's no better than yours! I know."

"Shut up, Danny." The rest of mother Daphne's response was muffled. Kate strained to hear the shouting that continued for a couple of minutes.

Finally, mother again. "Listen, principal, I'm not going to take this shit from you. You're dissing my little Desiree 'cause she's black, and Danny and me ain't going to stand by and let no bitch do that." Once into abuse, mother Daphne could really fly. "We're coming down, and you better wag your tail to get your fuckin' ducks in order! 'Cause we're going to shoot 'em all to hell."

The phone slammed down, and Kate let herself exhale. She was glad Danny was coming along, so she could see how they interacted. She looked forward to meeting this Danny, who claimed to know so much about her shit.

Kate used the outside door to exit her office, doubling back to the restroom off the teachers' lounge, where she scrubbed her hands hard, washing away the abuse.

In main office, she stopped behind Terri, whose long, blonde braid bobbed in time with her fingers on the computer.

"Terri, Mrs. Burnhart and her friend, Danny, are coming in soon to confer about Desiree." Kate nodded in the direction of the two girls, who were still looking out the window, waiting for the principal to reenter the way she'd left. Both stood less rigid. Kate needed to get to them soon, before they mellowed out. "Mrs. Jackson needs to be in that conference. Let her know you're coming to substitute for her class, so she can get down here right away."

Terri didn't break her rhythm. "Will do, Kate."

"And, Terri, would you find Theo and tell him—well, maybe not. Maybe I'll let it go—"

The tall blonde swiveled around on the computer chair, studying her boss. "You get a threat or something? Get Theo in here, that's what cops are for."

Kate shook her head. "No threat. Just rough talk. Nothing I can't handle—but we do need Mrs. Jackson."

"No problem."

The two girls were giggling by the time Kate got to them. Maybe that was the way Desiree made friends. Got in trouble and forged survival bonds. Just the way she'd seen adults do it, Kate would bet anything. Both girls blanched when the principal came up behind them. The attack from the rear unsettled them, and that's just the way Kate wanted it.

Gladys was sent back to her classroom, verbally repentant, but composed and cool to the core. Kate would have another go at four o'clock with her dad, but down deep this little gal knew she was right—right or wrong.

Desiree didn't pretend she regretted slapping or breaking the glasses, but she was sorry she got caught. Gladys listened when Desiree hinted that, next time, she'd take her revenge in private. Maybe Gladys would give her a wide berth. Not high quality character development, but low quality peacekeeping.

Kate settled Desiree down by the secretary, then returned to her office, unlocked her desk bottom drawer, moved the loaded .38 revolver out from beneath a pile of reports, and nested it in her top right-hand drawer. Now why did she do that?

She felt an uneasiness that had no basis in reality. She'd heard rough talk before, lots of times. Once the parent realized Kate was there to help, the abusiveness usually faded away. She'd even gotten apologies. No, it wasn't the content of the phone conversation, it was something else. Something she couldn't put her finger on. Maybe she should have Theo in the office. No, she didn't want him babysitting her.

Mrs. Matthews, a fourth grade teacher, interrupted Kate's nameless jitters with Harrison Alberts in tow. The fourth grader hung limply from the grip the small woman had on his elbow, unsuccessfully trying to be victimized by teacher brutality. Harrison's posture didn't arouse Kate's concern. What the teacher held in her left hand did.

The slingshot the teacher threw on Kate's desk landed with a clank. A far cry from the forked twig model of more innocent days, it was small, designed to be hidden in a coat pocket. A mechanical wonder, springs on both forks maximized its thrust. The sling was a leather-like synthetic that could deliver an accurate shot at fifty feet with enough force to take out an eye. David should've been so lucky when facing Goliath.

Kate kept the slingshot in front of her while she went through district protocol for handling weapons. Parents would be informed. Harrison wouldn't be allowed back in the classroom until he had a hearing before a district compliance officer. Actually, the policy stated that the student wouldn't be allowed back in *school* until the hearing that would probably result in a suspension. At Saguaro, they kept the child in school, but isolated before the hearing and during the suspension. Otherwise, any student hungering for an easy vacation would bring a knife to school and, voila, the vacation would begin.

After Harrison had been dispatched to the 'time out' room, Kate dropped the slingshot in the pocket of her blue blazer, keeping it handy for Mom and Dad's viewing.

She didn't notice him at first. Amy from Personnel was on the phone, wanting to know where Kate was going to get the money to pay for the bilingual aide Saguaro needed. Two sets of rascals, who had been giving two different substitute teachers grief, were awaiting their fate in the main office. A mother was complaining to the secretary about the teacher who'd made an error correcting her son's spelling test. A normal afternoon.

Kate was working on all eight cylinders until she saw *him*. Suddenly, everything stopped. Nothing else was important. The background voice over the phone. It belonged to *him!* Kate felt the hair rise along the nape of her neck and on her arms. A cold chill coursed through her nervous system. She suppressed a shiver and pressed her lips tight together, as her wannabe kidnapper's muscular form filled the door space. Black beard against black skin. Predatory eyes, cold and detached when they'd virtually stripped her at Allister's apartments, now sparked with rage.

"Little Chickie, your Big Daddies gonna take you for a ride."

His voice spoke out of her nightmares before he said a word. She slowly pulled out the top desk drawer from which, while her eyes were greeting Danny, Daphne, and Desiree Burnhart, she removed a paper. Then, she left it open a few inches, her hand never straying far from it.

The actress who'd guided her through her attempted kidnapping took over. Not for her sake—this time, for the sake of Desiree. The real Kate Mahoney's fingers ached from being denied the .38. The real Kate—horrified by the hiking shoes Danny wore even now, with the brand name, MERRELL, lettered in bold black and silver—saw three other sets of shoes alongside his. Forming a box around her high heels. The real Kate didn't want to run. She wanted to kill him.

The actress explained the infraction. The conference seemed to be taking place at a distance, in another dimension. Still talking and nodding to indicate she was hearing Daphne and Danny's complaints, Kate printed slowly and carefully in caps a few words on the piece of paper she'd withdrawn from the open drawer.

GET THEO. KIDNAPPER HERE. CALL POLICE.

The actress perused the message as if it were as harmless as an invitation to a baby shower. She rose gracefully, prepared to give it to her secretary in the outer office, when Kate's eye caught the leer in Danny's dark gaze and the sneer on his twisted lips. Kate froze, unwilling to leave the top right hand drawer. She stood, abandoned by the actress.

At that moment, Theo's face appeared in the door window. Bless Terri! She'd told him! He opened the door, never turned his back to the office's occupants and silently reached for the note Kate handed him.

Without reading it, he spoke like an efficient, if improbable, secretary, conveying a message to his boss. "Mrs. Jackson needs to see Desiree for a minute. She wants to hear Desiree's story first, then she'll join you."

Desiree rose. Her mother protested. Danny said, "Let her go." His eyes never left Kate's face. Did he know Kate recognized him?

Kate watched Desiree leave the room. Through the door's window she saw Theo read the note, beckon Allison and whisper to her. In slow motion, she saw the office empty. She sensed Danny's movement before he actually made it. Theo and Danny reached with their right hands into their jackets at exactly the same time.

Kate yelled, "Hands up, or you're dead!"

The .38 in her hand cried out to be fired. Cried out, "*Self defense!*"

Danny saw blood in her eyes and raised his hands, pleading to Theo. "Stop her. She'll kill me."

Kate wanted to. She stood, the .38 pointed at his heart until Theo reached over and took the gun away.

In the distance, she heard police sirens. Response time: two minutes.

Tired to the bone, Kate rejected Terri's suggestion to cancel the four o'clock conference with the Swensons, knowing consequences of fighting have to be immediate. The conference was a disaster, with mother and daughter pleading innocence, and Kate weak with guilt. Who was she to punish a shove, when she herself wanted to kill—to *kill*—a human being?

Gladys needed a strong principal. What she got was a rag doll. Kate let her get away with a scolding. Mother smiled, Dad squirmed, and Gladys smirked. Kate needed a double shot of Johnny Walker.

The office was empty when Theo found her, head cradled in her arms on her desk, crying softly. It was his "Geez" that jolted her upright. His discomfort at facing a woman's tears, his face flushed and hands opening and closing, made Kate lighten up.

"Geez, Kate. We got the son-of-a-bitch who almost took you out. He's down in the tank right now. And you're unhappy. You want him to get away, maybe? Or shoot one of us? Geez, Kate!"

"I wanted to *kill* him. Almost did!"

"After what he put you through, who wouldn't? So you've joined the human race. What do you think you are? An angel in an overcoat? Gotta go. I want to be at his interrogation."

Kate was suddenly re-energized.

In the Cannery...

It could have been a basement archive library with endless rows of shelves filled with dusty objects. Rows and rows of dusty gallon jars, most of them empty. Sister Katherine, calculator in hand, was inventorying the Congregation's cache of canned fruit: peaches, pears, applesauce, cherries. All from last year's harvest.

"It's taking you quite a long time, Sister Katherine." Mother Philippa donned a gray work apron to keep the dust at bay.

"Mother, you don't need to do this. I'm doing fine. Actually, I'm getting a perfect count."

"Don't waste your time making it perfect. Let me see. There are seven rows of shelves, each 60 feet long. That's 420 feet, or 5040 inches of shelf space. Each gallon jar is seven inches wide. That makes room for 720 gallons. But since they are four deep, you have space for 2,880 gallons. Which is about right, since we have approximately 60 nuns and 40 elderly guests. That makes almost 29 gallons yearly consumption per person. Sounds good to me."

"Mother, do you always micromanage?"

"Only when I can. I know these figures, because I authorized the expansion. Notice the shelves nearer the far wall are roughly made? Sister Colette and her novices made their extensions. Out of pine, but still... the finish is so much finer."

"Then you understand why Sister Jeanne Marie needs to know how many empty jars we have. It's near harvest time."

"How much fruit will the novices can?"

"The entire harvest. As we always do. The gardener novices think we have a bumper crop this year. Except the birds got some peaches." She tapped a number into the calculator.

Mother Philippa brushed against a shelf, then flicked the offending dust off her habit. "An approximation will do. This is busy work. Sister Jeanne Marie wants to keep many novices in her employ so, when canning time comes, she'll have a big crew. Bureaucracies do that, you know—pad their staff."

"I hardly think the cook runs a bureaucracy. We're doing it like it's always been done, Mother. I just want to get the blooming jars counted."

Mother Philippa dusted two stools with her handkerchief. "Sit, sister. Sometimes, you need to probe from different angles. Not just do it 'as it has always been done.' Take that unfortunate you almost shot yesterday. Whoever is killing district employees must be smart, because the murders haven't been solved yet. Put yourself in the killer's shoes. Would you employ a drug addict like Danny Beppo to work for you? I'd be afraid of blackmail."

"Then who tried to abduct me and why?"

"I don't know. Let's hope Danny sings…and it won't be Gregorian chant! Sister, go back to your real world. I'll handle Sister Jeanne Marie and her canning jars."

13

Danny Beppo. Was Beppo really his last name? Theo had been impossible to reach; probably still interrogating Danny. Usually, Kate's mornings flew by. This morning was painfully slow. She was having a hard time keeping her mind on her duties, so she decided to give herself a treat.

The classrooms she visited most often were those of beginning teachers, who were just learning how to manage a class. By "showing the flag," she would remind students that the principal backed up their teacher's discipline. Beginning teachers needed all the encouragement they could get, so she tried to help.

With time so limited, she spent little time in the classrooms of her excellent teachers. This morning, she thought she would take time to visit the fourth grade classroom of master teacher Craig Welsh. He had a class where children loved to learn. Opening his classroom door, Kate saw that half of the desks had been moved together in the center of the room to form a stage. Jeremiah, a talented mischief-maker, was leading the class in a rap song that was teaching the multiplication tables. Gyrating to the beat, he twisted about and turned upside down like a rubber puppet. The teacher sat adjacent to the stage, near the star performer.

Keeping his eyes on the rapper, Craig beckoned Kate near and whispered with a grin, "I know what you're thinking. There's no danger of him dancing off the stage, 'cause I've got him within reach."

Kate nodded. Concern had been Kate's instant reaction, but she trusted that Craig had things under control. The children's sense of fun was a delight. No wonder Craig's class did well in math. His creativity made things work.

For a few minutes, she rapped with them and forgot all about Theo…and Danny…and Jacqueline…until the intercom blared, "Mrs. Mahoney, please pick up the phone."

She moved to the teacher's office and closed the door. It was Theo.

"It's almost lunch time. Let Allison take care of the cafeteria. We need to talk. Let's meet at the San Francisco Grill in twenty minutes."

"I don't like it there."

"The S.F. Grill?" Theo sounded shocked. "What's not to like? Best sports bar in town."

"It's too noisy. All the TVs blaring. We can't talk there."

"Noisy. That's why we're going. Nobody can overhear us in that din. Best place in town to tell secrets."

The San Francisco Grill was as Kate remembered it, noisy enough to inhibit thinking and limit conversation. Four giant TV screens, each highlighting a different sport, blared full force. Theo's glance lingered for a long moment on a replay of the Forty-Niners against the Green Bay Packers, then, with a napkin he'd picked up at the bar, he wiped away wet circles left by previous drinkers. He seemed right at home.

"What did Danny have to say?"

"Good day to you, too. First, I want to show you the good news."

Kate wilted. The Danny news had to be bad. But it was Theo's show; she'd have to play along.

Like a jeweler displaying gems, he removed several eight by eleven photos from a manila envelope. Without a word, he placed building specs from five different construction companies, one at a time, in front of Kate. He was as proud as if he'd given birth.

Kate whistled as she viewed his babies. "You did good," she said, nodding, "but you did it without me."

Theo moved his lips to her ear. "We're not going to change that, are we? What we need now are pictures of Icarus's building specs. You were in the construction trailer looking for them. Tell me where you looked, so I'll know where they're not, when I go in."

"You're going in? I don't think so. This is mine."

"Hi, Theo!" The blonde waitress waved her shoulders and flashed a broad display of teeth. She ignored the lady with him. "The usual? A Michelob?"

"Ask the lady what she'd like."

The blonde's lips returned to a straight line, and she glared at Kate. "What would the *lady* like?" She said *lady* as if it were a disease that, fortunately, wasn't catching.

"Iced tea."

The teeth flashed as the waitress gazed benevolently on Theo.

"Diet coke and a large pizza with all the trimmings, but leave off the anchovies."

"Oh, my, my. Theo *is* keeping his head today." She turned and sashayed away.

"Girlfriend?"

"Wannabe."

Kate shook her head. The noise in the grill slowed her thinking, but it hadn't totally numbed it. "You're going to break into that trailer tonight, and I'm going with you, because I know where the building specs are. The other day, a couple of managers didn't know I was at Flora's desk behind the door. They were discussing some concrete that Wallace wanted poured. The young guy who got the job wasn't happy about the last minute request, overtime or no overtime."

Kate was getting increasingly annoyed at the need to either shout or whisper into her partner's ear. She choose shouting. "They couldn't figure out why, all of a sudden, the floor of a garden shed needed to be poured."

Suddenly, Theo became alert. "Think about it, Kate. Jacqueline was killed with a .45 on Sunday night. Suddenly, on Monday, the workmen get an order to pour concrete for a little shed that could be built anytime, and the job requires overtime. Wallace didn't get to be a successful businessman by authorizing unneeded overtime, so it must have been important to him. Why?" He leaned forward and lowered his voice. "A heavy-duty metal detector would reveal a gun in the concrete. With a jackhammer, I could retrieve it even if the cement had dried. I'll borrow a jackhammer from Alex. Okay, we go tonight. You take the trailer, I take the garden shed."

Kate nodded.

"But I go in first to handle the dogs and locks. You stay in the car while I take care of them. Jackhammering that concrete is going to be one hellava job." He grinned. "Ever use a jackhammer?"

"Can't say I have. But without a search warrant, the weapon won't be admissible as evidence."

"Our task is to see if it's there. If it's in the cement, we'll leave it and pour fresh cement that'll be dry by morning."

He caught Kate's raised eyebrow. "Don't worry, if we find the gun, an anonymous tip will alert the police. They'll get a search warrant and do their own jackhammering. It's going to be a long night, Kate. You need to know what you're in for."

"I'm in. Now, about Danny. What did you learn? Tell me it's good."

"Not good for Elijah. Danny sang like a birdie...really jolted him to be questioned by our undercover agent, whom he knew only as a lousy pool player. Danny fingered A. J. Rogers and Hiram Jones as his accomplices. Seems they were going to kill a witness to the superintendent's murder."'

"Jones...oh, no. Don't tell me he was related to Jacqueline and Tamoni."

"Jacqueline's brother. He wanted to help his sister's boyfriend. No connection whatsoever with Icarus Construction."

Kate shuddered. "This will help convict Elijah."

Theo spoke gently. "Kate, Icarus Construction is involved in a fraud, but it never did make sense to have them kill the goose that laid the golden egg. Larry Denton and Jacqueline Stanley...yes...their deaths probably are linked. But Julie Mason's murder is another story altogether. Knowing this, do you still want to help me tonight?"

"Yes, I still believe there's some connection. For some reason, they chose Elijah's room. Elijah didn't do it."

The stars shone as light specks glittering through pinholes in a curtain of indigo. Tens of thousands of pinholes. The breakneck speed of

Kate's life zoomed past simple pleasures like enjoying the stars, but tonight she had more time with them than she wanted. Where was Theo? When they'd arrived over an hour ago, he'd left her with instructions to hang tight and honk the horn if they got company. He'd be back.

Why hadn't she insisted on following him? On being his backup?

She strained to hear his footsteps. Instead, she heard Mother Provincial say, *You are David. Fear not Goliath.* Kate fingered the slingshot in her jacket pocket and chuckled. Her fatigue had frazzled her imagination. *You are David. Fear not Goliath.* There it was again. She wasn't dozing. What was the matter with her?

Maybe he'd started without her. She strained for the sound of the jackhammer he'd taken with him. The construction site was way out in the desert, so nobody but her would hear it. Still, no jackhammering. Had something gone wrong?

When Theo finally emerged from the black, following the wide beam of a heavy-duty flashlight, Kate exhaled with relief.

"You're okay?"

"Of course. I took care of the dogs and picked the locks on the gate and the trailer. Simple." Theo dug into the glove compartment and pulled out a miniature camera, a second flashlight and a pair of rubber gloves too large for her. "The camera's specially designed for this kind of work. When you're finished, leave everything exactly as you found it. Turn left to the outdoor shed site. You'll see the pad, about twelve by twelve."

Kate noticed Theo's energy surge and wondered why he ever left the CIA. This cloak and dagger stuff was his cup of tea. Not hers!

"Get it? When you finish in the trailer, come find me. You can't miss because of the god-awful noise I'll be making if I detect metal."

She nodded and followed him into the dark. The construction trailer was right inside the fence, not far from the parking lot. Though no one would see a light in the trailer, Kate felt more comfortable working by flashlight. Adrenaline charged through her as she opened the bottom right-hand drawer in Flora's desk. The building specs were on top, handy for frequent referral. After Kate photographed them, she rummaged through the drawer. This spy business had been too easy. She wanted more information.

Toward the back of the drawer, she touched a hard object about the size and shape of a square Kleenex box. She piled the papers for precise replacement and lifted the item into the light of her flash. The transparent Lucite case held the grandeur of a Fabergé egg! Even in the dim light, its elegant purple background showcased the intricate gold design that culminated with an emerald at its crown—like the one Jacqueline had on her mantel. A cold chill crept over Kate. *It was the one from Jacqueline's mantel!*

Either Flora or Wallace must have killed her. Here was the proof! The egg was worth tens of thousands. Why hadn't Flora put it in a safe deposit box? Or at least wrapped it in bubble paper for protection? Flora must have wanted it readily available, so she could enjoy its beauty. What kind of woman wants the fruits of murder at her fingertips?

"Beautiful, isn't it?"

Kate turned to face a blinding light. She would've dropped the egg had Wallace not taken it from her. He turned his headlamp away from her face. She blinked and looked past the business end of a pistol into cold eyes. "You killed her. Why?" As soon as she spoke, Kate knew she'd played her card too soon.

"So you've seen this egg on her fireplace mantel. Why Jaqueline? Denton was in on the scam from the start, and when he got too greedy he had an accident. We hoped his death would be a deterrent, but no! She kept demanding a larger cut. When she phoned that you were suspicious and she'd tried to kill you, I knew her greed had made her stupid. She had to be silenced."

Kate started to reach for the gun in her shoulder holster.

"Stand up, sweetheart. Naughty, naughty lady."

He reached under her jacket, removed the .38 and placed it on the desk. His eyes never left her face as he flipped his light and searched her pockets with his left hand.

"Been using this on your students?" He smirked and returned the sling to her blazer pocket.

"Did you kill her or did Flora?"

"Flora's my shadow. A twin joined at the hip. Great body, no brain. I make the decisions. She does whatever I want except for—"

"Except for?" Kate watched the pistol, hoping it would waver. She had to warn Theo. But the gun was too close, Wallace's grip too steady. She'd stall for time. The jackhammer hadn't started. Maybe that sound would distract him for a moment—but even then, what could she do? She had to think. "Where's Flora?"

"In my bed, sleeping like a baby. I came back to find the Fabergé egg. Damn foolish of Flora to take it, more foolish to leave it here. Tonight, with a little persuasion, Flora finally told me where it was."

Kate guessed the scratches on his face and his bruised knuckles were the result of persuading Flora. She knew Wallace was involved in Jacqueline's murder. He'd have to get rid of her.

"Why were you looking for the egg here?"

"The egg?" Kate fought to remain calm. Thinking was hard, like running through ankle deep mud, but she sloshed forward, telling lies. "Jacqueline told me that Flora lusted after her Fabergé egg. When Theo and I found her dead, I noticed the egg was missing."

"Did you tell anyone?"

Kate cast her eyes down, forging a guilty look. "No, it was worth thousands. I wanted it for myself, and Flora's office seemed a likely place to begin looking."

Wallace looked skeptical. "How'd you get past the dogs?"

"I drugged them. I can show you where they are."

"And the gate? Are you alone? Don't lie to me." He shoved the gun closer.

"I picked it. My dead husband was a cop and taught me quite a lot. Am I alone? To steal the egg, would I want company? Hardly."

"Now, for some unfinished business. No, not business." His eyes gleamed. "Pleasure." The cruelty in his handsome face shocked Kate. It seemed out of place. He kept it so well hidden, like the bruised knuckles and the scratched cheek.

"Did you kill Julie Mason?" she asked to gain time.

"No."

"You know who did?"

"Yes. You think I'll talk, since I'm going to silence you. Permanently. You've made your death necessary, sweetheart, but not until I have a little fun."

Sweat beaded Kate's brow.

"Juan Ramirez?"

"That one, my dear, I know nothing about. Nothing."

Kate believed him.

With a roughness that shocked her, Wallace grabbed her arm and pulled her through the door and down the steps. His headlamp illuminated the way as they trudged through the night. Where were they going? To an arroyo where she'd be shot and buried? Theo would hear the shot and come on cat feet. He'd be saved, and Wallace would be apprehended only if the jackhammer remained silent. But the jackhammer was her only hope for distraction. Her thoughts thrashed about, seeking a way out and finding none.

Stumbling through the night, she tripped twice and fell flat on the gravel. Each time, she scooped rocks into her pocket before Wallace yanked her up, impatient and brutal. The inner man so different from the facade.

Kate struggled to marshal her terrified wits. The side of the classroom building loomed in Wallace's headlamp, and then receded as they moved past it. He navigated around piles of lumber, steel beams, and clumps of hardened cement. Kate kept talking, hoping sounds would travel through the night air to Theo's ears. No jackhammer yet. Was he watching from the dark? Waiting to make his move?

"Why did you kill Julie Mason, if she was helping you?"

Wallace's answer was strained. "I told you; it wasn't me. She was essential to the plan. Besides," he chuckled, "she was a tiger in bed."

"If you didn't kill her, who did?"

Silence for a moment.

"She wasn't supposed to die—"

Kate waited, but nothing followed.

As they approached a mammoth structure, Wallace moved the glare of his headlamp up and down the walls. He lifted the yellow hazard tape with his pistol, so she could duck under it. For a second, the gun barrel pointed away from her, then back again before she could act. This hard-hat area smelled of raw concrete and sand.

Kate kept talking. "The walls must be forty feet high. What is this?"

"Fifty feet," he corrected her. "It's the gymnasium, has to accommodate bleachers and a stage." He spoke faster, with excitement. The light beam illuminated a crane inside the walls. "Seventy-foot-high crane—a bitch to get the main steel beam in place at that height." He sounded a little giddy. "Remember the main beam in the classroom wing? You were afraid to walk on it. Afraid to do what our hod carriers do dozens of times a day. Big, hotshot woman! You were afraid! I loved it!" His words echoed in the massive space.

As they picked their way around scrap lumber on the concrete floor, the shadows turned the scaffolding into a terrifying grid. Kate looked up at the night sky, punctuated with stars and intersected by the giant steel support beam that stretched the length of the building. A frightening déjà vu! No, he wouldn't relive that scene. Even Wallace wouldn't make her do that!

Her worst fears came true when they stopped at the hydraulic lift. His gun motioned for her to get in.

"No, I won't! You can shoot me right here, but I'm not going up on top!"

He twisted her arm behind her and forced her forward. When she kicked his leg and slammed her head under his chin, he smashed the butt of the pistol across the side of her face. Dazed, she slumped forward, trying to get her bearings. No hope. Theo wasn't out there in the dark.

"I won't do it!" she screamed. The hysteria in her voice alarmed her. She was coming apart—losing it! Deliberately, she took deep breaths and tried not to think of what the next minutes might bring. Maybe Theo would hear the hydraulic lift. No, it was too quiet. She pressed her legs against the side of the cherry picker cage to stop their trembling. Under his headlamp, Kate could see the sadistic eyes of her tormentor, eyes heady with the power to inflict terror. She looked away, but never down. He wanted to make this hotshot female fall apart, beg for mercy. She wouldn't give him the pleasure. *Mother Philippe, help me.*

Suddenly, her mental focus shifted. She became a nun again, observing Great Silence and modesty of the eyes. Feeling the security of the habit covering her from head to toe, she felt for her wimple and veil. They were there. The chapel ceiling, speckled with soft lights, loomed high overhead.

Kate's sudden calm upset her tormentor. He was losing his plaything.

"What the hell's the matter with you? Don't you know what's going to happen? I'm going to push you out on that beam, and you'll fall. Fifty feet! Land with a splat like a squashed bug. Big shot. Stupid bitch big shot!" His threats reverberated aginst concrete walls.

Kate kept her eyes modestly cast down. She prepared to walk the main aisle of the chapel. Carefully, with religious decorum. One foot in front of the other. Slowly and calmly, with Mother Philippe watching her move like a proper nun.

"Look up at me, bitch!'

A good nun with her eyes modestly cast down, keeping Great Silence.

"Look here!" Wallace screamed and slapped her.

Kate fell against the side of the lift, then calmly resumed her decorum. She'd turn the other cheek. That's what nuns did.

Even the jar of the hydraulic lift stopping fifty feet up didn't jolt her out of Great Silence.

"Look at me!" Wallace frantically grabbed her chin and forced her eyes to his. His glinted with frenzy, were red with rage. The eyes of Satan.

When she closed her eyes, he slapped her again.

Satan can't hurt me. I'll walk down the central aisle in the presence of God. Walk away from him.

"Once you get out on the beam, I'll see you beg. You'll be crying to come back." His voice was frenzied. He'd lost control.

Kate left the support of the cherry picker behind. *You know how to keep Great Silence in spirit as well as in sound, Sister Katherine. Carefully, as befits one who wears this habit, walk carefully and in grace. It's only the chapel aisle. You've walked it hundreds of times.*

"You bitch! You weren't afraid all along! You were fucking with my mind! Let's see how well you do in the dark!" Wallace's words shot like a gun.

When his headlamp went off, Kate paused for a moment, then remembered she'd walked the main chapel aisle in the dark to make her nightly visit. It was all right. One foot in front of the other. A string of obscenities came from the lift. That was all right. The devil had no power over her.

The walk was slow and careful, but it didn't take long. Just as long as it took a nun to glide up the main aisle and take her seat in the first pew. Suddenly, the light returned, and Kate was jolted into reality by the sound of a bullet whizzing past her into the black night.

Sister Katherine had stepped off the end of the steel beam, but it was Kate who crouched on the concrete block wall fifty feet above the cement floor. How to dodge the second bullet when it came? Any evasive action would insure her fall. Scrambled like Humpty Dumpty on the concrete below. She shivered.

Wallace began to walk toward her, .45 pistol in his right hand, his left arm reaching out for balance. To reduce glare, he'd turned his headband backwards, so the main light shot out behind him, leaving only a soft reflection to light his path across the beam.

Wallace's silhouette against the back lighting returned Kate to the night of Julie Mason's murder, when she'd cowered behind the bookcases, looking up, like right now. From her low position, Wallace seemed much taller than his six feet two inches. The full fashion style of his hair made his head look large. As if he had an Afro cut, like Elijah's. It had been Wallace, not Elijah, whose silhouette she'd seen against the street lamp! The relief sparked her vitality. *You are David. Fear not Goliath.* Kate loaded the slingshot with a rock. Carefully, she aimed between Wallace's eyes. An act of Kate, not a holy nun!

The missile whizzed by Wallace's head, surprising him. He paused and aimed the .45, left hand under his right, stabilizing the weapon. His balance wavered as he fired. The bullet hit Kate's shadow and knocked out a large chunk of the concrete block at her side. She could feel blood trickle down her cheek, where bits of concrete had nicked her. The kick of the .45 threw Wallace off balance. His feet left the beam, but his hands latched onto the steel support, and he hung there, feet dangling, arms and chest gripping the beam.

Kate overshot again. Closer this time. She was getting her range. Wallace pulled one leg over and straddled the beam, staying low. He used his strong arms to inch his way toward Kate.

You are David. Fear not Goliath. She fired again, hitting his right hand, and the .45 went clattering fifty feet below, its echo bouncing eerily through the enormous structure.

Wallace looked startled, then angry. His eyes glinted with determination as he continued to inch forward. The next rock hit him on the cheek.

"Who killed Julie Mason, if it wasn't you?"

Wallace rubbed his face and boasted, "Flora. My stupid broad set up the meeting in Elijah's room...saying it was Elijah's idea. Elijah didn't know anything about it. Julie wanted Elijah to take that Physical Resource job, so she came." Wallace was stalling for time. Talking until he got his bearings.

Where was Theo? He must've heard the shots. Or had Wallace taken him out before trapping her? Kate couldn't ask. Wallace must not know Theo was on site. Where was he?

"If you didn't kill Julie, who did?"

"I never would've killed her."

Kate waited, poised with a rock in the sling. When his silence continued, she sent a missile that hit him on the forehead. He swore and inched forward. "Put that slingshot down or—"

"Or what?" Wanting him to talk, she anchored the slingshot on the concrete wall with one hand. He stopped moving forward.

"It was Flora who killed Julie. It didn't take guts or brains, just passion, and Flora's got lots of that." He hesitated, then went on. "Flora set the trap. Premeditated. Hell, she even brought an iron bar in her tote." He started to inch forward again. Kate picked up the slingshot, and he stopped. "I was across the room when Flora started bashing her. Blow after blow. Julie pulled out her cute little Derringer. I knocked it out of her hand. Once the blows were lethal, I had to let Flora finish the job."

Wallace looked into the black vastness. "Afterwards, I beat the hell out of that dumb broad. She knew I was going to dump her for Julie. Flora is fading fast and dumb...dumb...dumb. Killing Julie was the only thing she ever did on her own."

From below they heard a woman scream. "And this is the second thing I've done on my own." It was Flora, brandishing the fallen .45.

"Flora! Take out Kate!" he yelled.

The first shot missed Wallace by inches. The second one knocked him off the beam, and the light from his headlamp marked the trajectory of the last seconds of his life. He hit bottom with a thud.

Flora walked to the broken body. The headlamp still beamed stubbornly upwards. She used her shoe to turn Wallace face up. Kate, feeling an acid taste rise in her throat, looked away.

When she looked back, Flora was still standing over him. Kicking him. After what seemed an eternity, the blonde reached down and took his headlight.

Please, God. Make her forget about me.

Kate's prayer went unanswered. Flora fixed the beam on Kate and fired.

The first shot was way off, but Flora had all night. Theo must be dead. Up to now, she'd refused to believe it. Theo was dead, or he'd have heard the shots. Theo dead! That thought took the life out of her, like a kite falling through dead air.

"All right, lady, if you'll just put that gun down, I won't have to blow a big hole in the back of your head." Theo's voice filled Kate's sails.

"Theo!"

He beamed his flashlight in the direction of her voice.

"You all right, Kate? What're you doing up there?" His voice rang in the gloomy tomb that the gymnasium had become.

"I'm okay. Wallace is dead."

"Yes, Kate." His voice was heavy with too much patience. "Humble homicide detective that I am, I can see that. He's splattered all over the floor." A pause. "Let me duct tape this female." His volume lowered as he advised Flora, "You have a right to remain silent—" Theo read Flora her rights and asked almost in the same breath, "Where'd you get the gun?"

"On the floor here." Flora monotoned. "I came out to get the egg—"

Another silence, then from above, "Theo, why didn't you come sooner? Didn't you hear the shots? Why weren't you jackhammering?"

"Alex doesn't take very good care of his tools. The jackhammer was jammed, so I had to find the tool shed, which wasn't easy in the dark.

It's way over on the other side of the campus. Had to break into it, which took all of thirty seconds. I was fixing the jackhammer when I heard the shots. Even running at top speed—which I did, Kate, I swear—it took me a few minutes to get here."

His attention returned to his suspect. "So you killed him?"

Flora's voice was empty. "Yes, he was going to dump me—then he would've killed me to keep me quiet. I wasn't so dumb. I got him first."

Kate wondered why she felt sorry for the murderess down below. Yes, Flora was dumb. Dumb to confess without a lawyer. Dumb to take out her rival. But, most of all, dumb to love Wallace.

Theo finished securing his suspect, then looked skyward. "Jump. I'll catch you."

"Will you stop that and get me down? I'm afraid of heights!"

Theo chuckled. Slowly, he withdrew a cigar from his breast pocket. "Just a minute. As soon as I have a cigar."

The rock from the slingshot came within inches of hitting him.

Elijah stretched his legs under his classroom desk until his feet popped out the other side. Theo and Kate sat atop first graders' desks, beaming like parents eyeing their firstborn.

"After that stint in the county jail, I'm never going to complain about first graders again. Not even at the beginning of school, when all the kids want me exclusively as their daddy…or mother…or both." He looked across the classroom at the monthly calendar: smiley-faced suns for sunny days, umbrellas for rain, puffy-cheeked clouds for wind. Today was sunny.

"Flora admitted that Julie didn't kill Denton. That was Wallace's doing. When Julie realized he'd been murdered, she upped her price." Theo scowled. "If he'd stopped his mistress from bashing her, he'd have to protect Flora from assault charges or pay more blackmail to Julie. Either one of his women might have blown the whistle on him."

"Wallace said he didn't want Julie to die, but he could've been deceiving himself." It gave her the creeps, being in this room. Her eyes strayed to the spot where the dead superintendent had lain. Even the new carpet couldn't erase the smell of blood from her memory.

Elijah fidgeted. "After Jacqueline and I are married, I'll have a brother-in-law in prison. He really thought he was doing me a favor, trying to take you out, Kate." Elijah shook his head.

Kate changed the subject. "You haven't been stuttering, Elijah. Come to think of it, you weren't stuttering when we visited you in jail."

"I stopped stuttering the second day in jail. I figured, if I can handle jail, I could handle anything. Even administrators." He turned to Theo. "Staying on as resource officer?"

"Since we cracked this case, my bosses want me to come back downtown. So, naturally, I didn't want to go. Anyway, I like it here." He glanced at Kate, and red crept up his neck and over the top of his bald head. "The football team, I mean. Lousy on the ground, but mighty in the air. I gotta stick with my kids."

"Our kids," Kate corrected.

"Our kids," Theo agreed.

That night, as Kate pulled her covers up around her chin, she did something she'd never done before. She willed Mother Provincial into her dream. *One more time, Mother, to say goodbye.*

Mother Philippe didn't come. Did she take orders only from God and Mother General? Kate's was a social invitation. Maybe that's why she didn't answer it. Mother Philippe Manning was all business. No time for chit chat, sentimentality, or unnecessary dreams. Elijah was free; her business was complete.

Still, Kate would've liked to say goodbye.

Epilogue

Kate folded her legs under her and snuggled into the wicker chair beside the peat fire smoldering in the bedroom's hearth. Absently, she smoothed the arm of the flannel nightie provided by her hostess. The mulled wine was soothing, and she caressed the mug to eke out its warmth.

Her thoughts drifted from the companion who was curled up in the recliner near her to the other nightie, the one in her suitcase. It was the exact blue of her eyes, with buttons down the front, a graceful collar with an open neck and sleeves that fell halfway down her arms. The material was soft and fine, not quite see-through, but almost. Maybe. Sometimes, in the right light. The granny gown, though, like the one worn by her friend, warded off the chill in this old castle-like structure with its stone walls and drafty rooms. More in keeping with the spirit of the place.

"So, Kate, why'd it take you so long to come and visit me?" The friend put down her own mug and nudged her chair nearer the fire. "And don't be telling me you didn't know where I live. Everyone in the Congregation knows where I live."

Kate looked over her drink at the impish grin that had cheered her in the novitiate years ago. With her unmanageable curly black hair and creamy complexion, Mother Casey Whitehall carried the title of Mother General lightly. She'd aged gently, but her laugh was as infectious as when she was a novice. Now, there was more confidence, more serenity in her manner.

Sometimes, a somber look would cloud her lively eyes, and Kate guessed it was the price she paid for being the absolute authority over both the American and Irish provinces. Kate felt the personal power of the Mother General. Had it always been there, or did it come from bearing the weight of the office?

That thought ushered in the question that had brought her to the Motherhouse on the Aran Isle of Inish Mor. "Whatever happened to Mother Phillippe Manning?"

"Mother Provincial when we were novices and a whole lot longer. She was provincial longer than any other leader in the Congregation."

"Twelve years."

"Now, how did you remember that?"

"Oh, I don't know," Kate lied. "Probably heard it somewhere."

"I'm not surprised you remember her. There was something special about her. Funny thing. She was in my dream the other night." Mother General shoved dark curls back from her forehead. "Kate, you goose, why are you looking at me that way? Do you think I'm daft?" She laughed.

Kate dropped her feet to the floor and leaned forward. "What happened in the dream?"

"It was so unusual, I wrote it down when I woke up. She was standing next to me as real as you are now. She didn't say anything, just looked at me with that funny little smile she'd get when things were going her way."

"I believe you, Casey." Kate controlled her smile so her friend wouldn't guess just how much she believed. "Tell me how things went for her after I left."

"She's dead now two years, you know, God rest her soul. You left just before Vatican II turned the religious congregations upside down. 'Let in some fresh air,' Pope John the XXIII said. Believe me, it let in a gale, and Mother Philippe kept us from sinking. She made sweeping changes in the Novitiate with a zeal that was almost fanatical. But aside from the Novitiate changes, it was hard for Mother Philippe to stray from tradition. She was still wearing the sixteen pounds of serge when she died, decades after most of us had switched to the shorter suits."

"Did she ever speak of Gene, a controller with her for many years?"

Mother Casey Whitehall paused, mug midair and stared. "Who have you been talking to?"

Kate looked away.

"Gene had been the accountant for Mother when she was superior at Saint Bridget's Hospital. The first black accountant in any hospital in Phoenix. When she became Mother Provincial, he came with her. As financial officer for the province, he made a lot of money for the Congregation in the stock market." Casey paused to reflect. "It won't hurt to tell you this. They're all dead and gone. Mother General Patricia Lynch felt his stock market ventures were too risky and asked Mother Philippe to replace him with a nun. She didn't do it. Mother General looked the other way until some of his stocks dived, and the province took a serious financial hit. Then Mother resigned as Provincial, but was immediately appointed Superior of Trinity High School in Phoenix. Her leadership was too good to waste."

"And what happened to Gene?"

"Gene—I don't remember his last name We just called him Brother Gene. He'd been around so long, it was like he was part of the Congregation." She took a slow sip from the mug. "He was replaced by a nun. Then he kept the books for some Phoenix resort and married in his late fifties. Even had a son. His son had a strange name. Something from the Old Testament. What was that name? Jeremiah? Joshua? It'll come to me."

Kate stretched her legs toward the flickering embers, soaking in their lingering warmth. "If I knew his last name, I could look him up when I get back to Arizona. I'd like to talk to him about Mother Philippe."

"Unfortunately, Gene and his wife were killed in an automobile accident when his son was a toddler. They say the lad stuttered ever after." Mother Casey's face betrayed a shrewdness that explained her station. "What is it with you and Mother Philippe?"

Kate shrugged. "Who would know more about that woman than you? Mother Generals know all the secrets. Besides, I wanted to see you. And Ireland." She changed the subject. "I have a friend, Theo, who's flying into Shannon in a couple of days. We thought we'd tour Ireland together." She chuckled. "Theo really wanted to take this trip, even claimed that Buloski was an Irish name. Way back. Generations ago."

"Elijah! That's the boy's name. Elijah!"

A wave of understanding flooded over Kate. No wonder the Gene in her dream had looked familiar. The tall lanky frame…the nervous striding…even the shape of his head. Of course!

"Elijah Stewart…"

"That's it! Gene's last name was Stewart. How did you know?" The questioning was insistent, pressed by one accustomed to having her questions answered.

"Elijah's a teacher now. A teacher in my school in Tucson." Kate beamed. It all made sense.

"How can you be sure? There are probably several Elijah Stewarts in Arizona."

Kate answered gently, "There are some secrets that are kept even from Mother Generals, Casey." She stroked the softness of her flannel nightgown, thought of the blue nightie in the suitcase, and smiled.

In her debut novel, *Provincial Justice*, Gerry Hernbrode traverses from cloister to inner city school with understanding. Her experiences as a pre-Vatican II nun, a public school teacher, an inner-city principal, and a member of the Arizona State Board of Education bring genuine authenticity to her characters and readers.

Ms. Hernbrode lives in the mountain hamlet of Portal, Arizona, where she's been an Emergency Medical Technician and a Radio Control Operator for Portal Rescue, the volunteer fire department.

CPSIA information can be obtained
at www.ICGtesting.com
Printed in the USA
FSOW01n2141150115
4471FS